JINN'S DOMINION

The Desert Cursed Series Book 3

SHANNON MAYER

Acknowledgments

Originally this series was going to be a trilogy, but the demand from the readers was so strong that I couldn't end it. (Seriously, I had people freaking out in emails not to end it at three lol) That and Zam, Lila and Maks were way too much fun to write, their personalities too strong for only three books. So thank you for loving these new characters as much as you do. Thank you to my team, my editors, cover artists, author besties, and ARC readers for always helping me put together the best books. 🖤

Chapter One

Grief is a beast I'd faced before, but not like this, not when hope had been offered, dangled like a sure thing. And then so cruelly snatched away while I reached for it, fingers aching to hold it tightly to my chest.

A slippery beast, grief slid under my skin and ran down my cheeks, stole the air from my lungs, burned the blood in my veins, and made my muscles ache, sucked the life out of me with each beat of my heart. This was a creature I had no way to fight, no weapon that would slay it. Some say faith was the weapon to fight grief, or maybe love . . . but I wasn't sure there was anything truly strong enough to hold the monster off me.

At least . . . not right away.

The steady staccato of Balder's hooves on the hard ground lulled me as we rode south, heading toward the Jinn's Dominion, continuing deep into the night.

Fatigue rode me hard, both from the battle with Corvalis, and the loss of my brother, Bryce. I let my eyes close as another wave of tears rolled down my face.

Eyes closed, my body twitched as my muscles spasmed here and there. I fell asleep, and that was the first mistake of the night.

But maybe *asleep* wasn't the right word because it felt like someone tugged my consciousness down deep, away from my own body, sucking me into a bottomless well with no ladder to escape.

My eyes opened to nothing but sand and sky, the golden glow overwhelming and familiar, the heat of the sun a welcome turn from the cold of the northern clime. Somehow, I was in the desert. Deeper than I'd ever been in a place I didn't recognize. I did a slow turn, the only sound, that of my boots against the sand.

"Hello?" Yeah, I know, classic dumb thing to ask, but I didn't know what else to do.

As I turned, the desert turned with me, spinning faster and faster until I could no longer stand, and the sand blurred my vision, stinging my skin. I lifted an arm to cover my eyes as I went to one knee, the other hand touching the ground to steady myself.

A voice finally answered me, deep, masculine and not one I knew.

"Hello, Zamira."

I put a hand above my eyes to block the sand as it slowly fell around me. The man who'd spoken stood in front of me. His body was thick with muscle from his feet up to his neck. His gray hair was braided back from his face, the tail of it flipped forward over one shoulder.

2

Beach colored clothing and cloak, and I knew why I'd not seen him right away. His skin was a dark golden tan from the desert sun and he blended in quite well. Dark brown eyes watched me closely.

The wind lessened, and I was able to push to my feet. This was a dream—if I listened hard enough, I could hear the sound of Balder's hoof beats—I knew that and yet it felt very real. And I'd learned to trust my instincts about weird shit like this.

I dusted off my clothes. "Who are you? How do you know me?"

He smiled, skin crinkling around his dark eyes, and I saw a flash of someone I knew though I'd only met him a few times. "Shit, you're related to Merlin, aren't you?"

His eyebrows shot up and the smile wobbled, nearly sliding off his face. "Unfortunately, yes. Merlin is my son."

Oh . . . fuuuuck. This was the *Emperor*? The one that . . . some people thought I would face and fight? I took a few steps back and found myself against a wall. "I was just leaving." I turned and he was in front of me, the invisible wall at my back again.

"You would deny me a chance to speak with you?" He tipped his head to the side. "I am not the monster some would paint me as, Zamira. I was a good ruler. I kept order and peace. The Jinn did not rule the desert as they do now."

I slid sideways, my back still against whatever surface was behind me, anything to put distance between us, and he kept pace with me. "Time to wake up," I said.

He laughed, and again, I heard a tone Merlin had in

his voice, both the hint of magic and true mirth of someone who knew they were free of any fear. "You will wake up when I allow it."

"Shouldn't you be . . . sleeping?" I didn't want to say dead. I didn't want to give him any ideas on what to do with me.

"My power is growing, Zamira. And in you, I see a strength I had not thought to see again." He reached for me and I slid sideways so fast, I stumbled and barely kept my balance. "You are afraid of me?"

"No shit, idiot," I snapped, my fear making me bolder than I really should have been. "You're the nightmare parents warn their children of before they go the fuck to sleep. The boogeyman." Oh, my gods, I just called the Emperor an idiot. I was going to die.

I tried circling to my left, but that barrier was still there. Fuckity crap on toast for breakfast, this was not good. *Wake up, wake up, wake up!*

If I could have slapped my own face without him seeing, I would have. Instead I clenched my hands, digging my nails into my palms. That pain felt very real, but it did nothing to counteract the dream I seemed stuck in.

The Emperor smiled at me, his eyes crinkling like he was nothing more than a kind old man, which I highly doubted was the case. "You may call me Shax. I give you that honor."

I stared at him. "Why the shit would you do that?"

He wrinkled up his nose. "Really, can you not come up with something other than such a simple question?"

This was insane. Insane was the only word I had for it. "Well, pardon my shit. I don't really feel like calling you anything, saying anything but goodbye." I turned again and tried to climb the invisible barrier, my hands splayed over it.

"You don't wonder if perhaps you could gain from this conversation?" he said. I turned slowly, seeing as I really had no other choice. There was no way out of this situation. The invisible wall followed me, as did he.

"Why would I think that?" I dropped my hands to my thighs, but my knives weren't there.

He spread his hands wide. "As I said, I see something in you that surprises me. Perhaps I wish to see what you're capable of. Tell me, if you could have anything in this world, what would it be? To have the shape your father's line should have given you, perhaps?"

"My brother's life." I spoke before I thought better of it.

His eyes widened. "You have a brother? The same parents?"

"What the fuck does that matter, asshole? He's my brother," I snarled. Forgetting again who the hell I was speaking to. His eyes narrowed and flashed with a glimmer of gold that was there and gone before I was sure I'd even seen it. "It matters if you want me to save his life. I can find his soul easier if I know more about him."

Bryce's soul? Was this even a possibility? With my back pressed against the unseen barrier, I was well and truly trapped until he decided to release me, and I barely dared to hope that I'd heard what I thought I'd heard. I fought to keep my jaw tight and not hang open like some village idiot. "We had the same father."

He eased back and a tension seemed to leave him. "Well, then, let me see." He held his hand out to the side, palm facing the ground. The sand swirled and danced slowly turning into a form I knew very well.

I dropped to my knees and reached for Bryce, but my hand hit a barricade around him, concealed like the one at my back. As if he were in a box that was clear, unseen but very much holding in away from me. He reached for me though, his hand against mine. "Bryce!"

He said my name. I could read his lips but couldn't hear him.

I looked up at the Emperor. "Why, why would you do this for us?"

He smiled down at me. "I want the Jinn, Marsum, dead as much as you do. But I see in you that you could use some—motivation, shall we call it? While you hate Marsum, your grief blinds you. And . . ." He waved his other hand over the sand, and it formed into a chunk of rock with gold and red lines coursing through it. The stone glittered; my heart pounded wildly as I stared at it. That stone called to me like none of the others had. I could almost feel it in my veins as if it would blend with my body. "I want the stone he carries with him."

I forced my eyes back to Bryce who sat with his legs tucked under his chin. He stared at me and shook his head. *Don't do it.* That's what he was saying. Only I knew there would be no way he'd leave me if the situation were reversed.

"You want Marsum dead and his stone," I said. Goddess of the desert, it was the same thing Ish wanted. The stones were important to more than her, apparently. Yet, while they held power, I'd not seen any power within those I carried that would make sense for everyone to want them.

"Yes." The Emperor tipped his head toward me.

I arched a brow at him. "I hear an 'and' in there. What else do you want?"

He crouched in front of me, still smiling. "You read people well. So you will know that I'm not lying when I say I can bring him back, but the cost is high. Which means your payment will be high."

Part of me knew I should be very afraid of this man in front of me, but I also had a feeling that if he'd wanted to kill me, he'd have done it already. For some reason, he needed me.

And that gave me the upper hand. Or so I thought.

The Emperor (I refused to call him by his name) clasped his hands together. "You are of a bloodline I wish to keep close to me. I want you to swear your life in service to me. I can give you strength you will never have otherwise, strength to defeat Marsum. Without it, I foresee your death at the hands of the Jinn."

Bryce slammed against the barrier, his mouth open in a roar.

I had to agree with my brother, as much as it cut into me. "Yeah, that's a shit deal. I want my brother back, that will never change. But I'm not a fucking dummy. I'll kill Marsum. Hell, I'll get you the stone, but that's all you get."

The Emperor's eyes hardened. "You would deny me?"

I grimaced. "It's called negotiation. Look, I get it. You're the big bad, but I'm really not interested in getting tied to you. I was tied to Ish. . .tar," I stumbled over her full name, "and she tried to kill me after I helped her for years. So . . . yeah. You can take all that magic you have and ram it up your too-tight asshole."

His eyes widened and then he laughed.

That was not the exchange I expected. "Yes, you are your mother's child, aren't you? Full of piss and vinegar, spitting and hissing despite your lack of size and strength. Do you know I was there when she was cursed to remain a house cat? A curse she moved to you as she died?"

His words hit me like a brick to the chest, but I made myself speak past the shock. "So?"

He leaned in, and his body fuzzed and faded. Grimace on his face, he was gone without another word. I dropped to my knees next to my brother.

"Bryce . . ."

He shook his head and smiled, and then he was gone just like the Emperor. Like Shax.

I groaned. I knew what this was. A deal with the devil.

A deal that I was considering. Because of one thing. Hope . . . stronger than faith, stronger than love, hope was enough to keep the grief of Bryce's death at bay.

Because if the Emperor could bring him back, and Merlin was the Emperor's son . . . then perhaps there was another way to save my brother. I drew a breath of the desert air as the dream faded and one thought rolled through me.

There was hope to save my brother. But that meant I had to find Merlin.

Chapter Two

The pre-dawn light barely brushed against my eyelids as I curled in tighter to Maks, a leg tucked between his, his arm over my hip, and Lila curled in between us, absorbing the heat the two of us threw off. Exhaustion had driven us the last two days as we put distance between ourselves, Dragon's Ground, and all that had happened there.

The dream of the Emperor had left me more tired than if I'd just stayed awake.

I had two goals now and they were as straightforward as they could be. One was to remove my new little pride from the lands of the Jinn, and the other was to find Merlin.

Merlin would help me bring back Bryce.

Damn it, hope was a deadly concoction.

Three days before, the three of us, Maks, Lila, and I, took the Dragon's green stone that helped them hold their portion of the wall, which in turn held the supernatural world from mingling with the humans. Lila had driven her father Corvalis away, and we'd escaped. But the cost had been higher than any of us knew until it happened. Bryce had been killed.

And now there was a chance he could be brought back. A chance.

In my semi-awake state, I let out a low groan and sucked back the tears that pooled in the corner of my eye before they could trickle down my face. Even with that hope, the pain of his death still hovered in my sleep.

Part of my head said this was what it was to be a leader, to claim the title of alpha. Losing those you loved and still moving forward to save others was just part of the job title. The other part of me was still that little girl holding her brother's hand while he bled out on the sand of the Oasis. Another tear squeezed its way out.

The interaction with the Emperor the day before was fresh in my mind. He wanted my help. Which made me wonder just what the fuck he really wanted. Mages with power like his didn't need help. Besides, he was supposed to be sleeping or trapped and unable to touch the world, yet there he'd been in my dream talking to me. In the last couple days, I'd considered a few options. There was a chance he was being impersonated. A chance it was Ish playing games. But I didn't think she'd do that. No. If she'd wanted in my head, she would have been far more devious.

No, the power he'd exuded had me fully convinced he was who he'd said he was. That and how fucking comfortable he'd been as I'd squirmed and tried to find a way out.

I'd not told Lila or Maks about my dream. Mostly because I hardly knew what to think of it myself. Shem had watched me closely, though. When I'd snapped out of it, yelling and shouting, my hands going for weapons, I knew he suspected something.

I pulled in tighter to Maks, wishing for thick down-filled blankets and a mattress that wasn't the cold ground. Something whispered against my cheek, as if brushing away the tear, and I lifted a hand to swat at it. Bugs in this cold weather? My sleep-addled brain attempted to make sense of what touched me. Another touch, this time against my forehead, not gentle but the flick of a finger being snapped on my skin. An ice-cold finger. I frowned and swung at him. Damn it, Bryce still hadn't grown up even all these years after childhood. It had been years since he'd flicked my head awake.

"Bugger off," I growled.

A low laugh and then a whisper that kickstarted my heart wide awake. *Wake up, little sister. We need to talk.*

My eyes snapped open to see Bryce's face in front of mine, his eyes wide, and a smile on his lips, though the smile looked strained. I could see a tree behind him. Not behind him exactly; through him was more accurate. I frowned and kept my voice low. "Why are you waking me up so early?" Maks's arm tightened around my middle, holding me a little closer, squishing Lila in the process. She groaned and shifted around, her claws digging into my back, the sharp pain waking me further.

I stared at Bryce, confused as to why he looked so . . . foggy.

Then I remembered. He was dead. Which explained the see-through business.

"What the hell?" I jerked upright, sent Lila flying into the air, and Maks rolling from me with a snarl as he settled into a crouch.

Bryce moved, his body fluid and indistinct. Again, I could see through him, and I didn't like it, because that meant . . . none of it was a dream. He really had died. He really had left me. I wanted to hang onto my anger, but I struggled to keep it close. I hurt too much to be angry.

"Zam, we need to talk about the Emperor. I was . . . wrong . . . take his offer. Bring me back. Please. I'll beg if I have to." He crouched, and his body shimmered and moved as though he were made of mist and clouds.

I stared hard at him. "Bryce, I . . . I don't know. He's like Ish, only a thousand times worse."

He grimaced, his white teeth not as clear as they'd been.

"I don't know if I'll be able to come to you again. Please, consider . . . I love Darcy, Zam, and I want a chance to be with her. Please. I wasn't meant to die on the Dragon's Ground, you know it too." He reached for me, his hand cold as it passed through my arm. I rubbed the spot.

I wanted to say yes. I wanted to tell him I would do it. "I'll find a way to bring you back, Bryce. If . . . he can bring you back, then so can others."

He lowered his head and his shoulders shook. *"He's the Emperor, Zam. He has power that Ish and Merlin could never have. I've seen it. His power is unmatched in this world. And I don't think he's the evil we've been led to believe he is."* He lifted

13

his head, sadness and fatigue curling through them. *"But I understand, Zam. I do. I will always love you. Take care of those who are left. Take care of them better than I took care of you."*

I reached for him, guilt and shame heaped upon my shoulders. "Bryce . . . you always took care of me." Which wasn't entirely true, but when we were younger it was. He'd been my protector, my friend and teacher even.

"Go. Save them." He put a hand to the ground and his body shifted from two legs to four until he was a full-sized male lion. He shook his mane and his whole body slowly dissolved along with his words. *"You've got work to do, so do it. Get our family away from the Jinn. Be careful of Marsum. I think the Emperor was right about that, you aren't strong enough. Not for Marsum. Do what you do best, slip in and steal them away."*

The sun rose, and its rays shot through where he'd stood only a moment before, the last of the mist that had created him evaporating with the day's warmth. I reached out and put my hand where he'd been, and despite the sun's heat, the air was cold as ice from a frozen river. I wasn't sure it was the cold from his spirit or the cold from his words.

I wasn't strong enough. Again. Would I ever see the end of those words? Would there ever be a time when someone believed I was strong enough? Hell. I'd be fine with them not believing, as long as they kept their fucking mouths shut.

I sat there with my hand waving through the air and stared at the place where he'd been only a moment before. Neither Lila or Maks spoke. I turned back to them. "Either of you see him? Or is this just me losing my mind?"

Lila spread her tiny wingspan and dropped to the ground beside me, her blue and silver scales catching the light like shimmering jewels. She squinted her big violet eyes at me. "See who, exactly? I mean, I heard you talking to someone, heard you promise to bring Bryce back. But . . ."

I grimaced and rubbed a hand over my face. That was what I thought—Bryce wasn't visible to anyone else. And damn it if he hadn't done exactly what I needed to get moving. My lips tightened. Between him and that fucking Emperor, whatever grief I had was put onto the back burner with ease.

If there was even a slight chance I could bring Bryce back, I was doing it.

I swiped my eyes with the heels of my hands, knocking the last of the salty liquid away, my resolve hardening.

"Yeah, Bryce paid me a visit," I said. "And . . ." I pushed to my feet with a low, drawn-out groan. I let the words *the Emperor visited me too* die inside my mouth. I wasn't sure I was ready to discuss that with anyone. Stupid maybe, but I couldn't seem to make them flow from my mouth.

"And?" Lila prompted.

I shook my head. "Nothing." I stretched again, groaning.

Sleeping on the cold ground was not my idea of a good time, even if there was a nice warm body behind me. Every joint and muscle in me ached even though it had been days since we'd done anything more strenuous than walk or ride at a slow pace.

Bryce had been the only one to die, but we'd all battled for our lives and it had taken its toll on us. Maks, as muscled as he was, stood up with difficulty, a twist of pain on his lips. "Damn, what I wouldn't give for even a bit of moss."

I smiled at him. "I'll put it on the list for the next campsite."

His blue eyes caught mine and he winked as he ran his hands through his hair, mussing it further. "You do that. Add on a pillow, chef, and hot bath and I might be your slave for life."

Lila snorted. "Aren't you already? Isn't that what being in love does?"

"You would know," I said. "Are you forgetting about Trick?"

Maks chuckled. "I bet she'd like you to forget how he made her blush in front of him."

Lila huffed and flew straight into the air, but not before I saw the skin around her eyes flush a deeper blue.

"Lila," I called after her. She tipped her wings so I could see her claw and flipped me off. I laughed. "Don't be like that!"

She barrel rolled and flipped me off with the other claw. Maks moved up beside me. "You were talking in your sleep last night."

"Did I say anything interesting?" I turned my chin up and narrowed my eyes. "Anything incriminating?"

He reached for me, and I let him tug me into his arms. Maks held me close and put his chin against the top of my head. "Something about Ish. And you called out for your father once."

I took a step back, not sure if he was reprimanding me.

He pulled me back into his arms. "I'm not upset, Zam. I'm just . . . worried about you. We're going into the Jinn's Dominion and it's going to get ugly before it gets better. For both of us."

I laid my head on his chest, letting him be the one to hold me up for at least right then. "Uglier than losing Bryce?"

He didn't answer, and that worried me.

"You two lovebirds," a gravelly voice grumbled, "it's too early to be awake. Lions are meant to sleep until noon."

I looked around Maks to where my crazy uncle Shem yawned. Even though he was on two legs, he looked like nothing more than an old male lion waking up in the morning, showing off his teeth and shaking his mane out. Literally. Shem shook his head, his tangle of blond hair flicking about his face. I snorted and Maks stifled a laugh.

"Yeah, well maybe the males sleep until noon while the females do the hunting," I said. "That shit is going to change with me in charge."

Shem rolled his eyes. "Promises, promises. But I can't hunt worth shit. My skills lie in other directions."

Maks turned with me, his arm still around my back. Since we'd decided that whatever we had going on was

17

worth fighting for, he'd been all about the public displays of affection.

I hated to say it out loud, but I didn't mind. Especially with what Bryce had added to my plate. For a moment, I wanted—no, needed—to pretend there was nothing more than a rescue mission.

I looked back at the lion shifter who was both new to our pride and very old.

Crazy Uncle Shem . . . I'd named him my seer, but I wasn't a hundred percent sure that had been wise. Let's call it a heat of the moment thing when all the adrenaline was running high and I'd been running on empty and I'd just lost Bryce and Shem was the closest thing to blood family left in my life. I'd wanted nothing more than to keep him close.

He smacked his lips and scratched his rib cage. "Your brother won't wander far. Not with all you've got going on." He yawned again. "And for the record, I saw him, too, though likely not as clear as you did."

Maks stretched an arm up over his head and rolled his head from side to side. "Gods, I'm sore." He brushed a hand across my shoulders and then down my back. As if checking for wounds without looking like he was checking for wounds.

I arched an eyebrow at him. "You think I'm wounded?"

He swatted me on the ass. "Maybe I'm just copping a feel."

"Not subtle either way," I said and shoved his arms away from me.

He might have been a Jinn—part Jinn, to be exact—

but that didn't bother me as it once had. He fit in my life, just like Lila did even though she was a dragon and I was a shifter. We were family and that was all to that conversation no matter what anyone else might've thought.

"I'll always look out for you," Maks said softly. I wasn't sure he had even meant to say that by the look on his face. I gave him a return swat on the ass when he turned from me.

Shem shook his head. "Feeling better then? Bryce showing up did the trick?" I nodded, but before I could say anything, he steamrolled on. "You need to pin down the rest of them. You got your dad's gift for finding your pride?"

I nodded again and opened my mouth. He made a waving motion at me. "Then get to it."

He wasn't wrong, but I didn't like the feeling of him bossing me. Not so soon after my taking the alpha position. "Don't push me, Shem. I'd as soon boot you out as put up with your chauvinistic shit. Got it?"

He held up both hands in surrender, though I wasn't entirely sure he wasn't mocking me. "Oh. Pardon me, mighty leader. Seeing as I am your seer, I thought you would be needing some direction from me. You go ahead. I'll just make you breakfast."

Yeah, definitely mocking. I stood tall and smiled at him. "I like my eggs scrambled. Don't dry them out."

His jaw dropped.

That's right, old man. There was a new sheriff in town, and she was done taking shit from the men in her life.

I turned and headed toward the horses hobbled on the far side of camp.

As soon as I was close enough, Balder shoved his nose into my belly. "Yeah, yeah, breakfast is coming."

I moved on autopilot as I fed the three horses and made sure they had enough water. From the corner of my eye, I watched as Maks and Shem pushed together the coals of the fire from the night before. Maks added fuel to it, and Shem got a pan and the few wild bird eggs we'd gathered. They worked with an ease that came from fighting side by side. That had produced an unexpected bond between the two men. They'd handle breakfast, and Shem would not dry my eggs out or I'd kick his ass just because. He glanced at me and I pointed at my eyes with two fingers, then back to him.

He barked a laugh. "Go, find your pride."

Damn it, I had been planning on trying that anyway, and with the added strain of Bryce showing up, I needed a few minutes to think. But now me heading off to try to find my connection to the pride would look like it was his idea. Bryce's appearance had made me think of it, and if I was going to save those left to my pack, I needed to make what few abilities I had work for me.

Even if Shem thought he was the one who'd suggested it.

"I'd already decided to do that." I took a step back. "Don't think this was your idea, old man."

He gave me another mocking bow, his hands in a prayer position. I rolled my eyes and caught Maks looking at me.

Unspoken words rolled between us. Not mind

reading in any way, just knowing each other. We'd been on the road together off and on for nearly three months and there had been times where words just didn't work.

You okay?

I nodded. *Good. I'm good.* Well, that was a bit of a stretch. Between Bryce's appearance and the Emperor's, I was being pushed in a direction I wasn't sure I wanted.

I'd already been going into the Jinn's Dominion. So, what was the point of the Emperor's midnight visit to me? Between that and the not-so-subtle guilt trip from Bryce, I struggled to make heads or tails of what the fuck was going on.

I rubbed my hands over my face. No matter how I looked at things, there were others that were still in trouble, others that needed me at my best.

And that meant I couldn't be distracted by the Emperor, or even Bryce. My heart twanged uncomfortably inside my chest. Bryce was not in immediate danger. Dead was dead. The Emperor . . . well, he'd done nothing but offer me things I wasn't willing to pay the price for.

As I started away from the campsite, Shem's voice tugged at my ears. "She might be okay, but what about you, boy?"

Maks muttered something too low even for my ears, though I strained to hear. More than the words I couldn't hear, his tone was off. Like he was brushing Shem's worries aside even while there was legitimacy to them. I made a mental note to talk to him when I got back, to see if he *was* okay. He'd had to kill two of his own kind, Jinn that had been coming for us while we'd been dealing with the dragons. I'd not thought until now how that might have affected him. What if he'd known them? What if they'd been his friends?

"Well, shit, I'm a bad friend," I said.

Lila dropped out of the sky and flew along beside me, bringing with her a rush of wind off her scaled wings.

"Why would you say that?" she asked.

"I'm not the only one who's been hurting, who went through shit the last few days. I haven't even asked Maks about the fight with the Jinn. What if he knew them? What if they were his companions at one point?"

She lowered herself to my right shoulder and settled onto what I now thought of as her spot. She wrapped a blue-and-silver-scaled tail around my neck to help herself balance and put one claw-tipped hand into my hair, kind of scratching against my scalp. "Well, I kind of doubt he had any friends within the Jinn. I mean, they tried to kill him at least once. For all we know, he could have been sent out of the Jinn's Dominion for the simple fact that he was expendable."

Lila had a point. But still . . . as soon as I'd seen Shem lean toward Maks while they worked to build a fire and breakfast, I knew in my gut something was wrong, and I didn't know what to make of it. I'd been so wrapped up in my own pain, I'd barely taken in anyone else's issues they might be dealing with.

For just a moment, I thought I heard my father's voice whisper to me.

You're the alpha now. You don't get to wallow.

My dad, whether I was hearing him or not, was right.

"I think Maks is holding back something," I said, acknowledging to myself that there was irony in what I'd just said considering all I was holding back. "Maybe he's worried about going back into the desert?" I tried to think of the last few days, of Maks's face as he spoke, of his actions, and through the fog of my own distractions, a slow pattern began to emerge. The way his eyes never stayed on mine, the way he looked to the south and then away, the way his body tensed when there was a sudden sound that didn't come from someone in our camp.

He was . . . nervous.

"I should have noticed." I shook my head.

Lila swayed side to side, throwing my balance off and making me stumble. "He's off, yes, but you're right. He could be worried about going south. I wasn't happy about going into the Dragon's Ground, you know. I knew that I could make you a target."

She was right. There was that possibility, but I didn't think it was *all* that bothered him. We were headed south into the Jinn's Dominion. The place where he'd been born and raised and tried to escape, and was now going back. That was different than Lila who'd been cast out.

That fear had to weigh on him. Fuck, it weighed on me going back to the desert. We'd have to go past the Oasis where my father was killed, my pride slaughtered, and the remaining members scattered to the wind. Yet as bad as that was, I suspected that whatever Maks was experiencing might be worse in its own way.

"I feel like we're on the edge of a sandstorm," I said. "One we can't see but that waits for us over the next dune." I grimaced, hating how those words sounded. Melodramatic much? Normally that wasn't me. But I couldn't help the way my gut twisted up and around itself. Seeing Bryce had only tightened that sensation. He might be dead, but he still needed me.

Lila grunted. "Well, you are nothing but trouble. For all we know, we could take a few more steps and fall into a deep hole. Or maybe something will explode."

"Ha!" I barked the word. "Please, I'm not that bad."

She drew a breath and raised one wing tip up as she spoke. "This above all: to thine own self be true. And it must follow, as the night the day."

I raised an eyebrow. "Polonius in *Hamlet*. But what has that got to do with me falling in a hole or blowing shit up, exactly?"

She grinned, flashing her sparkling white dagger teeth that could cut through me if she ever wanted to. "Trouble is attracted to you, whether you like it or not. Might as well own it. Use it for your benefit if you can."

I laughed again. "I am not trouble. I'm a house cat." I grinned and she snorted.

"Well, trouble likes you, which makes me think that perhaps cats are trouble in general. Maybe that should be your middle name instead of Reckless." She bobbed her head. "Yes. Zamira 'Trouble' Wilson. That's much better."

I dropped to my knees and spun out from underneath her, laughing as she screeched, reaching for my hair. I bolted forward, forcing her to fly hard if she would catch me. I pumped my arms and legs and let myself stretch out. Not because I had a great deal of excess energy, but I had to remember what it was to live for the moment.

To play for the sake of play, to laugh for the sake of the way the sound lifted my spirits.

Losing Bryce . . . I'd lost something vital to who I was, and I could feel the truth of that inside me. And I feared that without that vital spark, I'd be in trouble. Worse trouble than I normally dealt with.

I glanced behind me.

No Lila, so I slowed.

The whoosh of wings was the only warning I had—she was in a dive bomb. I did a limbo backward, not quite touching my ass to the ground, as she swept through where I'd been only a moment before. The balance was tough considering my momentum had been forward only a split second before, but I could pull it off. All my muscles tightened as I found that sweet spot of balance and held it just long enough to watch her swoop by.

Lila reached for me with open talons but missed by inches.

"Oh, you tricky cat!" she shrieked, laughing, as she pulled up for another round.

I twisted sideways from there, shifting into my four-legged form, then turned on another burst of speed, as I raced across the still-barren, cold ground.

The plains of the northwest side of the Caspian Sea were rocky and empty of life this time of year, leaving very few places to hide. But the small forested area ahead would work for what I wanted—a quiet place to settle my mind and connect with my pride. Assuming I could. The cat and mouse game with Lila was just a bonus that woke up my muscles and gave me a sense of freedom for a few minutes.

In my four-legged form, I was not much bigger than her, topping the scales at a whopping six pounds. My black fur rippled as I raced flat out for the trees, as low to the ground as I could get, zigzagging my way there as if avoiding a burst of rapid-fire bullets.

Not that I knew what that would feel like, but my dad had told us of fighting in the human wars. Of being hunkered down while the bullets flew, of not being able to shift into his lion form and give himself away if he wanted to protect the men he fought with. He'd had to play by the human rules all those years. A marine to the very end, he'd never stopped trying to protect those who needed him.

Strange to think that here, behind the wall, we were so stuck in a strange mix of times, a blending of the old medieval relics with bits of technology and current weaponry thrown in for good measure that had made it over the wall over the years. How long had it been since I'd even thought about the year it was now? Years. We had to be well into the 2000s by now. My thoughts distracted me and I got nailed for it.

A pair of talons wrapped around my middle as Lila hoisted me into the sky. "Gotcha!"

Laughing, I relaxed in her hold and turned my head and let my tongue hang out. "I'm dead."

"Yeah, you are!" She barrel rolled, still holding me, and my stomach turned in the opposite direction.

"Ugh, knock that off," I gasped.

Her talons tightened and she snaked her head around to stare at me, her eyes wide with horror and her face coloring a deeper blue. "Oh, my goddess, I'm sorry! I didn't even think about how insensitive that was!"

I shook my head. "That's not what I meant, and don't be sorry. Bryce actually had a decent sense of humor when he wasn't being a dick. Underneath all that bossy alpha nature of his."

She smoothed out her trajectory and quickly changed the subject. "The trees, that where we're headed?"

"Yes, that will work," I answered. She plummeted out of the sky, giving my guts another good drop and roll. I didn't have to point her to a clearing. She circled around a spot where we could land and let go of me when we were ten feet in the air.

I landed lightly on all fours and shifted back to two legs. For years, I'd avoided shifting, ashamed of my small form when the rest of my family were massive golden lions. But I'd found that my size, such as it was, had its benefits, too, if I let myself see it.

Shifting too much one time right after the other weakened me, but two or three shifts were easy enough now that I was doing it more.

A wry grin twisted my lips as I stood and walked farther into the copse of half dead, partially burned trees. Not exactly a fairytale garden. I lifted a hand and touched one of the branches, frowning at the brittle texture. Even for the plains, this was not what I would call normal.

"Lila, you seeing this? Does it look weird to you?" I asked as I walked among the bushes and trees. They were thicker now and tangled with some vine I didn't recognize. The stem was a deep red and it reached out with thin tendrils that curled and floated in the air as if testing it, or maybe even . . . tasting it. My feet slowed on their own.

Lila hopped into the air, flapped her wings once and was on the back of my neck, using my head to lean on. "That's very strange. I've never seen anything like it."

The vine shivered in the wind . . . only there was no wind. I took a step back. A tendril of the vine dipped to one side and then the other, circling around as if that creepy little fucker knew we were there. As if it were scenting the air, almost.

A voice whispered along the vine. *"Bow to me, Zamira."* Oh, shit.

"Well, that's a whole lot of nope," Lila whispered. "We should go."

I turned to do just that.

The vines had encircled us as we'd stood staring at the one that moved in front of us.

I reached back for the flail I carried, only I'd left it off to sleep and hadn't put it back on when I'd gone on this walkabout. The vines shivered and a low snicker rolled through them. *"Bow to me, or die."*

Laughing, talking plants? Yeah, that was a hard pass.

"Not the time to panic," I said softly, reaching for the kukri blades I carried on my thighs. The light

28

around us deepened as a cluster of clouds crossed in front of the sun. "If we have to, I'll shift, and you carry me out."

Lila squeaked, her tiny claws digging into my scalp. "Yes, it's time to panic."

She yanked my head back so I looked straight up at a perfect canopy of blood-red vines blocking us in.

"Well, fuck, that is not going to help," I muttered.

I tightened my hands on the blades. If the Emperor thought I was going down in a bunch of weeds, he was about to be proven sorely wrong.

Chapter Three

The vines tightened around us, the tendrils reaching slowly as they unfurled, revealing more and more tendrils. Lila wrapped herself around my neck so snugly, I saw spots and stars dance across my vision.

"Too tight," I gasped, but I wasn't mad at her—if I could have clutched at someone I would have done it too.

She eased off and I dropped to a crouch. The vines continued to make their steady approach. "I'm going to start chopping. Unless you have the sapphire with you?" Oh, please let her have it with her.

"I took it off," she whispered. Which I could see just by looking at her. The stone was no small thing. But it would have been really fucking handy right then. With the sapphire, she could have turned the vines to ice.

"Bow to me, and I will let you live," the voice that I was *sure* was the Emperor's said again.

"You see, this is why people think you're an ass," I snarled.

Lila shivered. "Do I want to know who that is?"

"Nope, you don't." I pulled both curved blades from their sheaths on my thighs and rolled them in my hand. One deep breath in and I lunged forward, still in a crouch, slashing with the kukris as hard as I could. They were designed to stay perpetually sharp and they cut through the vine in front of me, which was a relief. The bits of plant dropped to the ground, leaking juice in a spray that left droplets all over the ground and my clothes.

Lila screeched. "Blood, they're full of blood!"

I gritted my teeth and swung again. What was this madness? Was I still dreaming? Because this nightmare could not exist in real life—there was nothing like this that I'd ever come across. Unless it was a trap.

But for whom, for me or someone else? Hell, if that really was the Emperor we'd heard, then how did he know I'd come here? There was no way he'd have been able to predict this.

I cut through the vines in front and above us, my clothes slowly covered with sprays of the blood of the vine, more with each pass of my blades.

"Above!" Lila yelled as she ducked down, sliding partway down my back.

I dropped to a knee and swung above my head without looking. My right blade met some serious resistance and I tried to yank it free with no result. I looked up. The vine that had worked toward us was as thick as my arm and covered in a dark red bark that shimmered in the dull light. I jerked my blade out of it and a tiny drop of blood followed.

With my eyes up, I didn't see the vines coming for my feet. One of them wrapped around both my ankles and snapped them together, then pulled me down to my butt. I hit the ground hard and the shock ran up my spine, sucking a gasp out of me.

"Fuck you, asshole!" I leaned forward and cut through the vines holding my feet.

"Zam!" Lila screeched. I spun to see her fighting with teeth and claws as the vines pulled at her feet and wings, dragging her from my shoulder.

I reached for her, snagged the end of her tail and yanked her to me. She fought me until she saw it wasn't a vine that had yanked her. "Acid, Lila. You got any?"

She shook her head. "I used it all in my fight with my dad."

Sweet baby goddess, we were in trouble.

The vines laughed again. *"Claim me as your master, Zamira, and I will let you live."*

"Hang onto my front," I said, ignoring him. He didn't know me at all, so he had no idea what kind of shit he'd just stirred up. She dug her claws into the front of my shoulders and buried her head against my chest.

"If I was big . . ." she whispered.

"We'd have been caught already if we were any bigger," I said. "Call this a win for the small kids."

We had to get out of here, and out now. We had less than a minute if the vines kept up their creeping nature. The ground rumbled below us and I could only imagine just what other catastrophe was coming our way.

I had an image of the Emperor himself flash through my mind, his disarming smile, the way the laugh lines around his eyes crinkled. A mask for the monster? Suddenly I wasn't so sure.

There was no time to think. I slashed the vines in front of me, snarling as I fought my way through the mass of writhing things. Not vines. I would not call them vines as they bled, as they fought to get their tendrils wrapped around us. The ground rumbled again and the rocks and pebbles danced up and down with the vibration.

Lila clung to me and I pushed through everything. As the vines dropped onto me, I cut them off. As they reached to block our way, I sliced through them. Sweat dripped off my chin as I worked, slashing through everything that was even remotely in front of me.

The vines were there and then suddenly gone as I stumbled into the open plain, out of the copse of trees. I scrambled on my hands and knees to get farther away.

"We have to go," I said. "That thing will keep coming."

Lila crawled up far enough that she could peek over my shoulder. "Zam, the vines are gone. They aren't there."

I spun around, still on my hands and knees. All that was behind us was the same bush and scraggly trees that had been there when we'd landed, not a vine to be seen.

"That's impossible." I looked down at my clothes, half expecting them to be clean as when we'd gone in.

Blood splattered them, and I reached up to touch my face. My fingertips came away wet, covered in blood.

33

I sniffed at it to be sure. It was blood . . . and not just any blood. I wrinkled my nose.

"Lila, this is . . . the blood is from someone who carries magic. Like Jinn. Or witches. Or mages," I said softly.

She shivered. "I've never heard of anything like this before. Have you? And who was that voice?"

I shook my head. "No, I've not heard of it either. And I don't want to ever deal with it again. If we'd gone even a few feet farther into the copse . . . I don't think we would have gotten out." My first thought was to burn the place down. "As to the voice, well, that's a big fucking mess."

She shivered again, all the way down to the tip of her tail. I put a hand to her back.

"Why did you want to go in there?" she asked.

"I wanted to see if I could connect with the others in my pride, like my dad used to." I rubbed a hand over my face, wiping off the worst of the blood onto the sleeve of my shirt. "It would make it easier to find them if I could."

"You mean like you did with Bryce." She slowly pulled herself to my shoulder, but like me she didn't take her eyes from the seemingly innocuous bush.

"Yeah, that had been the plan." I made myself take a step, then another and another toward the bushes.

Lila scrambled back and launched into the air, flying ten feet above me. "Are you out of your gourd? Why in the world are you going back?"

I shook my head and then nodded. "Maybe I'm out

of my mind, but it calls to me." I just couldn't walk away from this place that had tried to kill us without at least making an attempt to figure it out. I mean, let's get real. The bush hadn't been about cuddling up for warmth. The plants didn't change as I drew closer, but there were spots of blood here and there on the ground where I'd fought my way out. I frowned and crouched while Lila groaned above me.

"Seriously, why are you doing this?" she yelled.

"Because it's not natural, even for our world of crazy." I touched the ground, brushing a thumb through a drop of blood. The ground rumbled and I lifted my eyes to see the dark red vines just suddenly there in front of me, tendrils unfurling as they reached for me. As if they had never *not* been there. I lifted my blades to my eye level. "I don't know what you are, but unless you want me to uproot you and salt the ground you live in, you'd better back the fuck off."

The vines wavered and slowly pulled back. Sentient, bloodthirsty plants with a taste for magical blood that were obviously connected to someone powerful. Most likely the Emperor.

Lila and I didn't have magic, though, so part of that made no sense. Maybe that was why the vines had taken their time in attacking us. Maybe we weren't the ideal food.

I stood and backed up, still holding my blades up until I was a good twenty feet back. "Lila?"

"Yeah," she called to me from above my head, "I'm up here, far enough away."

"Can you see any marker we can watch for in the next bit of bush we stumble on? A pattern or anything?" I wiped my blades on a scraggy tuft of grass and then stuffed them back into their sheaths as I circled to one side of the copse. The plants just looked like plants.

"Nothing." She dropped through the air, winging beside me as I started back toward the campsite. My stomach rumbled, reminding me I'd not been eating much the last few days.

But even with that, I couldn't help but look back more than once at the bushes. As if there were eyes on me still. I crinkled up my nose. "You feel that, Lila?"

"Yes, something is watching us," she said. "From the bush?"

I gave a quick nod. "Maybe Maks or Shem will know what it is."

She didn't answer, and she didn't have to because we both knew that answer. The plains and desert were my home stomping ground. If I didn't know what that freak of a bush was, there was no way Maks and Shem would know. The urge to go back and burn it down was strong.

I turned one last time, right before I stepped into camp.

For just a moment, I thought I saw movement, a figure walking toward the bush and then it—he—was gone. On my own, I would have gone back again and lit the vines on fire.

I was certain the figure had been the Emperor, as impossible as that seemed. The desert clothes, the hood covering his head. Who else would it be?

Who else had asked me to bow to him recently? Yeah, that's right, nobody.

But this wasn't about me anymore. I had a pride to take care of—to rescue from the Jinn before I could go after Merlin, before I could find a way to bring Bryce back. And that meant being more responsible than I had in the past.

Like a stick in the mud.

Shem cleared his throat as I turned back to the camp. "So, your walk went well, did it?" He stared hard, then fluttered his fingers on one hand at me. "Blood splatter already? Is that allowed before noon?"

Maks spun around and stood stock still, his eyes going to my once-white shirt. "Zam? What happened? Are you okay?"

I raised both hands. "I'm fine. Lila is fine. It's . . . weird is the closest word I've got for it." I quickly told them about the bush with the thick red vines, oozing blood, and our narrow escape. I did not mention the voice.

"I warned it I would salt the ground if it tried again." I sat against Balder's saddle on the ground and took a plate of food Shem offered me. "It backed off. Like it had a brain inside all those twisty vines." I took a bite of the eggs and grimaced. They were dry as the desert sands. I would lay money Shem had done it on purpose.

Maks stared hard at me. "If not for the blood, I would ask if you were seeing things."

I snorted and took a bite of the meat on the plate. Bird of some sort by the taste, maybe desert pheasant.

37

"You and me both. I wondered if it was a nightmare and I was still asleep."

Shem was quiet as he made up a plate for Lila and then one for Maks and himself. Too quiet. I narrowed my eyes. "Shem, you know something about that blood-thirsty bush?"

He sighed as he lowered himself into a crouch, easily balancing his plate on one knee. "I do. It's something of the Emperor's. Not unlike the standing stones, if you remember those from the stories I told you as a child."

I stopped chewing, the food in my mouth turning to dust. I shot a look at Lila and gave the subtlest of head shakes. We were not mentioning the voice. Not yet.

"We saw a set of the standing stones farther north. They ate two Jinn," Lila said.

Hell, they'd almost eaten Maks.

Maks paled, obviously remembering. He twisted around to look in the direction Lila and I had come. "And this bush, it's the same thing? Will it call to Jinn and others who have magic?"

Shem went from a crouch to sitting on the ground, his long legs out in front of him, crossed at the ankle. "The standing stones are the first marker the Emperor is awake. The blood vines, they are the second. While the standing stones take the magic and soul of those who carry that type of ability, the blood vines take just that. Blood."

I made myself keep eating though the food tasted like dirt. I swallowed with difficulty before I spoke again. "Two questions. One, the Emperor needs blood? And two, are there more signs like this we should be on the lookout for?"

"Yes, to the first. He needs blood to fully revive himself." Shem nodded. "And he needs a great deal of it. The vines are indiscriminate. The blood can come from any creature, though I suppose he might prefer one with magic humming in their veins. That would make more sense in terms of giving him strength to break the spell he's under." He looked past me in the direction where the bush was. "The signs are shadowed with his power so that you walk into the trap unknowing. That you escaped . . . that is surprising, to say the least."

Surprising. I put my plate down and noticed that Lila also had backed away from her food. "How surprising?" I made myself ask.

Shem leaned back and brought out a small pack that he carried with him. When we'd escaped Dragon's Ground he'd looked to have nothing but the clothes on his back. But under his shirt he carried a thin backpack that was very nearly empty by the looks of it. He unzipped the bag and reached in.

"I would say . . . impossible," he said, his eyes on mine. "Yet, with you, that seems to be a word you just ignore. Like leaping off the back of a dragon, falling, and yet somehow surviving what should have killed you."

Before I could respond, he pulled out a leather satchel from his bag that folded over and tied closed around a bone button. I frowned. It looked an awful lot like the satchel I'd taken off the Jinn from their camp—a satchel that had been full of nothing but blank sheets of paper. Lila caught my eye and nodded, but like me, she said nothing. The three of us watched as Shem untied the string that held the leather cover closed and pulled out a few sheets of paper. His paper was not blank like that in the satchel I'd stolen, but instead covered in strange writing. Pictures and letters, glyphs that drew me, and I found myself creeping forward.

"What is that writing?" I stared at it and the words shimmered and shifted around until they were pictures only, and not words or letters.

"What do you mean?" Maks leaned over from the other side of me. "I don't see anything but blank paper."

I lifted my eyes to Shem's and he raised both eyebrows. "What do you see, Zamira?"

Shit, I could tell him, but then would it be used against me? How? Fuck, I had to trust him, he was my uncle and I'd named him my seer.

I stared at the paper as it shifted and moved. "I see words that turn into pictures. Like a . . . TV." I knew that much about technology. We had a TV back at the Stockyards. Bryce had been trying to get it to work before he'd died. The best he'd managed was a flicker here and there of pictures, but I understood the idea behind it. Moving pictures with sound, just like life. Only on a box.

I looked back to the papers and the images cleared further. Were these like the papers I had snagged from the Jinn? Though they seemed the basic idea, I didn't think they were exactly the same.

Maks leaned forward. "What are these about?"

"These belonged to the Emperor's bastard daughter. A child born from a servant woman. She gave them to me for safekeeping. Her husband didn't want her to have anything to do with them as he felt they would bring about her death. As I have always been known for being crazy, she felt I could give warnings easier than she could and get away with it." He sighed. "In the end, she was wrong. Her life was snuffed out for these."

I stared at the papers. There was a distinctive feminine feel to the drawings on the papers. I had to clench my hands to keep my fingers from tracing them, and a part of my brain whispered that I'd seen them before. Which was ridiculous.

"Okay, so she gave you these papers, which means you found her in your journeying after you left the pride? Is she the one who told you about the signs of the Emperor returning?" Part of me fought that we were even having this discussion. Because despite what some people had told me, I was not interested in dealing with the Emperor. A mage of unbelievable power, he was a legendary terror among legends.

Especially after he decided to have a chat with me. That was a whole lot of nope right there.

Shem nodded, his eyes on the satchel. "She died not long after she gave them to me, but she knew she was being hunted and her death was written in the stars, is what she believed. She always told me it would come, but I didn't believe it—I thought I could protect her." His golden eyes clouded with old pain, like a wound seeping. Before I could ask him why the papers were worth killing for, he gave me the answer.

"You see, she knew how to kill the Emperor. That was her downfall."

Maks grunted as though Shem had punched him in the gut. "Wait, the Emperor has been asleep for over two hundred years. Even if there are signs showing that he's gathering power, it could be another two hundred years, long after we're gone."

Shem flipped through the papers as he spoke again. "The sleep was never going to be forever; she knew that, we both did. The Emperor's son put him to sleep, but the Emperor was savvy. He did something so he couldn't be killed. We don't know what, exactly. Hence the sleeping issue. Ah, here it is." He pulled out one of the sheets of parchment and laid it on top of the others. It had a single tick on it, like a page number. "Zamira, you have a bloodline that can read this, obviously. What do you see?"

The words slid and danced and finally began to form a moving picture. "I see a temple rising out of the deep sands, far to the east. It's shooting up like a mountain forming." I frowned and clenched my hands to keep them from touching the paper. "But that's it."

"That is where the Emperor sleeps." Shem pulled another paper and laid it out next. This one with several ticks in the corner. The next pictures were ones I knew.

This time I did reach out and touch the edge of the paper. "The standing stones, I see them all over the place."

"To catch the unwary," Maks said. "Damn."

I nodded but didn't look at him as the picture shifted. "The blood vine is next, weaving around the stones. But that isn't right. There are no stones here, none with the bush." I pointed my hand in the general direction of where we'd encountered the blood bush.

"Symbolism only, that they will come one right after the other," Shem drawled. "What is the last thing you see? I've never been able to interpret it fully."

Before I looked at the paper, I shot him a glance. "So, *you* are a bloodline that can interpret this, too, then?"

He shook his head. "I'm a seer. I have a knack for deciphering that which is hidden. But not enough to fully grasp what is here. I need you for that, apparently."

I dropped my eyes to the parchment again and watched as the vines pulled back and a dark mist flowed between the vines and the stones, eyes set inside of it, and then it blew away, into the vines and the stones. I shivered. "Eyes and mist. Like someone is watching. But then they are gone too." Gone, like water drying in the desert.

Lila groaned. "I don't like that. We don't need more people watching us."

I looked up at Shem, tearing my eyes from the parchment with some difficulty. "The Emperor is waking, sure. And while I realize this is like a case of the runny shits down the legs of life, what has that got to do with us rescuing the remainder of our pride from the Jinn and Ish?"

Lila cleared her throat and I shot a look at her. She widened her eyes and tipped her head as if to ask why we weren't saying anything. I shook my head. If we mentioned the voice now . . . then what? What would it change? Nothing.

We were going forward, end of that story.

Shem sighed. "A warning only is all it means. The old evil awakens, and we may inadvertently come across some of the traps he has as they spring up. The Emperor's power must be fed, and he will seek out blood and magic wherever he can."

"He sounds like a dick," Lila said.

I laughed. "Yeah, a floppy dick. Good for nothing."

She snickered, but I heard the anxiety in her laughter. Funny, but not funny. This was turning stressful.

Again. Surprise!

Maks rolled his eyes, but I saw the twitch on his lips. He didn't reach out for my hand, and much as I wanted to shift into my cat form and slide into his shirt to absorb the warmth of his body, I had a job to do. One that didn't involve letting Maks carry the bulk of my weight and responsibilities.

"Take these papers." Shem pushed them at me. "You can read them better than I can anyway. Perhaps you will be able to decipher more of them."

Before I could say yes or no, he'd shoved the satchel into my hands and forced me to take them. I clutched them to me. A smell of jasmine floated up. The Emperor's bastard daughter smelled nice. "You sure? You're the seer, not me."

"Yes, I'm sure." He didn't look at me again. "You should have them. She'd have wanted . . ." he muttered the rest under his breath.

I tucked them into my saddlebags, my thoughts

whirling. This whole transaction seemed odd, even for Shem.

"You never said if there were more traps to look for," Maks said. "Are there?"

Shem rolled his shoulders. "The Emperor has control of the Ifrit that are left. What does that tell you, Maks?"

Ifrit, I knew that word, but . . . the definition came to me slowly and I gaped like a fish out of water. "You can't seriously mean the underworld demons?" I blurted.

Shem nodded. "I do."

Maks's face was pale and he swayed where he was. "This is bad, Zam. Worse than even I could have imagined."

Lila buzzed between us. "I don't know what an Ifrit is. Will someone explain? And fast!"

I drew a slow breath. "The Ifrit, they are demons, and they rule the underworld. In the past, the Jinn traded favors with them and used them to their advantage."

"That was thousands of years ago," Maks said quietly.

"Then why the pale face?" Shem asked the very question I wanted to know.

"Because of Marsum." Maks sucked in a big breath and shook his head, almost as if he couldn't find the words. "Before I left, he was talking about waking the Ifrit and using them once more. He wants to rule, not just his section of the wall, but all of it." He looked at me. "He wants the Emperor dead. He wants to be the next emperor. The Ifrit would be a way to make that a reality."

I snorted, thinking of the man who'd taken me into a dream, and the power I'd sensed in him. "Then we should let that happen. Two birds, one big stone; they can just kill each other." Maks and Shem shook their heads in unison. I raised an eyebrow at them both. "Why not then?"

Shem held his hands out wide. "Because, there is always another big bad ugly. You know that, Zamira. Just like there is always someone stronger than you, faster, smarter. There is always someone more dangerous. Someone the Emperor in his own way has kept us safe from."

For just a moment, I stared at him, not comprehending. "What are you saying? That there is someone, or something *worse* than the Emperor and the Jinn?"

The twist of pain on Shem's face said it all. But he said it anyway.

"Yes, Zamira, there is."

Well, howdy fucking doody. How was that for a way to start the morning off right?

I stared at my uncle with my mouth hanging open and my brain stuttering over what he said. That something worse existed, something uglier than the Emperor.

"Are you fucking kidding me?" I sputtered the words.

Shem shook his head. "No, unfortunately, I'm not."

I wanted to put my head between my knees and take deep even breaths until this new twist slowed down. "Really, tell me you're teasing."

Shem sighed. "I wish I were, but the Emperor . . . he was not always the tyrant he became. He started out a hero, as so many tyrants do. He saved our world, Zamira, a long time ago. And the world worshipped him for it."

"Saved it from what?" Lila asked, her tail lashing with irritation. "What the hell could he save it from that was so bad?"

Maks surprised me by answering. "It's the falak, isn't it?"

Shem nodded, and I just let my body slump to the ground. "No, no, that is a legend. That is not real. Falaks are not real."

"Well, there aren't more than two of them, as far as I know," Shem said.

Two.

Lila tapped me on the head. "Tell me. What is this falak?"

I swallowed hard, but the two men didn't seem inclined to fill her in. "The falak is a giant snake-like monster that lives in the fire realm under the earth's crust."

The ground below us rumbled suddenly. I leapt up and stared at the sand and rocks at my feet. Lila squeaked and clung to me.

"Listen, much as this conversation is awesome, and the perfect fucking way to start the morning, I think it's time we go. I want distance between us and the blood vine," I said. "We can't do anything about the Emperor other than avoid his traps, and discussing the falak is not going to get us anywhere."

I held my hands up when Shem opened his mouth. "I get it. Things are bad. But I can only deal with one bad at a time. We are going south into the Jinn's Dominion, Shem, to get our family back. The land where our family's blood was spilled until there were so few of us left that we are close to the edge of being nothing. I think that's enough bad shit for right now, don't you?"

"As long as you understand that this conversation needs to continue." Shem stood and went to his horse, Ali. Well, she had been Bryce's horse before Shem's. I pursed my lips as I watched him tack her up. She was built thick, a heavier breed of horse for carrying the big men and pulling carts.

She was not built for speed. Which if we ended up running, we were going to need.

"We need to trade Ali in, much as I don't want to." I went to her and rubbed her velvet nose. Her big lips flopped around my fingers, looking for a treat. I smiled at her. "There are horse traders down the west side of the Caspian. We should go there. See if we can get you something with running legs on it."

"And avoid Ish along the way." Maks nodded. "Good call."

I backed away from Ali and went to my own horse. Balder watched me as I brushed him off and tacked him up carefully, checking that all my straps were straight and not pinching his skin. The last thing I needed was a saddle sore from being careless. I flicked a hoof pick through his hooves, checked his shoes that they were all nailed on tightly. While I could manage to fix a loose shoe, it was better to catch it early. So far, we'd been lucky not to throw any.

Balder nudged me with his nose as I finished attaching the last of his gear and mine. The flail sat on my cross-spine sheath I'd made for it. The weapon was light as a feather and I rarely noticed that it was even there. Until a fight broke out, then the urge to grab it and knock the shit out of my enemies was overwhelming. Which I did my best not to do simply because when I used it, the weapon drew my own life force into it. Basically, it tried to kill me.

I reached up and brushed two fingers along the wooden shaft, feeling the engraving of my family's crest in it. What were the chances that I found it in the giant's hoard all those months ago? That I'd seen it amongst the garbage and shit as if drawn to it? I shook my head as the wooden handle warmed, becoming tacky to my fingers. I snatched my hand away. "None of that," I said quietly.

The heat from the weapon's shaft pushed through my clothing and marked a line across my back as clearly as if I'd had Maks draw one there. Yeah, not sentient exactly, but there was power running through it I didn't fully understand.

Ignoring it as best I could, I slid a horse treat out of my cloak pocket and offered it to Balder. He took the treat and chewed contentedly, unbothered by eating around the bit in his mouth. That was our life, eating on the run. I sighed and mounted up, swinging my leg high over his back, then settled into the saddle.

His head snapped up and his ears pricked forward.

Something moved in the distance at a flat-out gallop. Balder let out a whinny welcoming the newcomer.

I frowned as the person came into view. Person, satyr, same difference. Goat from the waist down, man from the waist up, I'd sent him to Ish to get help for Kiara and her child. Maybe he had good news. But by the look on his face, I doubted it. Damn it, I needed to restart this day.

Chapter Four

Marcel the satyr slid to a stop, gasping for breath in front of me. I didn't dismount from Balder, but instead, urged him forward. "Marcel, you have news about Ish?"

I'd sent him in my place to beg for help from Ish when Kiara had been taken by the Jinn. I'd been torn in two directions—Bryce had gone into Dragon's Ground, and Kiara had been scooped by a fleeing Jinn as a prize. I'd hoped that by sending Marcel to Ish, she might consider doing something to save the young lion shifter. In a dream or a vision or some shit like that, I'd seen the meeting between Ish and Marcel, and the entrance of Merlin. But I didn't see it all and I was worried about what I missed.

Marcel bent at the waist, breathing hard, his hands on his furry knees. "Holy shit. Merlin showed up while I was there. Flounce me sideways for days, I do not want to ever see that kind of power thrown around again."

My eyebrows shot up. "What kind of power?" I hadn't seen Merlin since we'd forayed into the Witch's Reign, if you discounted the vision. What was he up to now?

Shem growled. "He's causing trouble, is he? No surprise there considering who his pap is."

Marcel stood and waved both hands at us. "He tried to calm Ish down. Said something about the jewels being what was making her mean again. Like she's been a bitch before. She flipped her shit and we ran for it."

I moved Balder beside him and handed him a skin of water. He took it and gulped it down. "Did she even mention Kiara? About helping her?" Again, I'd seen her response with my own eyes, but I was hoping that after I'd left the scene she'd changed her mind.

He nodded as he drank and a burst of hope climbed through me. He lowered the flask of water. "She said, and I quote, 'Kiara will have to save herself if she is to survive at all' or something like that."

Lila swung in close and whispered, "I think he doesn't know what a quote is."

I smiled, but it fled quickly. "Anything else?"

"Well . . . " He looked to the sky. "Basically, she said that *you* aren't safe around her. Something about the giants' jewel making her meaner than normal. And that they hate you and that is filling her up."

"The giants' hatred of thieves is nearly as strong as a dragon's," Shem said softly. "If she is feeling that, then the satyr is right, you should not go near her again."

I shrugged as if it didn't bother me, but . . . "We'd already decided to go to the west of the sea. This only reinforces that idea. Away from Ish. That's what we need."

Marcel grimaced. I frowned as I took my water flask back from him. "What else?"

"Merlin, he went to the desert. He said that the Jinn took someone, a woman named Flora. I never met her, but I think she's important to him." He shrugged. "The things people do for love, am I right?"

I didn't know what Merlin was up to, but I doubted it was as helpful as he would try to make it seem. Drowning me in a freezing stream in order to help me came to mind as his idea of helpful.

"Marcel, we are headed to the desert. I'm thinking . . ." I said, but he was already shaking his head.

"Yeah, that's a no from me." He rubbed his face. "I'm headed to cross the wall. I've seen a few satyrs headed that way. Long as I can avoid Stella, I'll be good." He grimaced.

Shem leaned forward in his saddle. "Wait, cross the wall?"

Marcel grinned up at him. "I know, right? Think of all the human women who need flouncing on the other side!" He ran his hands down his lightly furred chest and tweaked his own nipple.

"The wall . . . what do you mean you're going to cross it?" I asked. "We saw it, and while it's far from too tall to climb, it's got magic all wrapped up in it that electrifies you." Or something like that anyway. I wasn't dumb enough to try it to know for sure.

Marcel tipped his head. "I only know that there are places you can cross now. The wall is crumbling, along with the magic, and . . . well, there is a story already spinning around it. About a young female lion who is bringing down the wall. With a dragon at her side." His eyes flicked between me and Lila. "I mean, maybe they got the sizing wrong, but I . . ." He shook his head again, his nubby horns catching my eye. He reached up and took my hand, and brought it to his lips, drawing my eyes back to his face. He kissed it gently and then let it go. "Thank you, Wall Breaker. You are saving us all, you know that, right?"

My heart did a funny thump and my throat tightened. I managed a quiet "You're welcome." Maks and Lila wished him well and I was sad he was leaving us so quickly. Pain in the ass he might be, but it looked like he had completed his part in my story.

He trotted away, his tail flashing side to side as he hopped along, kicking his heels up here and there. Maks urged Batman closer to us. "What do you think? Is the wall down?"

"I have no idea. But if it is in places, it has to do with the jewels," I said.

We didn't watch Marcel for long before the three of us turned our horses to the southeast without another word between us. We needed to drop far enough to the south that the Stockyards was well out of range. And we needed a horse trader.

Riding for less than an hour, we came upon a small group traveling to the west. A few satyrs, a couple shifters, and behind them a wagon with several horses tied to it. I flagged them down and made a deal in no time. Ali would be traded for one of the finer boned riding horses along with other supplies that would see us through the next leg of our journey. I traded out my heavier winter coat as well.

Call it a hunch, but I did not see myself coming back to the cold ever again. Maks saw what I was doing and followed my lead, haggling for a better price on his coat. Of course, those headed to try and get past the Dragon's Ground would need heavier coats. Winter still held a grip on the land there.

The new horse for Shem was taller than both Batman and Balder by a few inches and his coat was a deep red auburn that made me do a double check under his belly. "What are you looking for?" Shem asked.

"Making sure it isn't a mare. You do not want to be riding a red-headed mare around," I said.

"Oh, I don't know about that." He winked and waggled his eyebrows, and I rolled my eyes.

The chestnut gelding was lovely, his dark brown eyes soft, and he seemed calm as could be. I checked him over quickly for any injuries before I put his saddle on. It fit well and in a matter of minutes we were off again.

"Why exactly did you need to switch out horses?" Shem asked as we rode away from the caravan.

I looked at Maks. "You want to tell him or should I?"

Maks laughed. "Have at it."

Lila landed on Balder's neck. "I'll tell him. Here's the deal." She lifted her head and paused for dramatic effect. "We've had to run for our lives more times than we can count now. That big mare, sweet as she is, would be left in the dust, which means you'd be left in the dust.

Consider it a compliment that Zam wants to keep you around."

Shem looked from Lila to me as if confirming. "You mean you run away when a fight comes?"

My eyebrows shot up. "You want to go back and stand your ground with the dragons?"

He frowned. "You did stand your ground."

I waved a hand at him, dismissing his words. "Never mind, bad example. We ran from the gorcs. We run from the Jinn."

"Not this last time," Shem pointed out again.

I gritted my teeth until the grinding sensation forced me to relax. "You are missing the point. More often than not, we have no choice but to bolt, okay?"

"I don't think I am missing the point. I think you are. You are learning to stand your ground."

Maks brought Batman between us. "The reality is that big mare would overheat in the desert. And when, not if, we need speed, she would have been a liability."

Shem backed down and my hackles rose. I pressed my heel into Balder's side, moving him sideways and forcing Maks and Batman to drop back. I kept him moving until my legs were pressed against Shem's and then I kept pressing forward.

My uncle looked down at me and I reached up for his face. He was dumb enough not to realize what I was doing until it was too late.

I grabbed his ear and yanked his face toward mine, my words low and hot as they bubbled out of me. "Do not undermine me again. I am your *alpha*. I gave you reasons why we switched horses but you didn't back down until Maks said something. You think because he's got a pair of balls and I don't that you don't have to listen to me?"

I twisted his ear harder until I got his eyes to lock on mine. "You got that, or do I need to remove you from the pride already?"

His eyes widened. "You . . . would do that?"

"My father obviously thought you were too much trouble. If you gave him shit like this, I can see why he did it." I let him go and he sat up straight in the saddle again. "I shouldn't have to have one of my seconds back me up when what I'm saying is perfectly reasonable. Bad enough I'll have to deal with Steve's shit when we find them. I don't need yours too."

I moved Balder away from him and rolled my shoulders, loosening the tension that had settled there.

Lila hopped along Balder's neck until she was on the pommel of the saddle. "Good catch."

I nodded to her but said nothing because I didn't need to rub it in. My father had always made one statement to the member of the pride he'd been correcting and nothing more.

Anything more and he removed them. There was not a three strikes rule, but two. Two strikes, and you were out.

The desert and the Jinn were too dangerous to allow for anything else.

I looked at Shem to see him . . . shaking? I frowned. "Are you fucking laughing at me, you dumb shit?"

"Yes." He tipped back in his saddle, his mouth wide enough to catch a damn eagle. I frowned harder.

"You want me to kick your ass out now? Is that what you're trying to—"

"No, no!" He raised both hands in mock surrender. "No, I wanted to make sure you would pick up on what I did. You are the first alpha female of a lion pride, Zamira. You are going to be pushed more than anyone else, tested at every turn." He looked at me, smiling and rubbing a hand over the ear I'd grabbed. "You caught it quickly and dealt with me. That's good."

I snorted and pointed a finger at him. "You almost got kicked out. Again. And I am not believing that you did that on purpose, not for one fucking second."

He smiled. "You remind me of both your parents, you know."

His words stole the wind from me as did the change of direction. "You knew my mom?"

"I did. She was a spitfire like no other. Which is, of course, what drew your father to her even though she wasn't a lion shifter." He settled into his saddle a little deeper. "She was young, barely twenty years old, when he met her, and though he was a fair bit older, she didn't care. They were pulled to each other like magnets. And they did try to stay away from one another, they really did. They knew it would be hard on them to have a cross-species relationship," he stared into the distance, "and they knew it would be hard on any children they had. There was no guarantee that a child would take after Dirk. A child could end up just like her. Small."

I found my eyes sliding to my left, to Maks. He was staring back at me. I knew exactly what Shem was talking about. That magnetism between Maks and me was too much to deny even though we knew it could end up hurting us in the end. We'd pretty much given up fighting it. For good or ill, we were in this together for as long as we could be.

He winked at me and I winked back before I turned to see Shem watching us, a soft smile on his lips. "I see you do understand at least part of that. Well, your mom won the other lions over. She was fierce, and she taught them to fight dirty when they were up against a superior force like the Jinn. Being smaller, she knew how to fight something that out-powered you, something the lions struggled with. She taught them how to take the Jinn's heads."

A chill swept through me from the crown of my head all the way down my torso and legs. I flexed my hands but said nothing. Shem was in storytelling mode, and from my childhood, I knew that the longer I stayed quiet, the longer he'd keep talking.

He sighed. "It was a sore loss not only to you and your family, but to the entire pride when she was killed."

I blinked a few times. "Wait, what?"

Shem looked over at me. "She didn't die of natural causes. I thought you knew that."

"My father told me she died after giving birth to me," I said softly. That guilt had been part of my life as long as I could remember. They'd never said when exactly she'd died, only that it had been after I was born. Maybe it wasn't my fault?

"The Jinn knew she was part of the pride's spine," Maks said quietly. "I remember Marsum talking about it."

I couldn't stop my head from whipping around to look at him. "You . . . were there?"

He shook his head. "No, I was a child, only ten years old when, well, I snuck close to one of the few meetings that Marsum held with the other Jinn. It's one of the few things I remember from my childhood." He frowned. "I haven't thought about it for years, but it just came to me in a flash. It was your mother he was talking about. How they took her down." His eyes were full of sadness when he looked at me. "I'm sorry. Do you want to know?"

I nodded. "Yes, the more I understand, the better." Even if it cracked open an old wound I'd rather have stayed shut.

Maks rubbed a hand over his mouth and then went on. "Marsum said if they could take down Dirk's mate, that it would only be a matter of time before the rest of the lions fell. He knew how important your mother was to the pride, and that she was training them to fight better, cleaner, and harder. Your father might have been the marine, but it was your mother who led the charge, I think." Maks smiled. "So maybe you take after her more than your dad in more ways than you realized."

My heart was doing weird things. I'd never known my mom, but I'd seen her twice now when I'd been hurt, close to dying. And she did look like me. But she wasn't a lion shifter, and neither was I, and my thoughts were all tangled in what I was learning.

The sound of water lapping against the shore caught my ears, a welcome distraction. I stared out between Balder's ears and caught the glimmer of the Caspian

Sea winking at us. "Thank you, both of you," I said. "I don't remember her so it's nice to know her better."

Shem reached over and patted my back. "She was strong and wise despite her years. And her gender."

I whipped around to punch him, but he was already racing his horse away from us, laughing. Asshole.

I grinned and urged Balder after him. I was going to knock that smartass right out of the saddle.

What was family for if not for keeping you humble?

Chapter Five

The edge of the Caspian Sea whispered across the sand. The horses danced sideways, tipping their heads at the water as if it were a monster reaching for their hooves. I sat quiet on Balder's back, letting him get used to the sound of the water. He actually liked to play in the waves, but it had been a long time since we'd been down this coastline and it was very different than the eastern side.

Shem let out a yelp as his horse gave a buck, the water scaring him most likely—very few horses were good with moving water right off the bat. A second buck and the horse sent Shem flying. He turned head over heels and landed on the wet sand on the back of his neck, legs in the air with a wet squelch. Lila screamed with laughter as she flew around us. "I thought cats were supposed to land on their feet! Oh, goddess, I could watch that a thousand times and not get tired of it!"

I laughed and reached for the reins of Shem's horse,

catching him before he could run back to the caravan. "I have to agree, that was a piss-poor landing."

Shem groaned and rolled to his feet. "I'm an old man now, nothing works like it used to." He knocked the worst of the sand off his clothing and took the reins from me. "Don't take this the wrong way, Zamira, but do you think Ish is going to let you just slip past her without making at least a token effort to snag you?"

I twisted in my saddle so I could look up the coastline that led back to Ish and the Stockyards. I stared as if I could see her pacing in her room, as if I could sense her watching for me on the horizon. For a moment, it was real, and I locked eyes with her, but it was gone in a flash. My imagination acting up again. My heart twisted and I shook my head. "No, I don't think she will. She thinks I'm weak, and she wants the stones more than she wants to protect me."

Maks brought Batman beside me. "You sure about that?"

I looked at him and a slow frown curled my lips downward. "Yeah, pretty sure."

Shem grunted. "I dreamed about her last night. She is not done with you."

My jaw dropped and I fought to snap it shut.

Maks let out a snarl. "You didn't think to mention this before we cut even this close to the bitch?"

'This close' was still a solid fifty miles south, and we were hidden by a number of hills, but still, I had to agree with Maks. I would have banked farther south if I'd known.

Shem shrugged. "Look, I only just remembered.

Being a seer isn't what I'd call an exact measure of life. It comes and goes, usually when it's seemingly the least helpful."

A hard wind snapped into my back and I slowly turned again to the north. A massive boil of pitch-black storm clouds crawled over the hills behind us as they formed a shape of a creature with clawed hands that dug into the soil to pull itself faster toward us, and an open, silently roaring mouth.

"Or like when you might be too late to give adequate warning?" I muttered. "Get on your damn horse, Shem. We're about to make a run for it. Unless you think we should stand our ground against that?"

He scrambled onto his horse and Lila shot down to my arms. "Under my shirt, Lila. That wind will rip you away."

She didn't question me, just shoved herself down the front of my shirt and then peeked her head out. "Nice bra. Maks seen it yet?"

Maks barked a laugh and I couldn't help but smile. "Not really the time, Lila."

"Just saying," she muttered as she settled herself.

The horses didn't need any urging to get them going as the wind smashed into our backs like a fist, bringing with it sand and stones, and even good-sized sticks. Balder grunted as a stick smacked him in the shoulder. He flicked both ears back as if asking me "what the fuck was that for?"

"Not me!" I yelled over the wind as I leaned closer to his neck. The roar of the wind picked up speed as we galloped along the edge of the water. Waves that had been small and lapping moments before, now washed over the horses' hooves. "Stay to the right, away from the water!" I yelled over the wind.

Maks and Batman stuck close to us as we urged the horses farther to the right, keeping them on solid ground.

Shem, on the other hand, either didn't hear me or didn't listen. Nope, the dummy went in the opposite direction, his horse's legs splashing through the waves, deeper and deeper. The horse rolled his eyes and fought to get back to us. Shem gave a hard yank on the reins to the left and the horse had no choice but to follow.

The roar of the wind caught up around us, and in the cacophony, there was a voice lilting and booming at the same time, chanting words I didn't know but which made my skin crawl. The words were rhythmic and they tugged at a part of me I didn't understand. My eyes fluttered closed as the words called me home, as they whispered they would protect me. I only needed to let go. My hands trembled as I loosened my grip on the reins.

"*Zamiraaaaaaa.*" Ish called to me across the miles and I swayed.

Blink.

I stood in her chambers. She was naked in front of a round, coal-filled brazier, flames coursing along them, her skin glowing with sweat. Under the skin of her arms and belly glowed the jewels I'd returned to her over the years. I knew without asking that the last four were meant for her body too. She gripped the edge of the brazier. "Zamira, bring me the jewels you have now and all will be forgiven."

I took a step. "Fuck off."

Her body shuddered but she never looked up at me. I found myself leaning over her to peer into the flames of the brazier.

In the waters of the Caspian Sea, Balder floundered as I swayed on his back, my hands limp to my sides. Deeper in the water, Shem was under the same influence.

I knew a dream or a vision when I saw one.

"Ishtar!" I snapped her name, and her head lifted slowly until she was staring at me.

Her eyes flickered. "Do you think you've found your strength then in the blood you despise?"

The words made no sense, so I ignored her. "Why are you doing this? You were my mother once, my mentor, my friend!" The emotions I'd held back for so long rolled up. "Why?"

"You are mine, a child I could never have." She shook her head and her hands tightened again, the brazier groaning under her grasp. "But you will bow to him. I see it in your future. And that cannot be. Give me my jewels."

I took a step back. "You cursed Bryce to remain crippled."

"It kept you close to me," she whispered. "I thought for a long time he was the one, but he was not. His weakness broke him. Your weakness gave you strength."

Her eyes were wild and the stones glowed brighter under her skin. I could name them all, I'd brought them all to her. Obsidian. Gold. Silver. Purple Quartz. Lapis. All gave her more power.

She let go of the brazier, stood and took a step toward me. Her face twisted suddenly, her lips in a rictus snarl.

"You will die. I will kill you myself. My hunters will take back the jewels." She held a hand out and from the shadows behind her came a snarling laugh. My skin chilled as the beast stepped into the light, its body dark, speckled, the hind end lower than the front, the teeth chattering as it snickered.

Werehyenas. They made Steve look like a sweetheart. Ish hated them. How she could possibly use them . . . it showed me just how far she'd sunk.

"Mistress, is that the cat you want caught?" He snickered and his body shivered.

Ish's eyes locked with mine and I refused to back down. I lifted my chin. She lifted hers. "It is."

I took a step back, snarling as the hyena scrabbled toward me, its claws digging hard for purchase on the tile. "Oh, I'm gonna like this," he yipped.

He leapt at me and I held my ground until the last possible second. The rancid hot breath was all over me as I twisted out of the way. I kept my eyes locked. Pain rocketed through my collarbone.

Blink.

A tiny pair of claws dug into my collarbone. "Zam, what are you doing?" Lila screeched.

I stared down at her and realized we were in the water, Balder lunging forward, fighting the waves and my legs as I turned him into the Caspian Sea.

"Fucking hell!" I yelled as I turned him back to shore. To my left, deeper out Shem still swam out ahead of us. Doing the same thing I'd been doing. His horse floundered, chest deep in the water as the waves built up alongside the wind, shoving us deeper and deeper.

"Shem!" I yelled at his back. He didn't so much as flinch as he let go of the reins and fell sideways into the water, his body stiff as a damn board.

His horse took its now riderless back as its cue to leave. He bounded out of the water and raced south down the shoreline. I pulled Lila from my shirt and wrapped Balder's reins around her. There was no time to think about what just happened with Ish. Shem needed help.

"Stay here!" I yelled at her. I dropped my stirrups and dove into the water after Shem as she sputtered. The water was not quite glacial, but close, and my skin seemed to shrink three sizes over my bones making it difficult to swim hard. If I hadn't had the same pull on my mind, I would have been cussing him out, but the truth was, I knew it wasn't his fault. Ish was fucking with us.

"Where the shit am I going to go?" Lila snapped her teeth in my direction as I came up, but I was already swimming—as it were.

Now, I wasn't the strongest in the water. Being raised in the desert will do that to you. But the water was not so deep yet that I couldn't touch bottom if I needed to. I swam hard for him, pushing off the bottom with my feet here and there to help propel myself forward. Moments later, I grabbed one of his feet, turned and headed for shore, dragging him behind me. "Come on, man. Help me out here!"

A bolt of lightning danced through the sky. I flinched but didn't let go of Shem. That was how this worked. My feet found the bottom again as the water grew shallower, and I pulled harder. "Shem, snap out of it!"

He is mine. The voice boomed out of the sky and rattled my bones. I clenched my hand over Shem's leg. That was not Ish.

That was the Emperor.

"Fuck off, he's part of my pride and I'm the alpha so he's *mine!*" I roared the last word into the wind and kept dragging Shem with me until we were on shore. The wind slashed at us, swirling faster and faster, building with each pass.

"Hurricane!" Lila screamed from Balder's back. I looked to her to see her clinging hard to the saddle, all four legs and sets of claws dug in hard and deep, her wings tucked tightly around her body.

Maks galloped up to us, Shem's horse in hand. He jumped off and helped me shove Shem across the saddle, lashing the bigger man down as best we could, considering the situation. He was going to have a bloody big headache when he woke up, but there was no other way to move him.

Balder and Lila joined us and I leapt onto my saddle, ignoring the cold as it sunk deeply into my bones. We had to get free of this storm or it wouldn't matter how cold I was—we would all die.

Maks and I moved in tandem, pinning Shem and his horse between our two horses. I reached up and braced Shem on one side. Maks did the same on the other. We galloped along the beach as the wind and weather snapped and howled. Lila shivered against me and I wasn't sure that it was all the cold water that poured down my body, or the fear of the storm and what drove it.

Ten minutes passed, and I knew because I was counting in my head. The storm kept pace with us, biting hard on our heels. A huge water spout shot up out of the sea, swirling and bobbing as it curled toward us. Because the hurricane-force winds weren't enough to convince us we were in trouble.

I looked across at Maks and shook my head. We couldn't keep this up. We had to do more than just ride south and hope to outpace this thing Ish or the Emperor had created.

A thought hit me. They'd been consorts once. What if they were working together again?

As if one of them wasn't bad enough.

Maks tipped his head to the west and I nodded. If we changed directions fully, we might lose the storm in the hills. Or at least find shelter.

Maks took the lead and I stayed next to Shem, keeping a hand on him where I could. We'd lashed him down good but if he started to thrash as he woke up shit was going to get real, quick.

The horses galloped over the first hill to the west and into the shallow valley below. Over and down, over and down. The foothills did help with the gusts of the wind around us. At least within the valleys.

Part of my brain said Merlin would surely show up with some magical shack we could crawl into and find safety. But my gut said that wasn't going to happen. Wherever he was, it wasn't here and we were on our own.

The wind shifted with us again, and this time shards of sharp rocks shot through the air, bouncing off our heads and shoulders, the horses' rumps taking the worst of it, making them leap and bolt in all directions.

"Hail!" I yelled. And no small amount, but large chunks of ice the size of my fist. One on the top of the head and you'd be sent flying. I leaned over Balder's neck to protect him and Lila as best I could.

The hand I had on Shem grew numb. Between the bath in the Caspian and the wind and hail, my body temperature had dropped to where I didn't feel the cold anymore. Warmth was going to be necessary in a matter of minutes if I was going to be of any use.

Or alive. There was that too.

Lila shivered against me. "Where are we?"

"Don't know." My teeth chattered, my eyes were locked on Maks's back. It was all I could do to keep him in front of me, to keep the horses moving. My focus was such that I didn't notice when the wind began to slowly, painfully slowly, abate.

Maks slowed Batman and circled around for us. "Up ahead in the foothills are some old caves."

I nodded, my teeth chattering. He led the way and a few moments later in the base of one of the rock-strewn hills, a cave appeared out of seemingly thin air. The mouth of the crevice was narrow and tall, but it looked like the horses could fit through if we pulled their gear off.

Maks leapt off Batman and handed me the reins. "I'll check it out."

He was gone before I could say otherwise and was back just as quickly. "It opens wide inside, so we can turn the horses around."

How the hell had he even known it was here? I realized that he'd led us straight to it and the understanding hit me.

It was a Jinn's hidey hole.

I forced my body to obey me as I dismounted. "Get Shem inside. I'll bring the horses," I said.

He nodded and helped Shem off his horse. Though 'helped' would imply that Shem was of any use. My uncle just kind of flopped into Maks's arms, forcing him to take all his weight.

I worked my fingers over Balder's gear first, breaking a nail in the process but hardly feeling it. Saddle off, I slid the reins over his head and sent him toward the cave. He went, good boy that he was, and I moved to Batman. Lila hovered around my face.

"What can I do to help?"

"Go sit on Shem," I said through clenched teeth. "We don't need him wandering off if he wakes up and is out of it."

The wind smacked me in the face with sand brought from the coast. I closed my eyes against the grit until it passed.

"You think he might?" she asked.

I nodded. "Yeah, he might."

She turned and was gone before I finished getting Batman's gear off. Like Balder, I flipped his reins over his head and sent him through the cave. I trained both horses and they trusted me when I asked them to do scary things. I eyeballed Shem's horse who danced at the end of his reins, neighing after his new friends.

He bucked when I moved to loosen his saddle girth.

"Don't be a shit!" I snapped, my patience not at its best. Not his fault, I reminded myself. He was as scared as the rest of us and with practical strangers. I forced myself to soften, placing a hand on his neck and standing as still as I could while touching him. We didn't have time for this, but it was what I had to do if he was going to stick it out with us. Maks appeared from the cave and scooped up the two saddles and disappeared once more.

"Easy." I slid one hand to the girth strap and loosened it, then pulled the saddle and pad slowly from his back. He let out a long low snort and I tugged him forward. I didn't want to lead him through the crevice, that was how you got trampled. But I didn't have a choice. I didn't have time to get him to fully trust me. Maks stepped out as I came to the crevice. Light flickered inside.

"Fire is going. Get in there and strip," he said.

Another time I would have smiled. Another time.

I tugged the horse after me and he leapt forward, ramming his chest into my back, which sent me flying into the cave. I fell to my knees and he trampled over me to get to his buddies, Balder and Batman, on the far side of the cave. I stayed there, breathing hard as I checked for broken bones. He'd clipped my right shoulder with his hoof, but otherwise I was okay.

Maks came through behind me and dropped the third saddle.

Without a word, he picked me up and carried me to the fire. Shem was already stripped and stuffed under some blankets near the fire.

"Lila," Maks said, "keep the fire going."

"You got it." She grabbed a stick and tossed it onto the flames, then fanned them with her wings. I wanted to ask how they had gotten so much stuff together, but my teeth were chattering again as the heat slowly made its way into my body. Maks yanked off his shirt and I just stared.

Lila snickered. "She doesn't need the fire, Maks. You just need to take your shirt off to warm her up."

He grinned. "Could be a worse reaction."

Even as cold as I was, I *was* blushing. "You'd think I was a teenager again," I muttered. I got my cloak off and my sodden shirt halfway over my head before he helped me with it the rest of the way.

He tipped his head to the side. "You're right, Lila, that is a cute bra."

I reached out to slap him but he caught my fingers and kissed the tips while Lila laughed, and then he was helping me out of my pants.

"We really have to stop meeting like this," I said.

"Nah, I like it. You need me, at least to keep you from freezing." He slipped his arms under my legs and carried me to the fire and sat, his back against the stack of saddles. He pulled a single blanket over us and I made a noise of displeasure at such light covering.

"Yeah, well, you either get all the blankets and I

cuddle up with Shem, or you get me." Maks held me a little tighter. "Please don't pick the blankets."

"Ohh, pick the blankets," Lila whispered.

Laughter shook out of me along with the shivering. "You two are horrible. We could have died."

"Yes." Maks nodded. "I think that's why it makes this whole situation even funnier. Death and laughter go together better than people realize."

I leaned my head against his shoulder and Lila crawled up behind me. Her claws slid into my hair as she deftly braided it back from my face. I wondered where she'd learned to do it, but then again, she'd seen me braid my hair back a few times. "You're a quick learner." I spoke through chattering teeth.

"It's hardly a complex spell," Lila said. "Three strands, over and over? Basic weaving."

I smiled, a laugh not quite making it past my lips. The movement of her untangling my hair, of her care for me warmed me as much as Maks's broad chest. He had one hand behind my back and the other over my legs with his palm resting against the skin of my outer thigh.

My shivering slowed, but I didn't fall asleep. I listened to the sound of the fire crackling, to Maks's heartbeat, to Lila's wings as they fluttered, the stamp of the horses' hooves and Shem's muttering in his sleep.

"That was Ish, trying to stop us," I said softly.

Lila squeaked. "The storm? You and Shem blacking out?"

Maks turned his face to me. "Wait, you blacked out?

75

I thought you were going in after Shem. And why would she attack him?"

I rolled my head side to side. "She wants the jewels back. She's sending hyenas after us for them."

Maks grimaced. "Fuck."

"My thoughts exactly. Which means we are running out of time. We have to hurry. As soon as that storm is done, they will be on us," I said.

"We can't fully outrun them," Maks said, carefully saying and not saying what was going through my head.

"I know. We'll have to kill them." I looked up at him. "They're the assholes of the desert. I don't feel that bad."

Lila tugged on my ear and I turned to her. "How bad can they be?"

"They are werehyenas," I said. "They're big, Lila. Not quite as big as the White Wolf, but big enough that a lot of them in a pack will pose a serious fucking problem."

Because we didn't have enough shit happening right then. "Ish has totally lost it," I went on. "Completely gone. There will be no convincing her to pull back, or that she's going mad. The jewels are under her skin. To take them . . . you'd have to cut her open." The image of her naked and feral gave me a shiver of fear that caught me off guard. I'd never been afraid of Ish before. No, not Ish.

Ishtar.

I would no longer call her by the name of the woman I thought of as my mother. She was Ishtar once again, a violent desert goddess whose mercy was fickle at best.

There was only one thing I could do now.

"I need to find the rest of our pride," I said. "I'm going to try to find them, like I did Bryce. The faster I do that, the faster we can get them and face the hyenas together."

Maks shifted me on his lap. "What can I do?"

"Just hang onto me." I curled in tighter to him.

"Easy." His face turned against mine and his lips brushed against my cheek.

For once, Lila said nothing. Then again, she'd been pushing hard for lion cubs to play with. Making those cubs would be something else. Assuming we ever found the time to do a test run.

A slow smile slid over my lips. Yeah, a test run would be rather nice.

"Dirty thoughts?" Lila leaned over and grinned at me. "I know that smile."

I shook my head. "Lila, you are far too smart for your own good."

"Ha, I knew it!" she crowed and Maks's eyebrows shot up. If I could have stopped the blush, I would have. I settled for closing my eyes and reaching out for the other members of my pride.

Chapter Six

The cave warmed significantly with the horses, the fire, and the rather lush man I curled against. I sighed and kept my eyes closed and my thoughts on the other members of my pride. I was supposed to be finding them.

But with Maks this close, all these unresolved feelings, pent-up sexual attraction, and frustrated wants were doing bad things to my head. And more importantly, other parts of my body that were not about to be denied. My hands crept up his bare chest, following the curves of his muscles all too easily.

Not what I was supposed to be doing. I clenched my fingers against my palms. This close to Maks, I couldn't focus. Which meant I had to leave him behind.

"Shit." I stood and held the blanket close as I walked to the back of the cave behind the horses. Maks didn't try to stop me, though I felt the loss of his heat keenly.

He was the desert that called me home in more ways than one.

Lila giggled and said something to him, and his low answering chuckle was all self-satisfied male. Again, he pulled on my body as if he'd thrown a rope around my middle he could tug at will.

I made myself ignore them as I sat well behind the horses. I folded my legs under me and tucked the blanket tightly around my body. My father had been able to reach all the members of his pride as the alpha. Or at least, that's what he'd told Bryce and me when we were younger. That he could find us anywhere, and that he would know if we were alive or dead. It was his connection as the alpha that allowed him this gift. He'd trained us as best he could, and I'd been able to use that training to find Bryce within Dragon's Ground. But would I be able to find the rest of them?

"Please let me have the same gift as my father," I whispered to . . . the desert goddess? No, never to Ishtar. Maybe to someone, or something that might hear my plea. I don't even know who I was praying to anymore, only that I needed to say something, that I needed help from a power far higher than myself.

I'd found Bryce with this technique, but he was my brother. My blood. And I was afraid I would fail my pride before they ever even knew I was their alpha.

I tightened my arms around my middle and kept the blanket snug around me as I slowed my breath. I focused on the intake and exhale of air in my lungs, the slowing of my heart as I let my senses open to the world. Minutes blended as the meditation tugged me deeper and deeper, as the cold left me and I found myself in a space of quiet.

The changes around me were subtle at first, barely there if I hadn't been in such an aware state. The ground below me embraced my legs and ass, drawing me into the stone the same as the forest in Dragon's Ground had done, but this was far more disturbing. This was stone melding around me, not moss and loose soil.

I pushed the fear back and kept at the meditation, sending my senses out farther and farther, deeper into the south as I fought to find those I was charged with protecting.

I focused on their names first. Kiara, Darcy, Steve . . . fuck, I really didn't want to find Steve, and the process hiccupped. Hatred was not something that would help me find them.

I snorted softly to myself and refocused on the girls. Kiara and Darcy. They might not be the friends I once thought, but they were mine to protect and they needed me to be strong enough to find them and bring them home. Wherever home would end up being after this was done.

That thought settled deeply into my bones, and as I accepted it, the light around me shifted behind my closed eyes. The threads of energy were different than Bryce's. His had been a deep gold like his lion's fur. Darcy's thread was a lighter gold, almost pale yellow and twisted, and Kiara's two threads wrapped around each other. A coppery thread woven with the palest of yellows that was feminine, for lack of a better word. She was carrying a girl.

Funny, I knew Kiara was pregnant, but feeling it was strange . . . like the unborn cub was already part of our pride. Even stranger, there was no gut twist on my part.

I opened my eyes and turned my head to the south, feeling them there, seeing their threads as surely as if they had attached skeins of yarn between us.

A slow grin crept over my mouth and I leapt up, blinking the vision away for now. "I can find them!" I ran from the back of the cave, past the horses and slid to a stop by the fire to see Maks staring up at me. I looked down. "Shit, I dropped the blanket."

"Yeah, you don't need it," he said.

I turned, blushing furiously yet again, went back to the blanket and scooped it up, wrapping it around my shoulders. I plopped myself down next to him, and my stomach rumbled, reminding me it was empty.

"How long was I . . . gone?" There was no other word for it. When I'd searched for Bryce, Lila told me later that I'd been out for an hour.

"A little over two hours," Maks said. He adjusted his seat. "Shem hasn't moved an inch either. He's alive, but so silent, I'm not sure he'll come out of this."

Lila and Maks shared a look. "What?"

Lila touched my leg. "We might have to leave him, Zam. If he won't snap out of this, that is."

Outside the storm still raged, battering and whistling through the crack that led into the cave. "We'll give him until the storm eases then."

I dug through my saddlebags and found dry clothes while my mind ticked over this problem. Ish had taken me in spirit to speak to her. Who knew what she had said to Shem.

Then there was the Emperor's booming voice . . . there was a chance he had snagged my uncle.

"Damn," I muttered. I was no closer to an answer.

I pulled my clothes on, then went to where my uncle lay. Dropping to my knees, I reached inside the blankets. "He's warm, that's better than the alternative."

"Yes, but out cold." Lila landed next to his head. "So now what?"

I frowned. None of us were healers, and far as I knew, there weren't many who could help him. If Ish hadn't lost her mind, I would suggest taking him to her. I rubbed a hand over my face. "If he doesn't wake up, I'll have to leave him here. There is no other choice I can see. We can't pack him like this into the desert."

Neither Maks nor Lila argued. Because they knew the same thing I did. There was only one option, as shitty as it was.

I didn't want to leave Shem behind. But Kiara, Darcy, and even Steve were in far more immediate danger than Shem, who had no apparent wounds other than whatever that voice in the storm had done inside his head. That was triage in a pride. Those who were most critical were saved first.

I sighed. "We'll stay the night and hope the storm and this spell on him drop at the same time."

Under his eyelids, his eyes moved back and forth at a rapid pace. Nothing short of disturbing.

I cringed and brushed a hand over his forehead in an attempt to soothe whatever demons clawed at him.

His eyes popped wide, pupils dilated, mouth open in a silent scream as he shot both fists straight up into the air, barely missing me.

"Shitfuckdamn!" I yelled as I scooted back, fell on my ass and rolled to my belly. "Not funny, Shem!"

My heart was in the back of my throat. I was sure of it, and I struggled to swallow or breathe around the heavy beating.

Maks grinned at me from the other side of Shem. "How do you like that? Being scared for no apparent reason?"

I tipped my head and narrowed my eyes as I pointed a finger at him. "I was *saving* us from walking into another trap, if you'll recall." We'd been underground, making an attempt to steal the Dragon's emerald gem, and a weird fog had started to come over me. I'd broken it by leaping into the air and screaming. Mind you, I'd also just about died laughing after I scared Maks so badly, I thought his heart would stop.

Shem let out a low groan and rolled to his side. I went to him, helped him sit up.

"Shem, back with the land of the living," I said. "Welcome. We were just discussing leaving you behind."

His hand wobbled as he lifted it to his mouth. "Goddess save us. Zamira, that was not Ishtar chasing us."

I looked at Maks and he shook his head and shrugged.

"Yeah, it was, Shem. Ishtar has completely lost it. I . . . saw her in a vision. She threatened me and has taken the hyenas as hunters." I moved closer to him and held out a hand. He took it and gripped it tightly. I tried to catch his eye, but he kept them closed, so I kept on talking. "She tried to kill me before, on our way to Dragon's Ground. I should have known, even without your warning that she was going to try for us again. For me." I patted his hand, albeit awkwardly. I didn't really know how to comfort a man who'd been my crazy uncle and tried to kidnap me when I'd been a little girl.

He put a hand to his head and tapped the side of it with his fingers. "Did you hear the voice, though?"

"The other voice? The one in the storm?"

Lila crawled onto my shoulder and leaned over to look at him. "Shem, if it wasn't Ishtar, who do you think it was?"

The Emperor. His eyes met mine and I looked away. My secrets dug at me. But I still couldn't speak them. The Emperor hadn't been trying to kill me.

He'd been trying to kill Shem.

"The Emperor. He is seeking out those who know of him, those who might know how to kill him." I turned back to him and his eyes slowly lifted to mine. Maks crouched behind me.

"Shem, you don't know that," he said.

Shem glared at him. "You, half-Jinn that you are, should be able to feel the Emperor wake. Do you not?"

Maks slowly shook his head. "As best I could, I cut myself off from the Jinn and their head games when I left the Dominion. It's the only way to escape them."

He said the words, but the tone was off. Like maybe he wasn't entirely sure that he'd severed the tie. "Then how can they find you? Wait, that's why you don't use your magic or whatever, right?"

Maks nodded. "Marsum can find me if I use my magic, yes. Which is why I don't use it because the second I do, it puts the rest of you in danger."

Shem snorted. "You could block him, you know."

"That's not possible." Maks shook his head and his eyes sparked. "So, don't speak about things you don't understand, old man."

There was more than a thread of heat in Maks's response. Shem didn't react but instead looked to me. "The Emperor knows I have the package, Zamira. I was able to keep him from seeing the memory where I gave it to you."

The package . . . "You mean his daughter's letters?"

He nodded. "Yes, he will try to kill me again. Something about your touch snapped me out of it, but . . . I think he will be back for me. I won't be able to hold him at bay again."

I sat beside him, thinking. "You are the seer for this pride. You gave my father advice on all manner of things from the running of the pride, to dealing with the Jinn until you took a ride on the crazy train and lost your marbles."

Shem's lips curled up. "Crazy train?"

"Kidnapping me. Remember?" I sat flat on my ass beside him.

"I was trying to protect you and . . . I thought you would be the one to stop the Emperor. I still do." He put two fingers under my chin and tipped my face up. "Kitten, you have it in you. Don't doubt it. This is only the opening gambit."

"Don't call me kitten." I jerked my face from his fingers. "It's fucking patronizing."

Lila lifted a wing, drawing our eyes to her. "If you are a danger to Zam, if the Emperor can find her through you, then you can't come with us. What will you do?"

Lila was right. And she was wrong. I opened my mouth to tell them the Emperor had found me already, that he'd gotten into my mind somehow.

"Ishtar was inside that storm too," I said. Why the hell hadn't I said the rest?

Shem pushed off the blankets and slowly stood. "She used it to hide herself, but that was the Emperor's power pushing it. He was talented with the weather and she was always good at riding others' coattails."

He closed his eyes a moment and a low humming starting in the back of his throat. As a child, I'd seen him do this more than once, try to scry the future so as to warn my father.

Shem stopped humming and looked at me, his eyes dilated. "Do not scorn your enemy. They will be the key to your survival."

I shook my head, confusion flickering through me. "You mean the Jinn?"

"All of them, not just Maks," he said softly. He stumbled to where his horse stood dozing. "I'm leaving now. It's the best thing I can do to help you survive. Lila is right about that. The Emperor will follow me."

"Where?" I stood and followed him. "Shem, we need to stick together, not spread out across the fucking continent." Still, I held my tongue about already knowing the Emperor could find me.

He grabbed his small pack of gear and led his horse past the fire. "Listen to me. I know what I'm talking about. I will head north and east, toward the far wall."

I stared hard at him. "The far wall is over three thousand miles away."

Shem quirked his lips into a smile. "Give or take. Be warned though, stopping the Emperor does not mean killing him. We cannot risk what would come from that."

I put my hand out and pushed it into his chest. "I can't let you just walk away now. Not when we just found you."

He put a hand over mine. "You don't really need me, other than the package I've already given you. And now that the Emperor knows I am alive, and the knowledge I have . . . he won't stop looking for me."

Lila flicked her tail back and forth. "How did he even know we were there? How did he know where to find you?"

Shem's eyes locked on mine and a shiver of fear started deep in my belly. "Because I belonged to him once, many, many years ago. It was through his power I became a seer. And I was trained for one reason only, to kill his bastard daughter."

Well, that was not the answer I expected.

Chapter Seven

Shem put a hand on my shoulder and it felt as though he'd put a literal weight on me, pushing me to the ground. Which was not what I wanted when he'd just admitted to being someone he'd hidden from all of us. I shoved away from him, stepping back far enough that the fire didn't warm me any longer. "You were a hired killer?"

He shrugged. "I sought power when I was young and stupid, and the Emperor used it against me."

"You killed the Emperor's daughter and took her papers?" I didn't know why that upset me so, but the idea that he'd killed a person who'd stood against a monster that had been a total tyrant bothered me greatly. Even if that monster looked like nothing more than a kind old grandfather.

He dropped his hand. "We all do stupid things when we are young, Zam. Save the others, but don't take the last stone from the Jinn. Whatever happens, the only thing I will tell you is to not take the stone. That will remove the last of the power imbued in the wall which is tied to his cage. Take the stone and the Emperor will be free in this world once more. As it is now, he can touch the world, but cannot be free. At least one stone needs to stay where it is." He tugged his horse forward. "And I will do what I can to draw his attention away from you, for as long as I can."

This was not happening. None of it. The whole fucking shit story had to be just a bad dream, one I couldn't wake from.

Shem stepped around me. "I'll ride hard and fast. Ishtar won't bother with me, I don't think, so I will go through the Stockyards, that will speed my passage."

"That's stupid even for you," I snapped. "She'll see you and draw you to her! She'll set her new pets on you."

He shrugged. "If she does, I'll chat with her and offer my services until she no longer sees me. I can play the chameleon if I must."

Shem walked out of the cave and into the suddenly still night. I followed him, my feet bare on the hard, cold, rocky ground. The stars glittered like chips of cut glass in the sky. The storm had passed. We all needed to get moving.

"Shem. You are supposed to be helping me! Not fucking off!" I said.

He turned to face me. "I *am* helping you. I'm buying you time, Zamira. You have the papers. Use them to guide you. I think you would have liked his daughter. She . . . was special." His eyes drifted shut and in a flash of insight I realized he'd cared for her. Maybe he hadn't killed her then? Or he'd killed her even though he did care for her. That was worse.

I swallowed hard. "I will get the rest of the pride, and then we are crossing the wall and getting the fuck out of here."

His smile was tired and sad. "I doubt that. Your life is here, Zamira. You are a protector of *this* world," he pointed to the ground at our feet, "no matter what else you might think, you know that is true. If the Emperor is freed, chaos will reign. And then . . . well, I don't want to think about what would have to happen then." He reached out and tugged me into his arms for a brief hug before he tossed his horse's saddle on and quickly cinched him up. I watched as he spun the leggy gelding and took off back the way we'd come.

There was no goodbye or good luck. Just gone with the night, not unlike the last time he'd left the pride. A hand circled around my waist. "You can't make him see sense," Maks said. "He believes in the stories of the Emperor."

"You don't?" I turned to him.

He shrugged. "Stories meant to keep us in line, meant to keep us from overthrowing those who have a hold on them. A falak is waiting if the Emperor is killed? The Emperor is free if we take the stones from those who make our lives miserable? It smacks of manipulating our fears as if we were children."

"I know." Except part of me believed Shem. Because I'd seen the Emperor. I'd felt his power against my skin, and he'd nearly killed Shem even though he was far from him.

And if he was right, then we were in more trouble than just dealing with a few Jinn. Not unlike Maks's reasoning, if the Emperor was real and I faced him, then there might be something worse out there he was holding back.

Fuck my life and give me a shot of whiskey. I needed a drink.

The sound of Shem and his horse racing into the night faded and a sudden spurt of energy flowed through me. "We go now. Those fucking dogs will be on us in no time." Like their counterparts, werehyenas had noses that outstripped just about any other animal.

Lila squeaked. "We barely survived that storm! And I want to stay warm for a little while."

"And if whoever it is that sent that storm thought they hurt us, they won't expect us to move." Damn the Emperor and his games. He was almost as bad as Ishtar. I could see why they'd been a couple. I strode into the cave, found my boots and yanked them on, along with a cloak that I cinched around my waist with a thick leather corset belt. That would keep it from flapping and give Lila a place to hang onto if she needed it.

"You're letting fear rule you. We need to be smart about this," Maks said.

I shook my head. "Nope, this is not fear. This is understanding my enemy. Behind and in front."

"Yes, you are letting fear rule you," he repeated; his voice had an edge to it. "You could have died out there. We all could have."

I turned to him. "Yeah, that's the thing, Maks. We are going to face death over and over. It's not going to end for us for a long time if even a small portion of what Shem said is true. Whether the Emperor is dealing in this or not, we have to move and move now. I know what Ishtar showed me whether she meant to or not. The werehyenas won't wait for light."

Lila's claws dug into my shoulder. "Don't the horses need to rest?"

"We aren't racing through the night, but we're moving now. We have close to three weeks before we hit the desert, and now we have dogs on our asses. You want to wait and fight them here, stuck in a cave with limited resources? If the pack is half as big as they can get, we'll be wishing for a herd of gorcs." I scooped up my saddle in one hand and my gear in the other. With a flick of my head and cluck of my tongue, I had Balder follow me out of the cave.

Once outside, I quickly tacked up. I was in the saddle before I realized that Maks and Batman had not followed me.

"Maks?"

"No," he called from inside the cave. "This is a bad idea, Zam, and as your second, I am putting my foot down."

My jaw dropped. Was he serious? Lila tightened her hold on me. "Zam, why is he doing this? That doesn't sound like him at all."

I shook my head. "I don't know." Was it possible that the Emperor had dug into his mind, too, in a different way? Was it possible that something had happened and

I'd not noticed in my own self-absorbed state as I searched for the rest of my pride? No, he'd seemed totally fine earlier.

I hopped off Balder and ground tied him. "Lila, stay here, please." I looked up at her sitting on Balder's neck. She bobbed her head.

"Okay, but if you don't come out in five minutes, I'm coming in."

I gave her a thumbs-up and ducked into the cave.

The fire was still going, and it lit Maks from the far side, his back to me. I bit my lower lip and approached him with caution. Just in case. The cave around us glittered with light from the cut walls. The stone held flecks of reflective glass that caught the light and threw it in a wider arc. I'd not noticed them before, but here and there I could see designs etched. The language of the Jinn.

I shivered, pulled myself together and put a hand on his shoulder. Moving with care, I walked around him until I was looking into his face. "Maks, talk to me. What is really going on?"

His eyes were closed and his body shook as though he were indeed fighting something. His throat bobbed up and down as he struggled to speak. "I can't do it, Zam. I can't go back to the desert. This cave . . . I should not have brought you here."

No other words could have rocked me so hard. "What?"

He reached for me, pulling me into his arms and burying his face in the crook of my neck, his lips against my skin. The trembling in his body slid through mine, scaring me in a way I'd never felt before. To know such a strong man, one who'd faced down the biggest and ugliest of our world, was afraid . . . it cut my own strength. I held him tightly while he shuddered.

"Maks, talk to me."

He did a hell of a lot more than talk to me.

He lifted his head and kissed me, salt on his lips, heat in his mouth as he took the kiss without asking, demanding that I give over to him. I slid my arms around him and hung on while he plundered my lips and mouth with his tongue. His hands clenched me, to the edge of pain but not quite. I bit his lower lip, tugging at it as he moved his mouth away from mine to my jaw, down my neck to the top of my shirt. He pressed his forehead to the top of my chest and rubbed his face side to side . . . marking me as any cat would do to its mate. A flush of warmth spread from my lower regions all the way up to the tips of my ears. "Maks, much as this is hot as hell, I need you to talk to me."

He kept his head down, his breathing ragged as he rubbed his face against my bare skin. No lips, just that smoothing motion side to side, as if he could make the mark visible. I caught his face in my hands and tipped it up so I could look into his eyes. "Maks. Please. I know the Jinn are going to be tough to get by—"

He shook his head. "It's not that. I'm fine. I just . . . had a moment of weakness is all." He smiled, but I saw the strain behind it and that set my alarms off. He kissed me gently once more, then turned away. "I'll get my stuff."

I stood there staring at his back as he grabbed his

saddle and gear, took Batman by the reins and led him out. He didn't look at me again.

Moving on autopilot, I put the fire out, kicking dirt over it. The darkness that fell as the flames died was heavy as if eyes were in the shadows the light kept back. I shook my head, knowing my imagination was running wild.

My eyes adjusted to the dark—perk for being a cat shifter. I made myself stand and stare into the void of the cave. "I'm not afraid of you, whoever you are."

The words echoed and bounced as if the individual letters were rearranged as they moved.

You will fear me. The voice was a whisper, a ghost of a man's voice as if coming from far away, and I knew without a doubt who it was.

That fucker Marsum. I wanted to say it was all my words jumbled up inside my head that gave me the voice speaking to me, but that was a lie. Son of a bitch, this freaky ass shit was not the way to start the night after losing Shem. After seeing Maks lose his courage.

I stumbled back. I couldn't help it and reached for the flail before I even thought of grabbing a weapon.

The handle warmed, but I knew there was nothing to fight even though my senses were screaming like crazy that I was in danger. There was nothing in the dark.

I kept my ass moving toward the opening and my eyes on the back of the cave . . . just in case I was wrong and there was something or someone sitting in the depths of the darkness. I slid out, and the second I was free of the cave the words faded from my ears.

As if they had never been. I closed my eyes and

swallowed hard. Maks was already on Batman, his face flat of any emotion.

Lila cocked her head to one side. "What happened?"

"Nothing." I forced my fingers to let go of the flail as I walked to Balder. "Nothing."

Maks did look at me then and I couldn't meet his eyes. Maybe he had his own secrets, maybe I had mine.

Long as they didn't end up getting us killed, did it really matter?

We got the horses moving at an easy trot, following the natural flow of the hills around as we headed straight south. At some point, we'd turn east again, but not for a long while. Not until we had to.

Silence ruled the night air and we made good time. Hours slipped by in complete silence. Maks and I had ridden like that before, on our first trip into the Witch's Reign. But that had been a comfortable silence of people who didn't need to talk to each other, but could if they wanted to. I wanted him to talk to me. To tell me what was freaking him out.

Lila slept as we rode, curled in between me and the pommel of the saddle with a chunk of my cloak covering her. I kept one hand on her tiny body, making sure she didn't fall off.

After four hours, I couldn't stand it a second longer. "Maks, are you angry with me?"

He shook his head. "No, you are doing the right thing for the pride. I . . . didn't think about what your next step would be when you named me your second. I should have."

I frowned and moved Balder beside him. "Why does it matter?"

His shoulders tightened. "We are going into the Jinn's Dominion. Is that not enough for me to be concerned about both your safety and the others?"

I reached out and grabbed his arm. "I know you, Maks. You don't run from a fight, but back there you not only wanted to run, you wanted me to run too. Why?"

His jaw ticked, but he didn't pull his arm from me. "Because I love you, Zam. And that . . . is a dangerous thing in the world of the Jinn."

Holy shit, had he just said what I thought he said? "You love me?" Okay, that came out like a needy whisper, but who cared? Lila was asleep.

He looked at me, those blue eyes of his piercing even in the darkness. "I don't know if I can protect you once we are there, Zam. I don't know if I can protect you as we travel there. And that guts me like nothing else. I know you have to go. I know your pride is there, but Marsum . . . he has a long memory. Has it not occurred to you once that since you've removed the necklace that kept his curse from you, nothing terribly bad has happened?"

His words made me blink. "You don't think a hurricane that almost sunk me and Shem was something bad?"

"Yes, that's bad. But nothing little has gone wrong. You've not had your saddle strap break, or lost a weapon, or gotten unexpectedly sick. Nothing out of the ordinary for what we are doing. And you are driven to get to the desert as if a madness has taken hold of you.

You didn't for one second think of waiting on Shem to get better. You agreed to leave him. That's not you." He shook his head as if he could shake something free. "I can't put my finger on it, but I think this is Marsum again. He's changed the curse. We know that. What if it is no longer about making your life miserable? What if he's done something else? What if he's drawing you to him?"

I sat deep in the saddle, thinking. "Can he do that? I don't know Jinn magic." And to be fair, my mind was still stuck on the fact that he'd so casually thrown out that he loved me. How could he know that? How could he love me?

Did I love him?

Yeah, you do. Say it! My inner voice screamed at me and I kept my mouth shut. Much as I trusted Maks, the last man I'd loved had broken my heart into a million pieces. I wasn't ready to throw myself at the next man with as much abandon.

"Zam, are you listening to me?" Maks said. "Before we go into the Jinn's Dominion, you have to know what I know. Okay?"

"Sorry, say it again." I smiled, but he didn't smile back. Which made my smile slip off my stupid face. Shit, how bad was it, whatever he had to say?

"When Marsum put his hands on you, as a child, he made a connection with you that can't be broken until one of you dies. He made you . . . like his familiar, is the best word I can come up with. He's connected to you, the same way he's connected to me. And his magic is such that if he takes note of you being alive—which we know he has—he can change his hold on the curse. He could remove it completely if he wanted." Maks stared hard at me. "Do you understand? He has a hold on you, Zam."

Lila yawned and stretched. "What am I missing?"

"Marsum can change the curse on me," I said softly. "But that doesn't explain why he would suddenly make my life easier."

Lila crawled up Balder's neck. "Maybe because he wants something you have? If he knows you would come and rescue your pride, they are perfect bait, aren't they?"

"He wants the jewels," I breathed out the words. "He wants the jewels. Maks, do you think that's it?"

I turned to see Maks staring at me. "Maks?"

"The jewels are secondary, Zam. I think he wants you, and he will do whatever he has to do to get you into his hands." His eyes tightened and narrowed suddenly, flashing a blue so bright that it seemed they glowed for a moment.

I reached over for him, touching his arm. "Maks?"

He pulled away from me and shook his head. "Sorry, what?"

My eyebrows shot up. "You said he wants me."

Maks closed his eyes. "No, I want you. Marsum wants to kill you."

Except . . . I didn't think that was what he meant at all. I bit the inside of my cheek to keep from speaking. Lila looked at me with her eyes scrunched up as if she were trying to figure out what the fuck was going on too.

Maks held his hand out and I took it, weaving our

fingers together. Balder and Batman rode happily side by side through the night, content.

But I was not content. Something was wrong with Maks. Something was very wrong.

And I had no idea what it could possibly be.

Chapter Eight

The next few days passed so quietly, it was almost pleasant, and I could *almost* forget that Maks was acting strange, not letting me far out of his sight, or that Shem had fucked off on us, or that the Emperor was reaching for all of us, or that we had werehyenas on our asses. Lila didn't stray far, not even to hunt. But I suspected her reasons were the same as mine. Shit was weird. We did not need to be split up. At the same time, I needed to speak to her without worrying about Maks overhearing.

We kept our pace up, steady, never resting for long.

The second day, I managed to get Maks to talk, but he would only speak about things long past. Sort of.

"You didn't know your mother at all?" I asked, prying as carefully as I could.

He shook his head. "Marsum told me she sold me to him when I was a child. I don't remember anything about her." There was something in his voice though that made me think otherwise.

"No siblings?" I tried a different tactic.

He shook his head again. "No. I dreamt once I had a brother." His eyes slid to me, sadness filling them. "He was an unusual-colored lion. But that was just a dream. I don't recall my childhood, Zam. I dream sometimes, but that's all they are. Dreams."

After that he shut down completely and I got nothing more out of him.

On the third day, near dusk I called an earlier than normal halt, which had me looking over my shoulder more than once. "Maks, do you think you could snag something for dinner? I'm exhausted." I slumped in the saddle for good measure. Goddess, I was a bad actor.

He nodded and pulled out a small crossbow from his pack. He put it together quickly and then helped me with the two horses, and even got me set up with the fire. As if I were helpless. I let him, closing my eyes as I slid under a blanket he gave me.

His footsteps receded, and I opened my eyes. "Lila!" I hissed her name and she crawled across the saddles.

"Yeah, this is fucking weird, Zam. What's going on with him?" She craned her neck, watching the foothills for his return. "He's barely talking to us, and he's treating you like a freaking glass egg."

"His eyes, have you seen the flashes of blue?"

She nodded. "I thought it was just me." She let out a little whimper. "What are we going to do?"

"I tried talking to him. I tried to get him to tell me what was wrong and in the middle of it, his eyes flashed blue and he forgot what he'd said before. Or he changed it to sound less ominous. He said that Marsum wanted me. And I don't think he meant to kill me." I realized as we spoke that we were whispering even though Maks was nowhere to be seen. "And now he could have gone hunting as a caracal, far easier than with the bow. Why the bow, Lila?"

Her tiny claws reached up and she put them on my cheeks. "The Jinn are master manipulators, Zam. What if . . . Marsum has his hooks back in Maks? What if it's not Maks anymore?"

She said exactly what I was terrified of—Maks was being drawn back into being the kind of Jinn I thought were the only kind before I met him. My heart thumped hard because I knew what I had to do.

We had to leave him behind. This was why I hadn't told him I loved him. Maybe I'd known no matter how we felt, it could never be. He was Jinn. I was a lion. The idea of star-crossed lovers had never been so fucking poignant.

"We have to outrun him," I whispered. "Balder can do it. But we can increase our odds." I stood and crept to Batman's gear. Slowly I pulled my kukri blade from my thigh sheath and cut through the thick leather cinch strap. Maks would have to fix it first and that would slow him down. I couldn't bring myself to hurt Batman or take a shoe off him, which would have been smart. If Marsum was controlling Maks now, then there was no telling how far he'd go to get what he wanted. As it was, Batman's front left leg swelled off and on, an old injury that haunted him.

I took a step back, my eyes on the hills where Maks had disappeared. Lila squawked and I spun, my kukri raised by my head, ready to strike.

Maks stood behind me, the small crossbow raised, his eyes flashing that freaky fucking electric blue. He motioned at me with the bow. "Put the knife down, cat."

Cat. Not Zam.

"Maks, this is not you." I didn't lower my blade and he didn't lower his bow. "Please listen to my voice. You've got to fight whoever has a hold on you."

"Come on, toad!" Lila yelled. "You have to fight Marsum!"

Maks's face twisted into a snarl. "How do you know that all along my job wasn't to take you to Marsum? How do you know that I'm not just a fucking amazing actor, unlike you? How do you know, Zam? You don't. You don't know. Do you?"

Horror of the deepest kind flowed through me and I fought it, but I couldn't help the sensation that I was living my worst pain again. Betrayed . . . this time by my heart and a good act rather than another woman.

Lila snarled. "No, this isn't you, Maks! Stop this stupid shit! This isn't you! You stop it right now!"

He spun and pulled the trigger on the crossbow. I screamed and lunged, trying to intercept it with my blade. I missed.

The bolt flew through Lila's right wing, tearing it open wide. She screamed and I launched at him while his eyes were on her, my blade going handle first. I hit him hard, and tackled him to the ground, barely holding back from driving the blade into his belly.

"You fucking Jinn!"

He slammed hard on his back and I pressed my blade against his neck until blood welled around the razor-sharp edge.

His eyes flashed that bright, strange blue again. "You are weak. Weak enough to think I loved you, that a Jinn could love *anyone*. We take what we want, and when we need something done, we make it happen. Any way we must. You're a fool, cat, to have believed a single word that came out of my mouth."

His words cut into me and all I could do was stare at him. Because it wasn't Maks. Nothing about his words or what he was saying was him at all. "No, that's not true. It's not, Maks. I know you. Lila is right. This is not you."

"You don't know," he growled. "If you knew me, if you understood who I was, you'd kill me now without hesitation. Do it! Kill me!"

I couldn't move. I'd thought I was done with indecision, but I could feel nothing but uncertainty rocketing through me. Lila cried out from my right. Maks bled under my blade.

My two closest allies were injured, the two I loved the most, and I couldn't help either. Maks glared up at me, his lips twisted in a cruel snarl . . . and a tear slipped from the corner of one bright blue eye.

The decision became easy with that single tear. This was not Maks talking to me. Whatever was going on, it wasn't him.

I turned the handle of the blade fast and slammed it into the side of his head with a thick thud. His eyes rolled back and he slumped into the ground, a groan sliding from him.

"Lila, hang on, I've got to immobilize him first," I said.

"He shot me! That piece of shit Jinn shot me!" Her whimpers tore at my heart, because they were heavy with more than physical pain. She sucked a shaky breath and cried out, a sob slipping from her.

I flipped Maks over and grabbed some of the leather binding from my gear, then wrapped it around his wrists with a slip knot that would only tighten more if he struggled, then did another set around his ankles.

For good measure, I covered his eyes with a blindfold and stuffed his mouth with a gag before I turned to Lila. Every movement to bind him broke another piece of my heart and I pushed it away. I had to—Lila needed me.

Her wing bled in tiny little drips across the hard ground. I picked her up. "I can stitch it, then we can use the hacka paste. It'll heal if you don't use it for a few days."

She nodded, but her jeweled eyes were full of pain and hurt of a different kind. "He said he wanted me as a sister. He's just like my other siblings. He tried to kill me, Zam." She buried her face against my belly, her tiny body shaking with her sobs.

I bit my tongue while I worked on her wing. Steady hands were what I needed here, and Lila's pain kept my own right at the surface.

I blew out a slow breath and threaded a needle, focusing only on the task in front of me. Using the thinnest line I had, I stitched the hole in her wing together, keeping each stitch as small as I could.

"There," I snipped the end of the line. "Just the paste and you'll be good as new."

I reached for my bag and dragged it across the ground to me. It bumped into Maks and he groaned.

I flipped open my bag, my eyes on his body as he woke and realized he was bound and gagged. He grunted and thrashed, and I recalled all too easily how he'd been bound by the Jinn before. How they'd pinned him face down in the mud and left him to die and Lila and I had saved him. But how the fuck did I save him now?

I dug around, blindly found the hacka paste and opened it before I turned to Lila. Her eyes were on me. "You can't save him. Not this time. If they have his mind . . . there is nothing you can do."

I gritted my teeth as I smeared the red sparkling paste over the stitches, then grabbed a match from my bag and lit it with the flick of my thumbnail. "Hang on, Lila. This will sting a little."

She closed her eyes and clamped her mouth shut as I put the match first to one side of the wound, then to the other. Bright sparkling puffs of smoke rose into the air that smelled like cinnamon. Lila twitched only once, then she slumped, her legs wobbling. I caught her up into my arms and held her tightly.

"We have to try to save him, Lila. This isn't Maks. I'm sure of it." I had to be sure. There was no other way for me to move forward. Even when I'd caught Steve with Kiara, I'd not been totally broken—I could look back and with perfect hindsight see that I'd always known Steve was not really for me. He'd been my first crush, my first love, my first heartbreak. But he had never been a part of my soul. He'd never understood me, never fought at my side. Instead, he had always fought me.

Maks . . . he was the other half of my heart and soul, and this pain was beyond deep. It ran all the way to the center of my bones, making me ache in a way I'd not felt since I'd been a child, since the Oasis and the loss of so much life, since my father's death, since Bryce's injury.

I turned to where Maks lay on the ground. He'd yanked the leather bands tight and his hands were going red with the constriction over his wrists. "You'll end up with no hands if you keep that thrashing up," I said.

He muffled something through the gag and slowly relaxed. Lila climbed to my shoulder and I carefully made my way to Maks's side. I took the gag out and lifted the blindfold.

Maks raised both eyebrows. "What the fuck is going on?"

Lila glared down at him. "You shot me through the wing! Is your brain as dry as the remainder biscuit after a voyage?"

Maks looked to me. "I'm lost."

"That's from *As You Like It*," I said. "That help?"

"No! I know what play the line is from," he growled as he shifted onto his back. "Why am I tied up? Wait, I shot Lila?"

I shared a look with her. "This is what I was talking about. He doesn't even know what he's doing."

She frowned and snapped her teeth at him. "You're lucky I want cubs to play with, or I'd rip your balls off and eat them with my breakfast. Wrecking wings is only like the worst thing you could do to a dragon, you know."

Maks stared up at me as sweat rose all over his face. "Zam. I would never hurt you. Either of you."

"Except that you shot Lila and threatened me," I said softly. "And you said everything was a manipulation, that you were sent to take me back to the desert. That was the goal all along."

He closed his eyes, but not before I saw what crossed them. Pain and embarrassment.

I scrambled back. "You were sent to find me?"

"I was sent to find the last lions," he said softly. "The children of Dirk in particular, though I wasn't told why."

"Witch's Reign?"

His throat bobbed. "Initially, yes, I was to take you back to the desert, but that changed! I realized that the farther I was from the Jinn, the less hold Marsum had on me. The more I could block him." He opened his eyes. "Zam, it wasn't all a manipulation. I stayed because . . . I'd never loved anyone before. I didn't know . . ."

His back arched suddenly and the leather bands creaked.

I scrambled away. "Lila. Back up."

But it wasn't Lila who answered me. Maks did. "Oh, little cat. You love him, don't you?"

"Marsum." I snarled his name and my skin crawled.

"You can't kill him, can you? This is too rich. You make this too easy." He laughed, only it wasn't Maks's laugh. It was deeper, uglier, and I knew it even though I hadn't heard it in years.

Marsum had full control of Maks.

He rolled to his belly, his hands and feet lifted behind him as he pulled on the leather. "The cave, if he hadn't taken you to shelter in the cave, I would never have found his mind. But it is one of my places. Now, the more important question. Do you know why he is so connected to me? Have you guessed yet?"

I took a step back, bent and grabbed my bag of gear and gave a low whistle for Balder. Engaging Marsum was not smart. I'd seen how that played out for my family before.

The barking howl of hyenas lit the air.

Well, wasn't that just fucking peachy. I cocked my head and counted the beats between the howls. At best we had fifteen minutes before they showed up.

"He's not just a Jinn," I said. Damn it, I couldn't help myself.

"No, he is not. I found his mother fetching and couldn't help myself despite the fact she was a mere shifter," he said.

Lila gasped and I froze in place. His mother . . . was a shifter. I chose to focus on that instead of the rest of what he'd said. Marsum's son. Maks was Marsum's son.

"He'll never truly escape me. His blood is mine."

I made myself turn to face Maks as one of the leather wraps on his wrists snapped. He quickly untied himself and stood. He tipped his head to one side. "Why aren't you running?"

I dropped my bag of gear while Lila tugged at me. "You have Kiara, Darcy, and dumb ass. You want me to come to the desert, and you have the bait. Why the fuck are you doing this to him? You don't need to do this to make me show up on your doorstep."

He smiled slowly and took a step toward me. I refused to back down. "Lila, on Balder," I half threw her toward my horse as Maks stopped right in front of me. Not Maks. It wasn't, yet I couldn't stop seeing him as the man I loved. Damn my heart.

"I do this to remind him who his master is," he said. "He was away too long and has a sense of freedom that is false. You are not for him, Zamira of the Bright Lions. He is a mutt." He lifted a hand and brushed it across my cheek. The same hand had touched me before, but this time was different.

A ripple of unease followed it, but I refused to back down. I would not run. I would not.

"Let him have his mind back. I'm coming to the desert, you dumb fuck. You don't need Maks like this."

He grinned. "No. *This* is my insurance policy. You would come for your friends, but . . . For Maks? To see if you can save him . . . I believe you would go to the ends of this world and back. That is what love does to you mortals; it makes you foolish and stupid."

Anger flared brightly within me and it took all I had

not to punch him in the balls. Because it wasn't Marsum who would be hurt, but Maks.

He grinned and a low laugh rolled from his mouth. "Oh, the look on your face is precious. You want to kill me but can't because that would hurt your precious Maks. I should have done this years ago." He grabbed either side of my face and yanked me to him, kissing me hard enough that our teeth clinked together. Skilled, he was not.

I pushed hard against his chest as he plundered my mouth. This was not Maks, and I was not about to let it happen. Heat snaked from his mouth into mine—not desire, but the heat of the desert sands lighting within me, setting off something in my blood I didn't understand.

Power.

Magic.

Fire.

I screamed and he swallowed the noise down as I pushed at his chest, finally snapping a fist up between us, slamming into his jaw despite knowing I was going to feel it too.

He bit my lip as his teeth snapped together and I stumbled backward, free of his hands and mouth, the coppery tang of blood on my lips. My mind whirled with that heat he'd shoved into me as it coursed through my limbs with a tingling not unlike bugs crawling over my skin.

"What did you do to me?" I flinched and twitched like a horse covered in flies.

He wiped his mouth with the back of his hand. "I lit

a fire in you, cat. You are not only a shifter any more than Maks is only a Jinn. For now, I will give part of him back to you—not the part you want, likely. But at least you will know it's him and not me."

He grinned and his body sagged where he stood as if something left him, and then he shook his head and looked at me. Blue eyes, just blue eyes. But they were hard, and there wasn't an ounce of laughter in them.

The heat in my limbs wasn't slowing and I didn't know what to do with it. I clenched my hands into tight fists. "Maks?" I wasn't really hoping it was him. Not really.

"I am your escort to the desert, cat," he growled and turned his back to me. "Nothing more."

The hyenas cackled again.

Lila launched from Balder to me, a whoosh of air across my face, drying tears I'd not even noticed.

"What do we do?" she whispered as Maks sat with his back to us, his face turned to the south.

My body felt as though it were on fire and my heart was breaking into a million little pieces of glass that cut me from the inside out.

I didn't have it in me to be brave in that moment.

"We run."

Chapter Nine

Merlin stood next to Marsum while the Jinn came back to his own body. "Goddess, that was the most fun I've had in a long time, old man. You were right! Taking Maks away from her will drive her right to me."

"That's not what I suggested doing at all," Merlin said, fighting not to snap at the powerful Jinn. They were on par with one another in strength, which was the only reason Merlin hadn't just barged his way in to rescue Flora. That, and Marsum had a gaggle of Jinn following him.

There was not a day that went by that Merlin didn't regret giving the Jinn the sunstone, the strongest of the gems. It had made the Jinn's leader sadistic in a way he could never have known possible.

"No," Marsum opened his eyes and grinned wide, wild lights flickering in his eyes. "No, you said that I should try and gain her trust. Do you see what I did? I told her the truth about him. He didn't really love her." He snorted and turned to Flora who sat on the floor at his feet. "What say you, priestess of Zeus? Did the cat love my wayward son?"

Flora was dressed in a long white slave gown split up both sides, her hair twisted into intricate braids on either side of her face. Beautiful, if not for the look she was giving Marsum that said she'd like to put his balls in a stew pot.

Electricity danced in her eyes. "Unchain me, and I'll show you exactly what I think."

Merlin shook his head ever so slightly.

She pointed a finger at him. "Don't you shake your head at me! This is all your fault!"

"That's not true—" Merlin said but she cut him off.

"It is! You told Marsum there were lions left in this world! He thought they were all dead! You basically sent Maks right into this and now look at all of us! I thought you'd changed, but you're just the meddling bastard of the Emperor you've always been, hidden in better fitting clothes!" She drew a breath and Marsum waved a hand at her. Her mouth clamped shut; Marsum's magic doing the trick.

If she'd been angry before, it was nothing to the fury that lit up her face when she realized she'd been forced to shut her mouth. The sky above them rolled with an unseen storm. If Marsum pushed her much further, she would break her bonds and then they'd all be in for a shock.

Literally.

Marsum rubbed his fingers over his brow. "Gods,

that could give even me a headache if I let her go on. You don't mind, do you, Merle?" He tipped his head and smiled at Merlin. Merlin did not smile back.

"You are testing my patience, Marsum. I am only here to make sure the Emperor is dealt with. You are his pawns and he is drawing power again through the stones and the blood vines—" Again, he was cut off.

Marsum growled, his features twisting into something less than human. "I am *not* his pawn."

Merlin snorted. "Your Jinn are going missing, are they not? The standing stones are calling them, drawing their lives to feed his. I believe that makes you pawns."

The other Jinn around the room shifted on their feet, a soft shuffling that had Marsum's head whipping around to glare at them. "We are not his pawns. He sleeps, and he will remain sleeping. The cat will bring me the last jewels and I will make sure she is kept very safe." He grinned. "She will not bring down the remainder of the wall."

Merlin wanted to bang his head on the wall. "That is not how this works, Marsum. You are simplifying things far too much. I know you struggle with complex ideas that are above your pay grade. But let me spell it out to you. The Emperor is waking. With or without the wall coming down, he will rise again."

"Then why does it matter if I let her live?" Marsum tipped his head again. "You told me my best bet was to keep the cat alive. To keep her safe from the Emperor."

Merlin pinched the bridge of his nose. "Gods save me from fools. Yes, because she is the only one able to kill him should the need arise." That, and of course, he, Merlin, was playing all sides of the field, working his own manipulations as fast and as cleanly as he dared.

Marsum was right up in his face in a flash, so close that Merlin could smell the grains the Jinn had eaten for breakfast.

"I don't think I like your tone." Marsum breathed the words across him. The Jinn around the edges of the room slid closer. Merlin shot a look to Flora. Her eyes gave him nothing but the anger of a woman he adored.

Damn his life and all it brought. It was time to leave, no matter that he wanted to stay with Flora. That he wanted to be her hero.

He held up a finger. "Pull my finger, would you?"

Marsum looked down at the finger and then back at Merlin. "Have you lost your mind?"

Merlin grinned, grabbed at his own finger, deep red sparks flying from his skin as he snapped his fingers. He closed his eyes, knowing Flora would hate him for this, but he had to go. Zamira needed him, and the world needed her.

Except that as his body dissolved, something took hold of him. He fought the sensation as he writhed and worked to flee to Zam.

He blinked and found himself in a small glass box. An infinity box, just like the one he'd placed his father in. Un-escapable unless someone who knew what they were doing freed you.

He was good and royally screwed and it was his own fault. But the sorrow he felt was not for his own dilemma, but for those who'd followed him into this. For

Flora, Zamira, Maks, and even Lila. They would pay the price for his efforts.

On his hands and knees, he stared out at Marsum as he grinned down at Flora.

"What do you think? Should we kill him now?"

She turned her face away from Marsum to look at him. Merlin put his hands on the glass and lowered his head.

Their voices were muffled, and it didn't matter anyway. Marsum was an idiot when it came to other magics—Merlin was, for all intents and purposes, trapped for eternity. What that meant was he couldn't be killed. There was no threat to his body. Just his mind as he slowly went mad.

What a way to go.

"You see," Marsum strolled in front of him, "the blood vines are not working for the Emperor. I've attached them to my own strength." He grinned. "I am the recipient of all that power as it is absorbed from supernaturals too stupid to live. I am the one who controls them now. I almost had Zamira a few days ago. But . . .she slipped my grasp."

Merlin didn't dare move and give away the horror that rocketed through him. "That will not go well for you when the Emperor rises."

"Which is why he won't." Marsum grinned. "You see? I keep the kitty cat safe. I keep all the jewels, and the Emperor's power, and he will never rise."

Merlin knew it was not so simple. But for now, he wasn't arguing.

He closed his eyes and let his mind take him outside

the box. Not an easy trick, but he could follow the ether to somewhere else. Wherever he was needed.

The light flashed around him and as suddenly as he'd been on his knees in Marsum's throne room, he was sitting next to a tall, slim man with golden hair and eyes.

"Shem?" He stared at the lion shifter he'd thought long dead. Or maybe he was, and Merlin was just seeing a ghost. That was possible.

Shem turned to him. "Well, damn, Merlin. Thought you'd be fucked up shit creek by now."

"I am. Infinity box." He shrugged as if it were nothing. It wasn't and they both knew it.

Shem sighed and then grinned. "Good thing I still *had* the girl's notes."

Merlin's eyes popped wide. "What? You have my half-sister's papers? Wait, you said had."

"I told you I'd look out for her." He frowned. "I loved her, you know. Would have done anything she asked and then some even though I knew what it meant."

Merlin couldn't stop staring at the shifter in front of him. "I don't know what you did with those papers, but you need to get them to Ishtar. She is the only one strong enough to free me now."

Shem shook his head. "No way. I promised I'd give them to Zamira when she was old enough. She has the bloodline to read the glyphs. Not many do, you know."

Merlin's jaw dropped. "You . . . gave them to Zam? What is she going to do with sheets and sheets of spells? She's a shifter, Shem. Not a damn mage!" He could not believe Shem. Then again, part of him said he shouldn't be surprised. Shem's time with the Emperor had given him cause to be not right in the head.

Shem grinned at him and leaned back in his seat. "Well, that's a matter of opinion. You don't do genealogy much, do you? Because our little kitten has a whopping powerful bloodline that even you haven't noticed yet. So . . . I'm not so sure Ishtar is the only one who can free you."

Merlin lost his hold on the real world. His mind whirled at such a rate, he slammed back into the infinity box as if he'd really been gone and not just his mind.

Shem's words swirled until they settled softly on his shoulders, and he let himself really look at Zam . . . through the eyes of a mage. Not the eyes of a manipulator. The dark hair, the green eyes . . . a powerful bloodline . . . "No way," he whispered as the answer came to him. But even as he denied it, he knew exactly what Shem was talking about.

Zamira was far more than she looked to be.

Chapter Ten

The sounds of the early night I would consider normal in the desert were cut off by the howls of the hyenas drawing close.

"We can't outrun them," Maks said, reaching for his bow. I moved so Lila was behind me. Maks rolled his eyes. "My job is to protect you and take you to Marsum."

"Yeah, well, that didn't go so well for Lila earlier, did it?" I snarled.

He gave me his back as he pulled his weapons clear of his gear. Shotgun in one hand, small crossbow in the other.

"Lila, stay on Balder. Do not use your wings at all," I said as I reached for the flail on my back. I paused, grabbed my bag and pulled the sapphire out of its hiding place under the one flap. I handed it up to her. "If they get close, freeze their scrawny asses."

"Damn it," she snarled but took the stone from me and rested it on her neck.

I whistled for Batman and he trotted to me. I positioned the two horses nose to rump, able to protect each other if the hyenas came at them.

The sound of heavy breathing and big padded feet on the sand snapped me around.

Two werehyenas crested the rise above our camp, tongues lolling out of their long snouts, their bodies with dark speckles and darker coats blending into the night so they looked like shadows come to life. There was a pause where they looked us over, looked at each other and snickered, and then they came at us.

There were no words between us as I moved beside Maks. I trusted him more than I trusted the hyenas, and that was about all I had at that point. "Lila, call out to me if more show."

"On it," she yelled back and then there was no more time for speaking. I yanked the flail out, the handle humming under my palm.

Here we go again was all I thought.

The werehyena on the right went for Maks and the one on the left came at me. I swung the flail, spinning the light weapon hard and fast. The werehyena dodged, zipped around me and went straight for the bags of gear.

"Oh, no you don't, you fucker!" I was after him in a flash, shifting into my house cat form before I really registered that what I was doing was stupid.

I raced across the distance between us and leapt up onto his back, digging my claws in for purchase. The werehyena spun, snarling and snapping at me as I dug in hard. I hissed and spit right back at him as he whipped around in a circle, fighting to get to me.

"Get off me!" he roared as he fought to reach me. But I was just beyond the end of his teeth. I curled my claws deep into his flesh until I felt bone under one of them. Oh yeah, I had him now.

"Look out!" Lila screamed, and I turned my head to see a dark body slam into us, bowling us over and over. I hit the ground hard and the bigger animals landed on top, crushing me. I couldn't breathe, couldn't hear anything beyond the sound of my heart pounding in my ears.

I tried to shift back to two legs, but my body wouldn't budge. Under all this weight, my skin and bones refused to do anything for me. Panic laced my mind and heart as I fought to breathe, fought to do anything but lay there under the big body.

It went cold suddenly, gone from the heat of the body to a block of ice, and as quickly as it was cold, the body shattered around me.

I scrambled out, favoring a front leg as I gulped in a breath of air that had never tasted so sweet.

"Get on your horse," Maks said. My eyes found him, a spray of blood across his face and his hands glowing with a pale yellow light. He clenched his fingers and the light went out. "I said, get on your horse."

"She almost died, toad. Give her a chance to catch her breath," Lila snapped.

Maks snorted. "More of those werehyenas are coming. You want to be here for them?"

I did not.

I forced my body to shift even though it hurt like hell when I was injured. There was a chance the shift itself would help the pain. I pulled myself through to my two-legged form with a cry of anguish, my right arm throbbing as though someone had taken a hammer to it.

Maks took a step toward me and then stopped, went and grabbed the horses and saddled them up quickly. I saw his hand flick over the cinch I'd cut and it was whole once more. So much for thinking that would slow him down.

I mounted up and Lila slid down Balder's neck to rest between me and the pommel. "Are you okay?"

"I'm fine." I leaned forward, urging Balder into a gallop. There was no sound of hyenas behind us, which meant we'd killed their two scouts. But with them dead, they would be able to find us easier with the scent of their pack mates on us.

We rode through the night; it wasn't until after the sun rose that we finally stopped. At this rate, it wouldn't take us three weeks to reach the Jinn's Dominion. Then again, that was assuming we didn't get eaten before we got there.

"We'll stay here for a few hours," Maks announced. As if he were in charge.

I arched a brow but kept my mouth shut. For the moment. He had Batman untacked and a fire going so fast I was sure he'd used magic.

"Think you can blur our trail?" I asked him. "Seeing as you're going to be using your Jinn powers out in the open."

"Not one of my talents," he said, and then he turned his back to me. Just like that, done with talking.

"You really are a dick when you're a Jinn," I growled.

Maks never moved from where he sat with his back to me, to us really. I stood there for the longest time staring at him. Because what the fuck was I supposed to do with this twist in my story? It was as if some sadistic author was laughing at me while she turned my life inside out. Knowing my luck, that was probably the reason for this stupidity.

I forced my hands to relax, to soften the death grip I had on my palms. Lila paced on Balder's saddle that sat next to my foot. Her eyes said it all.

There could not have been a worse turn to our journey. We'd lost an ally and gained an enemy in one fell swoop. An enemy we couldn't even kill because we both loved him and knew that Maks was still in there. Somewhere.

This was the first time since the night before that I'd let myself think on the change in our fortune.

My stomach rolled so hard, I had to clench my teeth against the rising tide of acid and bile. I fought that sensation and the prickling that announced an onslaught of tears.

No, I could not break down, not now. There were more things at play here than just losing Maks.

Kiara, Darcy, and the camel's pizzle still waited for someone to save them.

The Emperor had taken an interest in me.

As had Marsum.

I had to finish what I started with Marsum. That was the only solution I could come to. And maybe . . . that would free Maks? I had no idea. The Jinn were a mystery to the rest of the supernatural world in many ways. We knew they were some of the strongest mages alive, that they were mean as one-eyed snakes and liked to hold power, but other than that, what we knew was based on observation in many cases, and not actual facts.

Basically, I had no way of knowing what would help him, or if there was anything I could do at all.

There was a chance Maks was gone forever, and that soured my belly in a twist that made my gorge rise.

"Lila, we need to eat." I forced the words from my mouth. "And we need to rest a little before we move on."

She bobbed her head. "You want me to stay here?"

I shook my head. "I don't want you alone with him."

He didn't so much as flinch as I spoke. Before I thought better of it, I shifted to my cat form. I could hunt the smaller desert animals this way.

Despite her wing injury, Lila launched into the sky. I wanted to yell at her, but I was in no place to make orders. She knew her body best. If she thought she could fly, I wasn't going to stop her. She shadowed me as I ran into the hills, the wind rippling my fur and whipping the tears from my eyes. Damn it, this was what I got for putting my heart out there.

Smash and trash.

I wrinkled my nose as I caught wind of small prey. A covey of birds launched in front of me, wings fluttering as they tried to gain altitude. I leapt and caught one around the middle, my mouth on its neck in a flash. I snapped the bone with a quick crunch, and before we hit the ground, the bird was dead.

Lila swept by with her own catch and we headed back to the campsite. I shifted back to two legs partway there, stumbled and went to a knee to catch myself. Lila swooped by and dropped her bird to me.

A flicker of white caught my eyes from between two hills and I found myself walking toward it. Like a white flag of surrender waving at us. Lila flew ahead of me.

"Whoa, Zam, you aren't going to believe this." She swung back and held herself in midair with only a slight hitch in the beat of her wings. "Seriously, come see."

I picked up my speed and then jerked to a stop as I rounded the edge of the dune. Spread out across the ground were white feathers the length of my body fluttering along. I only knew one bird with feathers that white and that big.

The Ice Witch's Raven. "She must be close. This does not bode well."

"Yeah, no shit. Then again, she did bring you the flail back," Lila said. I nodded and backed away.

"If the Raven is hunting, then we need to keep moving. Giving me the flail back means nothing as far as I'm concerned."

I turned and headed the way we'd come. I couldn't even bring myself to care that much about the Raven or the Ice Witch. She wasn't the power she'd been without her jewel, and the Raven had returned my flail to me as Lila said, so . . . they weren't out to get us. That being said, I wasn't going to just sit by and hang out in their territory if I didn't have to. Just because we'd escaped them once didn't mean we could do it again.

"Let's hope the Raven likes to eat werehyenas," I said. Lila bobbed her head in agreement.

Still clear of the camp, I stopped, moving on autopilot as I gutted the birds and threw the warm innards to Lila. Even with the situation as it was, she hummed happily as she gulped her dinner down.

Her belly swelled with the amount of guts she slurped back and she ended up walking back with me the last distance, waddling side to side. Much as this was a total clusterfuck with Maks, Lila, just as she was, made me smile.

It was good to have a friend I could depend on.

As soon as that thought crossed my mind, I banished it. Because I didn't want to jinx myself.

I'd lost enough friends in the last few years to know that nothing was forever.

Firelight flickered in front of me as I slid down the last dune to the camp. Maks faced the fire and was eating something off a plate. Dried jerky, by the look of it.

I tossed both birds into the fire. The smell of burning feathers cut through the air with a sharp tang. "You can have one if you want."

"I don't," he said.

Lila bumped into my leg and I looked down at her. She had the edge of my pack and had opened it to show me something.

The top of a bottle peeked out at me. Țuică.

She shrugged as if to say it couldn't hurt. She had a

point. How much worse could it be? At least if I were buzzed, the pain might not be so sharp.

I grabbed the bottle and sat, poured Lila a cup, and then sat back against one of the saddles and stared into the flames.

"You think you are safe enough with me to get drunk?" Maks asked, his voice a deadly soft reverberation.

I shrugged and found that mean streak that resided somewhere along the edge of my spine. "You're controlled by Marsum, and he wants me alive. Which means your job is to keep me alive, as evidenced by the fight back there. You better keep me alive or you'll face your daddy's wrath." I tipped the bottle at him in a mock salute and then put the opening to my lips and chugged back a swig.

The sweet, far-too-strong plum liquor burned a pleasant trail all the way to my toes. Empty stomach, right, that was something to remember when drinking.

I closed my eyes and held onto the bottle. I wasn't afraid of Maks hurting me. Him hurting Lila, yes, I was concerned about that. She snuggled against my side and put her head on my thigh, her breathing coming in slow, long draws. Healing her wing with the hacka paste would still draw on her energy, and sleep and food were the best things for her.

Maks broke the silence, surprising me. "Why would I . . . care about you at all?"

I opened my eyes and looked across the fire at him. The buzz of the liquor wasn't doing what I wanted. I wasn't getting numb at all.

"Because I'm fucking amazing." I grinned, but it was hard to smile because my lips wobbled. "Because you're like me, outcast and looking for a place in the world. Because . . . I have a great ass."

I raised the bottle again, then leaned forward and dragged one of the birds out of the fire by a foot. I felt the heat but didn't care as I bit into the flesh. Not quite cooked. What did it matter what he thought of me?

It didn't.

I ate my bird and that helped to settle my stomach and the buzzing of the țuică in my veins. I should have made a sleep schedule to wake Lila and watch for a bit, but somewhere between my last two chugs of țuică, I finally stopped caring about everything.

Hallelujah.

Not what I'd call my finest moments, but there you go. I was as broken as the rest of the world and handled it about as well when the chips were down. At some point, I managed to cap the bottle and stuff it back in my bag and then curled around Lila, my head on the ground, my face turned to the fire. I couldn't stop the shivering, though; the daytime temperature was cold and the only spot of warmth was Lila and the fire. My back twitched and spasmed but I didn't have it in me to get up and find a blanket.

Distantly, I heard Maks moving around the fire, and then something settled over me and I remembered nothing else.

* * *

THE AFTERNOON CAME AROUND with a dull rumble of a distant storm. I groaned and pulled the blanket up over my head. "Lila, tell the storm to go away." I whispered the words.

She mimicked my noises of discomfort as she shifted beside me. "Oh, my head. I drank too much."

I managed to push to a sitting position. My hair was wild, tangled and sticking out in every direction.

The fire was gone, the bird I'd thrown in for Maks was gone, and he sat across from me, as still as if he'd never moved.

The blanket slid to my waist, pooling in my lap and over Lila.

I frowned, my fingers on it. I didn't remember picking up a blanket, but then again, the hours between dawn and now were somewhat fuzzy, to be fair.

Maks said nothing to me as he stood and went to Batman. The horse shied from him, his ears flicking back and his eyes rolling.

I just watched, saying nothing as Maks stopped and held out a hand. Batman shook his head as if he knew something was off with his friend. The horses were always the first to see someone for who they really were.

Maks spoke softly to the horse. Batman slowly approached and then shoved his nose in Maks's chest, shoving him hard. A reprimand.

Lila crawled partway up my leg and I reached down for her. "No flying today," I said.

"Agreed. Even if not for my wing, my head is throbbing," she whispered, her eyes locked on the scene in front of us, just as mine were.

Maks made his way around Batman, saddling his horse.

I wrapped my blanket and stuffed it into my bag, then went to Balder. I fed him, gave him a quick brush, and then tacked him up. Every movement soothing to my battered emotions because it kept my mind busy and away from the previous day's events.

We mounted and Maks led the way now.

I held Balder back, farther and farther, until there was a good forty feet between us and Maks. He looked back but didn't drop to ride with me. Lila curled around my neck, half hidden in the hood of my cloak.

"What are we going to do?"

"Question of the day," I muttered. "I'm not sure, but I'm trying to figure it out."

"You think Marsum really has a hold on him?"

I rested my hands on the pommel of the saddle, thinking. "Yes, but Maks is still in there too. I'm sure of it. He put a blanket over us, after we were out."

"He did?" she whispered again, as though she thought he might be able to hear us. Hell if I knew, he might be able to.

I nodded. "Yeah, he did. That's Maks. Not the Jinn Marsum has a hold on."

She flicked her tail back and forth, like an irritated cat. "Then we have to find a way to fix this. We can't lose him. The others . . . I know they are important, but isn't Maks . . . more important?"

To me, yes, he was more important. But . . . he also

wasn't in mortal danger, and I was the alpha of the pride, which meant I was stuck with the shitty fucking choices like the one in front of me.

"Yes, he's the most important to me, Lila. You know that."

"But he can't come first. Can he?"

I shook my head. "No. Which means we need to lose him somewhere along here. He'll take us straight to Marsum and hand us over. We have to find a way to outrun him and his magic without hurting him."

"Just how in the world are we going to do that? I know Balder can outrun Batman, but his magic could catch us easily if he's any sort of a Jinn. And if we make a break for it and screw it up, he'll be watching us close from here on out."

"Yeah, I know. If I thought it wouldn't hurt you, I'd suggest sizing you up again and having you carry me and Balder, but I don't want to chance you getting trapped," I said. She'd used my necklace that for years had held my own curse back, and when she'd put it on, she'd no longer been the tiny dragon that could rest on my shoulder. Her body had grown, and with it, she'd fought for her place in the Dragon's Ground as I'd fought to save my brother.

We'd both missed our goals, but it had been a glorious thing to see her spread her wings and be who she was always meant to be, if only for a little while.

The cost had been high, though, and the necklace had hurt her in the end. I still had it, tucked in my pouch I carried tied to my belt.

She shivered. "What I wouldn't give to have made

friends with that white Raven of the Ice Witch's. She's big enough to carry a dragon if she wants to. Full sized even."

My eyes popped wide as a rush of possibilities cut through me. "Wait . . . do we know if they went south? Do we know where they went?"

"Who went south?" She turned her head to look up at me. "What are you talking about?"

I closed my eyes, thinking back to when the white Raven had returned the flail to me. What the hell had she said? That the Ice Witch wanted to see me succeed or something like that? Damn it, my țuică-fuzzed brain didn't want to give up the memory easily.

"Zam, what are you thinking?" Lila dug her claws into the edge of my shoulders. "Talk to me."

I opened my eyes. "I think we might be able to get that ride, just a matter of finding the Ice Witch."

Lila's mouth gaped open and I didn't blame her. The Ice Witch had tried to kill us all on multiple occasions.

But she had a big bird, and that big bird could get us out of Maks's way. And if those feathers meant anything, the Raven and her witch were close.

The trick would be finding the bird, and finding the Witch, and making them see that it was a good thing to help us.

I almost smiled, imagining how that scene would go. Almost.

Chapter Eleven

Lila, Balder, and I slowly dropped farther back from Maks. Step by step, we increased the distance. The Caspian Sea was still far to our left, and the rolling hills and flat plateaus around us were bleak and held no cover.

As of yet, the werehyenas had made no further push to catch us.

But even with all that, we didn't make a break for it. Not yet.

When Maks stopped for the night, we caught up and I stripped Balder of his gear, rubbed him down and fed him. Lila and I brought down a couple more birds and repeated the same meal and situation as the night before. Minus the țuică.

After we'd eaten, I curled by the fire, Lila tucked in by my belly and my back to my saddle.

Once more a blanket was laid on me by morning,

only this time I knew it was Maks. I'd still been awake when he'd laid it over me. And I'd thought he whispered something to me under his breath but so quietly that even my ears, as good as they were, didn't pick it up. But my name was in there, along with a heavy dose of pain.

The next day, I got up early and did everything with little thought process. Again, Maks led the way and I held Balder back.

"You ready, Lila?" I asked. "Don't range too far. If you find the Raven, don't engage. Come back."

She bobbed her head. "I'll be back by dinner." With nothing else to say, she launched into the air, going high enough that a bank of cloud covered her. I kept my hood up and when Maks looked back, I knew what he'd see—my head down, and hopefully he'd think Lila was tucked away inside it as she so often was.

This could take days, even weeks to find the Raven and the Witch. But we had the time. The desert was weeks away.

Goddess of the desert, don't let it take weeks to find the Witch and her bird.

The day seemed to crawl, and with each step of Balder's feet, I wanted nothing more than to ask him to run, to bolt forward and go for a gallop that would leave this whole mess in the desert sands where it belonged.

A pool of water between the hills appeared ahead of us, and Maks stopped for a drink for him and Batman. Shit.

He twisted in his saddle, waiting for me to catch up. If I held back he'd know something was up. I just had to keep my hood up and hope he didn't notice Lila was missing.

I urged Balder forward and he broke into a trot, happy to be moving a little faster.

The water that burbled up out of the rocks was clear and I could smell the different minerals in it. Good, clean water was a rarity around here. I slid off Balder's far side, away from Maks, took my water canteens and refilled all three. Balder dropped his head and took a deep drink, slurping the water back until his belly was full. He and Batman were working horses. They knew to drink deep when they could.

"Where's the dragon?" Maks growled.

"She went for a flight, to test the wing you shot," I snapped. I looked at him over Balder's back, glaring hard for good measure.

He didn't glare back at me, but he was obviously weighing my words. I could see it in his face. Shit, that was not good. He was suspicious already.

"She'd better be back soon."

"Or what?" I was around Balder in a flash. "You think you're going to threaten her again? Hurt her again? You'd better believe you've got to come through me first, *Jinn*." We were nose to nose, and each word I punctuated with several fingers jammed into his chest. He grabbed my hand and yanked it above my head.

"There is no one to help you here, cat."

"My name," I growled, "is Zamira."

And then for no particular reason, I swear I had no plans to do this, I kissed him.

He grunted and I wrapped my free hand around his

neck and held him to me. His whole body stiffened and then the hand that held my jabbing fingers wove with mine. He kissed me back, and a tremor started through him that reverberated through my own.

He pulled back, his forehead against mine. "Run, Zam. You have to get away from me. Now. I might only have a few minutes."

My heart beat wildly with hope and love and a weird rush of relief. "No, you're still here. I'm not giving up on you."

"He has me too tightly bound. He knows how much you mean to me." He rubbed his face against mine. "I'm fighting him. I swear it, but I can't . . . I can't hold him off." Those pretty blue eyes of his locked with mine. "I love you, Zam, more than I thought possible. Tell Lila I'm sorry. I didn't want to shoot her. I'm . . ." His body shivered and I kissed him again, and the shivering softened. We were wrapped around each other and I was terrified. Because it felt like a goodbye.

He kissed me hard, his arms wrapped around me, and then he pushed me away, half shoving me up onto Balder. "Go. Run, Zam. I'll hold back as long as I can."

I bit my lower lip, and I knew he was right. This was the chance I needed. But I couldn't stop looking at him.

I couldn't stop loving him.

He closed his eyes and lowered his head. "Please, don't look at me like that. I always knew this was a chance, that he could take me again. You . . . showed me what life could be like outside this prison." He still didn't lift his eyes. "Please, I don't want to hurt you or Lila. I love you both, and . . ."

The howl of a hyena behind us cut him off.

I didn't hear the rest of what he had to say. I turned Balder and give a low hiss, sending him from a stand into a flat-out gallop. I couldn't help myself. I looked back.

Maks's head was up now and his eyes followed us. I stared until I couldn't see him anymore. The distance or the tears, I'm not sure which blinded me first. I rode hard to the south, keeping Balder at a pace I knew Batman couldn't match. But it wouldn't buy me enough time. Time. Yes, but not enough. And then there was Lila.

Fuckity camel farts. I needed to find Lila.

The werehyenas were silent and that slowed me. They'd found Maks. What if . . . what if they'd killed him?

It took all my will power not to spin Balder around. Sobbing, I screamed for Lila.

"LILA!" If she'd gone very far, we were screwed. Shouting for her into the wind was somewhat ridiculous, but then again . . . what else did I have? Every five minutes, I hollered for her again, on the off chance she'd clue in and come find us. Damn it.

All that noise and no werehyenas. Had Maks killed them all, had he survived, was he hurt? The questions rolled through me in a nauseating loop.

Balder and I galloped for a solid hour, and while he slowed as he fatigued, it wasn't by much. He was built for this kind of travel and he thrived on the flat distance running we were doing. I wished I could give him a burst of energy, like the Jinn did for their mounts to keep them going.

I shivered as a warm curl of energy seemed to pool in my belly and spread outward, down my arms and into my hands. This new sensation had me moving automatically. I needed Balder to be able to outrun Batman if Maks gave him a boost of energy . . . desperately needed him to be able to keep going. I placed my hand against his neck and the warm energy zinged through my fingers. He gave a grunt as if I'd shocked him.

His body surged below me.

Renewed, refreshed . . . "Holy baby goddess, what was that?"

He ran as though he were fresh, as though he'd not already been galloping as fast as he could for the last hour.

Which was great. Except for Lila. She was fast, but even she couldn't keep up with Balder at top speed.

I had to find her. I couldn't just keep running like this or I'd lose her, and I couldn't do that again.

I eased Balder back, and he reluctantly slowed. Of course, he wanted to keep running now that he was powered back up.

"LILA!" I shouted for her, already knowing that it was probably wasted breath. I frowned, frustrated beyond belief. Maks had given us the break we needed and we'd screwed it up by being proactive in our own escape. The irony was not lost on me.

"ARG!" I yelled to the sky. "Motherfucking Murphy's Law. You fucking suck!"

While that did nothing more than make me feel a little better, I'd take it.

If Lila had been one of the lions in my pride I could have found her. The thought rippled through me. I'd made Lila one of my seconds. Which meant she was part of my pride, the same as I'd done to Maks. Only they were tied to me by the heart, rather than bloodlines and species. I swallowed hard. I didn't have time to get off and sit on the ground for two hours to find Lila's threads.

I needed to find her now.

I closed my eyes and let Balder keep up a quick trot. Lila was all air and fire, even though she wasn't a fire-breathing dragon, she was fire. Maks was like me, earth and fire. The thoughts fumbled through me and I was not even sure where they came from. I only knew they were true. The lions were of the earth . . . that was why I had to find them by touching the ground.

Lila . . . air, fire . . . I peeled off a glove and held it palm up. Part of my brain told me I was being fucking ridiculous. The other part told that half to shut up and let it do its job.

The air was warm on my hand, dry and soft, the breeze coming from the south and meeting the wind that drove at my back from the north. The two together wrapped around my fingers, tingling and dancing between them.

"Come on, Lila, show me where you are." I spoke out loud, and Balder snorted his agreement. There was a tug on my fingertips and I opened my eyes. Woven around my fingers was a bright silver and purple strand, the same jeweled tones as Lila's eyes. It tugged me to the west and I didn't hesitate.

We'd intersect and then head south. The good thing about this hard ground was that maybe Maks wouldn't see my direction change.

I let Balder gallop as fast as he wanted as I kept an eye on both the footing and Lila's threads. An hour passed with no sign of her other than the silver and purple lines. She wasn't injured. I could tell that much. But . . . where was she? She shouldn't have flown that far away.

The plan had been for her to check quadrants. To the west first, and then slowly moving south. I doubted the Ice Witch would have wanted to be all that close to her sister, Ishtar. I mean, considering they were trying to kill each other, that seemed logical.

West, west, west. I rode the rest of the day and finally had to slow Balder as night fell. Riding in the dark was dumb, especially on a night with no moon, and on ground that was rough and unfamiliar.

Lila's thread still pulsed happily. At least she was not hurt. Not until I'd stopped for the night did I realize something integral about the threads that led me to Lila.

"You haven't moved all day." I sucked in a sharp breath. "Fuck, what happened?"

A single bark of a werehyena sent my heart rate up. Shit eating dogs were still coming. Even if Lila's position hadn't changed, I would have to keep moving.

Forget not riding in the dark. I remounted and slowly followed Lila's threads. There would be no stopping now, even if I had to ride all night.

Lila was not moving, which led me to believe one of two things. Either she'd run into trouble and had to hide . . . or worse . . . the Ice Witch and her Raven had her.

Don't ask me why, but I had a sinking feeling it would be option number two.

Chapter Twelve

Balder and I rode through the night, carefully, slowly, with nothing more than Lila's threads to guide me and the werehyenas behind us to drive our feet. Exhaustion tore at me, but fear for her kept me moving and my eyes open.

Whatever the extra juice was I'd shot into Balder had faded and he yawned repeatedly as we walked through the last hours of the night and into the morning. The only good thing I could think was that Maks would have stopped for the night—assuming he was alive—and I'd gained a lot of ground on him.

But at what cost? It wasn't like I was able to push hard through the next few days, and Balder surely wouldn't be able to after going hard for nearly twenty-four hours.

"Fuck!" I yelled the word to wake myself up as much as to express my displeasure at the circumstances I was looking at. Fuck indeed.

Ahead of us, a big hill blocked our path. Lila's threads hummed right on over it. I slid from Balder's back—not for the first time during the night—and held onto his saddle as we walked up the slope together.

He dug in hard and half pulled me up, but the movement woke me some. Not as much as the sight that greeted me at the top of the hill, though.

We stumbled to a stop and I just stared at what lay in front of me. I couldn't wrap my brain around it. I couldn't make myself believe that I wasn't dreaming. The Ice Witch's castle stood in front of me. A river around it. A forest and . . . snow. There was freaking snow in the desert.

My jaw dropped. I'll admit it. Dropped, and I sucked in a breath that tasted of ice and snow and . . . "What the ever living fuck is going on?" I yelled the words. Yelled them because I suspected the Ice Witch was watching. I could almost feel her eyes on me. "Seriously? Is this your idea of a joke?"

There was a deep caw from the castle turrets and a wingspan that would put any dragon to shame stretched out as the Raven rose into the air. I didn't know if I should mount or stay on the ground.

I mounted. I wasn't about to let Balder take the brunt of anything bad happening if I could help it.

I didn't ride down to greet the Raven. Balder danced under me. He was no fool. He knew a predator when he saw one and . . . the Raven was a predator. She had eaten young dragons in the past.

Distantly I wondered if she would know who was stealing the dragon younglings. The dragons thought it was the Jinn, which was likely, but I doubted they kept the dragons for themselves. Another time, I reminded myself. One problem at a time.

Speaking of . . . behind us rose a cacophony of laughing howls. I twisted in the saddle to see four were-hyenas racing toward us, jaws open. There was no way I'd be killing all four.

"Any time, big bird!" I yelled at the Raven.

The whoosh of the huge feathered wings rushed through the air as she closed in and I held up one hand in greeting. Best I could do at that point.

She cawed and swooped down, her talons outstretched. Balder tried to bolt and I held him fast with my hands and my legs. "Hang on, my friend. It'll be just like riding with the dragon Trick again."

He let out a long snort and pawed at the ground with one hoof. Yeah, I wasn't so sure either.

Goddess, let me be right about this. It was either go with the Raven or face the werehyenas. I was betting on the bird as our safest route, which was a crazy fucking thing.

I held my breath as the massive talons wrapped around us with room to spare. My chest burned as I clung to the air and my hand went to the handle of the flail. Just in case.

But the Raven didn't squash us or tear us apart. She only scooped us up and rose into the air. Balder grunted and flicked his head up and down in obvious irritation, but he didn't thrash about. His ears swiveled and beneath me I felt his legs moving as if he were running. Maybe he was getting used to the idea of flying. After all, this was not his first flight with an oversized predator.

I could only hope it would be the last. I didn't like trusting these big winged creatures—bird or dragon—not to drop us for shits and giggles.

The werehyenas screeched their displeasure as we were lifted out of range. I twisted around and stuck my tongue out at them. "Neener neener, stupid mutts!"

The Raven banked to the right and swung toward the castle. The snow below us sent cold gusts of air up around my face, whipping my hood back and tangling my hair.

The distance between the hilltop and the castle was short, and in only a few minutes, we were coming in for a landing. The Raven brought us to the center court-yard, her wings sending up flurries of snow and bits of dirt as she neared the paved stones.

Balder's hooves just touched the ground and she opened her talons and let us go. He stumbled only a step or two and then he was jigging away from the big bird, his tail flicking side to side as he danced. He wasn't the only one glad to be back on solid ground. I released a long-held breath and some of the tension left me. Until I looked to my right.

The Raven landed next to us, her wings tucking back sharply against her body. She was easily as big as some of the largest dragons I'd seen, if put together differently. Her dark beak was twelve feet or better in length with a wicked sharp curving point at the end. Her black eyes were hard to read, and that spiked my heart rate up yet again.

"Thanks?" I said. "For not dropping us. And taking us away from the mutts back there."

"My mistress would speak with you. Now that she is free of the jewel, her mind is more her own." The Raven pointed with her beak at a narrow doorway set into the castle at the far side of the courtyard. The wooden door had large hinges and a circular iron handle, and as far as I could see, it was the only door leading out of the courtyard.

Backed into a corner, I had no other choice but to go through that door.

"Talk or kill?" I asked.

"If she wanted you dead, I would have dropped you over the snow field and pecked your bones clean of flesh myself," she said with only a slight tremor of excitement in her voice. "She commanded that I should not do that."

Her eyes widened and I thought for just a second I could see my broken body in them, blood everywhere. She blinked and the image was gone.

"You are one creepy-ass motherfucker, you know that, right? But you could eat those werehyenas. If you're hungry, that is." I pressed my leg against Balder, scooting him sideways. I realized that if the Raven launched at us, we wouldn't be able to avoid her, but I couldn't help but put distance between us and a creature that wanted to peck our bones clean.

Color me cautious if you want. I liked being on this side of the dirt and not in a raven's belly. A thought caught me off guard. I was not the only one in danger of being pecked to death.

"I'm being tracked by a Jinn," I said. "But I don't want him dead. He's not himself, but if he comes, let him come."

Her eyes narrowed and her head swept toward me. "I obey the Witch, not you. I will kill whoever else I like, whether it is a hyena or a Jinn."

My hand shot to the flail and I pulled it free before she could get too close. She paused. "You would use that weapon on me?"

"If you force me to. Don't kill the Jinn. That's all I ask, not command."

"That weapon would devour you if it could." She cawed a laugh that hurt my ears and made Balder whinny and dance even farther away.

I kept him steady with my legs. It was the best I could do. "The flail and I have come to a working relationship. It doesn't suck the life out of me, and I let it feed on whatever I'm battling."

The Raven hopped backward, horror written clearly in her eyes. "Fuck my feathers, are you serious? That is not possible."

My eyebrows shot up. "Yeah. But back to my Jinn tracker, can you not kill him, please?"

She ruffled her feathers and scooted a few more steps back.

"He won't find you while you are in this place. You could only find us because of your connection to your dragon," she said. "Rest your horse." She tipped her head at a set of stables. A troop of little gnomes scurried out, one right after the other. About four feet in height, they were chubby creatures with gentle faces and some form of beard on each, in a variety of colors. As they approached, they made soft clicking sounds that had Balder lowering to them so he could nuzzle their heads.

Ice goblins had been the Ice Witch's minions before when she'd been the Ice Witch in truth. With the jewel gone from her, and out of the goblins' lives, had they become the more helpful cousins to the goblins?

What did that say about the Ice Witch? Was it possible she wasn't the psycho I'd met before? I wanted to believe that, especially since she'd helped me by returning the flail. I wanted to believe it more because she had Lila with her, and I was afraid for my friend's life if the Ice Witch turned out to be fooling us.

The troop of gnomes hurried forward. As they drew close they bowed repeatedly, whispering something under their breath.

"Hail the Wall Breaker."

I grimaced and slid off Balder's back. They reached for his reins and he calmly followed them toward the stables, ruffling his lips through their hair and beards.

"The Witch waits for you," the Raven said.

I stared up at her. "Do you have a name?"

"You may call me Raven. I will not give you my name. It is enough that the Witch has it." The white feathers ruffled down her back in a shiver.

So that was how she'd been captured, by her name. Names had power in our world, which was why so many of the supes didn't give their real name. Unlike me, who had no reason to hide behind a moniker.

"Raven, then. You caught Lila looking for you?" I asked.

She bobbed her head. "I did. She begged to go back for you, but the Witch wants you here for a time. And I must obey her." A flash of irritation snapped through her eyes. The emotion was there and gone so fast that I might have thought I was seeing things, only I knew I wasn't.

I felt bad for the big bird because I knew what it was to be trapped, to be told you couldn't fly free. "I'm sorry for that. I know what it is to be . . . held down."

She snorted. "Doubtful. You have no idea what you ride into, reckless one. You think you know, but you don't . . ." She lowered her head until her beak was only a few feet from me. "The Witch is not who you think she is. She is not who she was and she is not who she will be, so take what she says with caution." She shivered again and pulled back. "I can say no more."

"Why would you even say that much?" I frowned up at her. "Why help me at all outside of what you are commanded to do?"

"I knew someone like you once. I did not help her and I regret it." She turned her head away and her wings spread as she pushed off the stones. Into the air, she rose with three effortless flaps that took her to the edge of the castle wall where she sat facing outward. Guarding her mistress again.

There was nothing I could do for the Raven. I kept telling myself that while I wondered if I could convince the Witch to let her bird go. I turned and strode toward the door in front of me. No time like the present to say hello to an old friend and find out just what the fuck was going on.

The thick iron circle was ice cold against my hand, and heavier than I'd anticipated. I had to use both hands to pull the door open. The iron hinges creaked horribly as I pulled. They needed to be oiled, and badly. Stupid thoughts, I know, but I was avoiding thinking about all the possibilities that waited for me on the other side. A nice witch. A bad witch. A dead friend. A live friend.

The interior smelled of ice—yes, ice has a smell—and pine tar. Sconces set in the walls lit up as I took a step, leading me on a pathway deeper into the castle. The flames burst into life as I drew close and went out as I passed. I made myself stop and back up, but the flames didn't light again behind me.

Forward it was then. I lengthened my stride. The faster I found Lila and dealt with the Witch, the better. So far, her actions spoke of someone trying to help, but I was no fool. I'd been duped more than once by friends and lovers to know that rarely were people out to help you. More like out to help themselves. I put a hand on the stone, not because I was losing my balance but to see if it was real. I still struggled with the idea of snow and a castle in the middle of the desert.

My hand came away warm, not cold. I frowned and stared hard at the stone. "What are you really?"

For just a second, I thought I saw the red rock of the desert cut to mimic the stone, and then it was gone, and the black and gray stone was back to what the original castle had been.

The sconces twisted to the right and then lit up a winding stairwell.

"Shitty fucking place to fight," I muttered under my breath. I could all too easily see someone come down from above, forcing me into a fight in the narrow space. Bad, bad juju rolled through me. I'd fought the Ice Witch before to a standstill, but I'd not killed her. And part of me thought I should have. Then again, the flail would not have been returned to me if I'd killed her, and the weapon had saved me more than once.

I counted the steps as I went up, gauging how high I was. The stairs were at least four flights and in my head, I tried to map out where I was based on my brief look at the castle from above. There had been a room at the top of a huge turret. That had to be where I was going.

I put a hand to the kukri on my right thigh, the handle ready for a quick pull and slash. I took the last corner carefully, peering around to see an open door at the top, my eyes just above floor level. The door was oversized in width and height, and it was wide open.

The room beyond it—at least what I could see—was draped in fabrics, and the sound of a fire crackled merrily. A waft of heat blew out to me, the smell of wood smoke tickling my nose.

Voices floated to me as if they had suddenly come to life. That was interesting, since I'd not heard them sooner. With my ears, if they'd been talking I should have heard them halfway down the stairwell even if I'd not been able to decipher what exactly they were saying.

"Lila, you are sure you do not have a curse laid on you?" The voice reminded me of the Ish I'd known as a child. Soft. Kind. Worried about my well-being. Of course, it wasn't her. It was her sister. But they were close enough in tone that my defenses slid a little.

"My grandmother never said it was a curse. She said it was something to overcome. A challenge," Lila answered. "Do you think the Raven will have found Zam yet? I'm worried about her. Maks is not himself. I should go and find her."

Part of me thought I should wait and see what the Witch said in response, but I didn't want Lila to worry. I made my way up the last few steps. "I'm here, Lila."

She gasped as I took the last step and a blur of blue and silver slammed into my chest. I reached out to catch my balance on the wall before we both tumbled down the many flights of stairs I'd just come up.

I hugged her with my other hand. "You're okay?"

"Yes. Maggi has been very kind. Surprisingly enough." Lila pulled back from me, her eyes worried despite her words. I knew how she felt. Trusting someone who'd tried to kill you in the past was not a natural thing.

I made myself take the next few steps into the lair of the Ice Witch. "So, Maggi is your name then?"

"It is the name my mother gave me, yes." Maggi stood and clasped her hands in front of her body. Slim, tall, long white hair, pale blue eyes as piercing as any hawk's, but there was not fury in them as there was the first time I'd met her. Neither was there any blood lust. She was just the sister of Ish now, and had no vileness attached to her.

Of course, I couldn't let it ride at that.

"How is it that you are so different now? Why are

you helping me? Why would you return the flail?" I asked, not letting go of Lila.

Maggi sighed. "You have not noticed that the jewels bring with them not only power, but madness too? They were never meant to be held by anyone. My sister . . . she stole them a millennium ago from the very waters of creation and used them to rise to power."

"You mean Ishtar then, don't you?" I needed to be sure. One hundred percent that we were talking about the same person.

I found myself in the room, drawn to the woman in front of me. She had answers to questions I'd asked for years.

"Yes, I mean Ishtar. She is ancient, as am I, I suppose." A smile twisted her lips. "The jewels allowed her to imbue a pantheon of gods and goddesses. She helped to create many of the supes as you know them, but the jewels . . . they broke her mind, even as strong as she was. Too much power took her mind to a dark place, a place of chaos. That kind of power will always corrupt." She sighed and sunk into her chair.

"Wait, are you actually going to tell me what the fuck is going on with all this?" I waved a hand through the air as if to encompass the world. "No tricks like Merlin? No manipulations like Ishtar? No games like the Emperor?" I still struggled to believe Ish was Ishtar, that she was *that* one, the desert goddess we'd feared and loved in equal parts. A consort to the Emperor. A demon goddess whose fury could be felt even thousands of miles from her.

Maggi gave me a weary smile. "As much as I am able

to, yes. I will tell you what I know. There are parts that are hidden even from me. But you are the Wall Breaker, and you have a heavy journey ahead of you. That is why I'm helping you. I . . . there was much wrong I did as the Ice Witch. Perhaps this is something I can do to make amends."

Like killing three of the members of my pride. Like trying to kill the rest of us. But I kept those thoughts to myself.

"Oh, well that's just fucking fabulous, isn't it?" I grumbled as I lowered to the floor, choosing to ignore the part about her amends. I didn't know what to do with it. I needed whatever help I could get, even if it was from someone who had at one point been an enemy.

My legs were tired, and I was exhausted from the amount of time Balder and I had been running. I wanted nothing more than to shut my eyes, but the idea that I might actually, *finally*, get some answers kept them open. "Let's get this show on the road then. I'm on a time crunch."

Magi's eyes swept over me. "You should sleep."

I shook my head. "No. Tell me what you need to tell me and we'll get the fuck out of here."

She sighed and bowed her head. "Reckless as always." With her fingers to her lips, she nodded, more to herself than me, I think. "You can rest your body. Sleep before you fall over, and I can dream walk with you both. It is a talent I have. That will speed up your stay. If it is agreeable to you?"

I wasn't sure if it was agreeable. Especially after my

last two jaunts into dreamland. "You would be inside my head?"

"In a manner of speaking." Maggi nodded.

"How can you possibly do that?" Lila asked. "Linking dreams is not an easy thing between two minds, never mind three."

Maggi smiled at Lila. "Did you not wonder how Zamira found you? She followed the threads of your life. You are part of her family as far as she is concerned, and that simple truth allowed her to do the impossible. You two are bound together as tightly as any siblings I have ever seen. Perhaps even more so." A twist of pain slid over her face and I wondered if she and Ishtar had been close at one point. "Close your eyes to the world, and I will bring your minds together, then I will join you there in the dream world."

I shouldn't have trusted her. I knew that in the logical part of my brain, but my instincts on people were generally spot on and they were saying she'd changed. She was not the same woman I'd battled before. Maggi was no longer the power-mad Ice Witch. She was just Magi, a witch who had strength and knowledge that could ultimately help us. I hoped.

Lila leapt up, flew to a pile of cushions near Maggi and brought one back for me. The velvet material was a deep gold like the desert sands. I dropped my head onto it, lying flat on my back. A sigh slid out of me as my eyes closed. This was not what I would call the most comfortable sleeping arrangement, but I'd had worse. Hell, I'd slept through ice storms, so this was damn near tropical.

Lila circled on my chest, then settled down, laying so that the tip of her nose touched my chin. I put a hand over her body and let sleep take me, trusting we were making the right decision. Warmth whispered through my veins, not unlike the warmth of the țuică.

There was no discernible moment between wake and sleep. I was just . . . there, inside a dream that looked a great deal like the room where I'd gone to sleep in, including me flat on the floor, Lila on my chest, a velvet pillow under my head.

I sat up, Lila slid off me and rolled to her feet. "Is that it, are we there?"

I looked around us. "I think so."

Maggi sat in her same chair with her eyes at half-mast as if she were dozing. "You are both fully here. That is interesting. Most don't dream so deeply into this world."

"This is another *world*?" I couldn't help the question.

She gave a single nod. "It is. And in many cases, what happens here is reflected in the real world. So, you must be careful if you find yourself here. Death is final in these dreams, and not a game."

"Awesome," I muttered. "One more place that can kill me."

She smiled. "I doubt it will ever come to that. But be wary."

Lila trotted in a circle. "I feel awake. Are you sure we are not awake?"

"Yes, you are bound to Zamira, and she is here fully, so you are as well." Maggi looked at me again. "But that is not why you are here. You want to understand what is happening. Why all this is coming at you, all at once."

I didn't dare hope for that much. "And why you're helping me. You really haven't answered that one yet either."

She smiled, but the smile slipped as she settled into speaking. She waved her hand in front of her and the wooden floorboards turned to sand and a miniature Oasis I knew all too well. The water sparkled a clear blue, the trees around it were thick with foliage, but none of that held my eyes. The sand was covered in red spots and golden-furred, unmoving bodies. My throat clenched at the sight of one of my worst memories.

"This is where the world turned on its head, Zam, not only for you, but for all of us. The Jinn and Marsum, in particular, believed he could become the super power the Emperor had been for so long. You see, even asleep, the Emperor still draws on the Jinn. He uses their power to keep from being put too deeply into stasis. That is how he kept his son from killing him. He knows his time of escape is coming, and he is banking on not being weak when he emerges."

I stared at the bodies of my family as the memory, the smells, the sounds, rolled through me as if I stood there again. "What has that got to do with my family?"

Her eyes lowered as she stared at the water of the Oasis. "Because the lions held the Jinn in check. Your mother held the Jinn in check. She taught the Bright Lions to fight in a way that allowed them to battle with the Jinn on a more even field. She led them into battle, not your father." She swirled her hand and the scene changed to one I didn't know. This one was frozen too, a still picture cut out of time.

A woman with black hair and green eyes fought from the back of a huge chestnut horse with a flail I knew all too well in her hands as she clashed with a Jinn. Her eyes were narrowed and mouth open in a scream of what I could only think of as defiance. My skin prickled. It was like looking at myself, but I had never fought in the desert with the flail from the back of a chestnut horse.

"That's . . . your mother?" Lila whispered. "She looks just like you, Zam."

Maggi swirled her hand through the image, turning it and showing all sides of the action. "She was determined to see the lions live for more reasons than that she loved them and your father. She knew there would be one with the blood of a lion in their veins that would become the Wall Breaker. She believed the wall needed to come down, that the Emperor needed to be freed."

She swirled her fingers and the scene shifted to another I didn't know, one that made my heart freeze in my chest. A little girl with dark hair and bright green eyes sat crying in the sand, her chubby legs not yet able to stand on their own. In front of her stood the woman who was my mother. My whole life I'd been told that I was the cause of her death. Shem had said I wasn't the cause, that I was older, but I'd not really believed him. Because that would mean the truths I'd lived with and carried as a weight for so long were in reality, lies.

What I was looking at put that belief and those

truths into question in a way that Shem's words could never have done. Unless it was something worse that had stolen my mother from me. For the first time, it hit me that my childhood was nothing what I'd thought— what I'd been trained to believe.

My breath came in little gasps. I couldn't help it as understanding flowed through me, what Maggi was going to show me. . . "Do not make me watch my mother die."

Maggi lifted a hand and gave a single nod. "I will spare you that. But you need to see what comes before, the pieces of the puzzle that may help you understand who you are."

The image swelled until I stood within it behind my childhood self. My mother's back was to me and she faced someone I knew.

The man in front of her was Shem—a younger version, but Shem without a doubt—and he was arguing hard. The action and sounds went from nothing to full-on in the single beat of my heart. My child self cried softly, and the two adults raised their voices.

"You must run. Take the girl and go. The Jinn know she's the one," Shem said. "They will come for her and what then? You must go, for all that is holy in this land, you are not strong enough to protect her here. If you run, you'll have a chance."

His words were like a slap to my face. My mother had been weak, and everyone believed her incapable too. Just as they believed of me.

She shook her head. "They *don't* know any such thing, Shem, and neither do you. You are speculating once again. The Jinn might suspect, but there are others who could be the Wall Breaker. There are others who could fit the prophecy."

"No." He snapped the word at her. "There are not. You might cast doubt on those here to protect her and you might make it look like another cub has the potential, but you and I know the truth, and so do the Jinn. You are a fool if you think she will make it to adulthood without some sort of protection. Without continually running."

"Ishtar has agreed to take her if something should happen to me," my mother said. "She will raise and protect her."

"Then send her there now!" Shem roared, and my little self cried harder. I wanted to stop the noise, but my mother didn't look back at me. She couldn't turn her back on Shem. That was a sign of submissive behavior in the pride and I understood she couldn't do that even for a crying child.

"No. She is my daughter, and if we are to be separated, I would have as much time as I could have with her."

"You are a dead fool then." He spun on his heel and stalked away, his shoulders hunched. She watched him go and then turned and dropped to her knees, holding her hands out to me. I'd been told my whole life that she'd died shortly after my birth.

I had to be at least six months old in this memory, assuming it was true. I didn't know if that was better, knowing I'd had her love for a little while. But why then tell me I'd been the cause of her death? That my birth had taken her life? The guilt I'd lived with for as long as I could remember was not easy to let go, but I pushed it aside.

Maybe it was not my fault she died.

Of course, I was wrong. My birth hadn't caused her death. But my life had.

"My little Zamira, can you crawl to me, lovely girl?" She wiggled her fingers at me and I obediently flopped forward into the sand and squirmed my way to her. She scooped me up and held me to her face, her eyes closed, and more than one tear tracking down her face. "What can I do to protect you, my darling? What can I do to help you survive until you are old enough to stop that old bastard? You are the only one who can. Such a heavy burden for one so young."

She held on until the little me squirmed and squawked to be put down. My heart thumped wildly as the light around the scene changed, shifting to an early twilight. What old bastard was she talking about? Who could she possibly mean?

Marsum . . . it had to be Marsum.

As if thinking his name had summoned him, a dark mist flowed along the sand and through the trees until it formed into a man. A Jinn. My throat clenched because there was nothing I could do. This was a dream, a memory that couldn't be changed.

Marsum's dark eyes and white-blond hair marked him clearly as a Jinn even if the mist he floated on for legs did not.

My mother spun and let out a hiss. "You wish to die today, Marsum?"

"Not today, princess," he grinned at her, "but you carry with you the child that will ruin my plans. You and I both know she will be a powerful lioness, that she will lead this pride, and as such, I need her. Give her to me, let me raise her, and I will let the rest of your lions live— hell, I will even let you live. All of them. Surely a single life for the lives of so many is worth it to you?" He arched an eyebrow at her and I put my fists to my mouth.

Lila tightened her hold on my shoulder and it was only then I remembered she was with me. I reached up and put a hand on her, using her for an anchor. I wasn't really here. I could do nothing to change what was happening.

That didn't mean I didn't want to change it, that I wouldn't have given anything to stop what was coming.

"No," my mother said softly. "She is not the one you believe her to be, Marsum. She will be small, nothing like the lions who are destined to take you down. She will be nothing more than a house cat at best. Just like me."

He shrugged. "Do not ever say I was not generous, princess. Do not ever say that I didn't give you a choice to save her now. To save yourself now."

His words hovered in the air and the tension grew until I thought I would scream with it. She clutched my little self to her chest, her lips pressed to my cheeks as the tears flowed down her face. The scene exploded into action. Arrows flew from every direction and my mother dropped, curling her body around my much smaller one.

The scene froze in that split second before any of the arrows hit my mother's curled frame.

Maggi walked between the still form of Marsum and me, drawing my eyes to her. "She died protecting you and protecting what she thought you would become. You are the Wall Breaker, but I do not believe you will be the one to face the Emperor as some believe. That was meant for a lioness of great strength. That has always been the understanding."

I swallowed the lump in my throat, not giving half a shit about the Emperor. "Marsum killed both my parents."

"He did." She nodded.

"I'm going to kill him," I whispered, feeling the truth of those five simple words to the core of my bones.

Maggi sighed softly. "But do not be quick to kill him, Zamira. He has a part yet in this story of yours. And I do not think you will like what will happen if you kill him. His son would be forced to take his place as the leader of the Jinn, and Marsum's power would go to him."

My knees wobbled and I locked them in place. "But then Maks would be free, and he would stop the Jinn from doing so much harm." If anything, killing Marsum would solve a great deal of our problems.

Maggi grimaced and she held both hands up, wiping away the scene in front of us. "No. That is not how the succession works with the Jinn. Marsum carries his father's cruelty, and his father's father's cruelty. When one leader dies, the next absorbs not only the power of his predecessor, but his very energy and memories. Maks as you know him would be lost." Maggi looked at me. "Assuming you do not free him of the Jinn before that happens."

My eyes snapped to hers. "What? Is that possible?"

Part of my mind said that Maggi was distracting me from finding out more about the truth of my life, and of my world, from answering my questions. The other part of my brain reminded me that I had asked her. This was the direction that my questions had taken us.

She clasped her hands in front of her and slowly nodded. "There is a way to free your Maks, if that is what you truly want. If it's what *he* wants. Because you don't know, Zamira, if he wants to be free of the Jinn. They are all he's known his entire life. You've known him for a year at best, if you count the time he spent at the Stockyards. How do you know he even wants to be free?"

Her words could not have hit me harder. "He said he loved me." I whispered those words, hating how weak they sounded. How frail. Because love was frail, love was dangerous. I knew that better than anyone else. It could be the worst of any weapon when it came to cutting someone.

"Perhaps he does." She held her hands out, palms up, and in them swirled a new image. Maks riding Batman hard to the south, his face scored with cuts. At least he was alive. "He rides now at the will of his father, and his father will not let him go again."

"How do we free him?" Lila asked.

Maggi looked from me to her and back again. "The only way is one you will not like."

"Tell me!" I yelled at her, anger making me bold. "Tell me how to free him!"

She took a breath and held it a moment before answering. "There is no way to untangle a Jinn from his herd. To free him from his fate, you must kill him."

Chapter Thirteen

The Ice Witch was right. I didn't like her answer. And even though we were in a dream world, I couldn't pretend that it was only a dream answer. I felt it in my bones.

Saying there was no untangling a Jinn from his herd sounded weird, and I let that weirdness keep me from absorbing the rest of what it meant. Her words settled into me slowly and I repeated them to myself under my breath before I let it reach the front of my mind.

Maggi was saying there was no way to save Maks. That he was lost to me. To us. That his freedom from a fate where he would absorb all his father would come only on his death.

As quickly as the understanding hit me, I balked.

No, I refused to believe that. There was always a way to save someone. Like Bryce. Like Darcy.

I clamped my teeth together, took a sharp breath between them, and shook my head before I spoke.

"Nope. That's not the answer I want. Fuck you, that is not the only answer!"

Lila grunted. "Me neither. We can find a way to save him. If anyone can, it's us."

Maggi smiled, but it was sad and full of a deep pain. "I believed I could save someone once. I believed I could save the man I loved. I could not, Zamira, and I am a powerful witch. You have power, but not the kind that could break spells. Your mother was a weak shifter with a fierce fire in her belly—the same fire you carry and that has brought you this far. You saw her. She died for love and it gave you nothing but a childhood without her."

The words were like slaps. I took several steps back from her until I was no longer in the desert dream and once more stood inside her room with the fire crackling. My body slept. I could feel it resting while I sought the answers I needed in this dream world.

Lila let out a hiss and her tail lashed a warning. "You said you would help us. All you're doing is being mean."

"The truth often hurts, Lila," Maggi said, not unkindly. "That is not my fault. I am but a messenger."

I didn't know what to say. I didn't know what to do. Part of me wallowed with indecision rearing its ugly fucking head.

I wanted nothing more than to kill Marsum, but if I did, then Maks would be bound in ways I could never free him from, unless I was willing to kill him too. But if I let Marsum live, Maks would never be free either. There was no winning this new game laid in front of me.

I shook my head. "I won't give up on him. I won't."

"Me either," Lila said. "He called me his sister. Family sticks it out through the worst. Even if he thinks we've abandoned him, we'll keep on hunting for a way to free him."

Thank the desert gods Lila saw and felt the same as I did—I was not sure I could find all those words in that moment. Because Maks was . . . he was the other half of me, and I couldn't imagine him not being in my life. Even if we couldn't be together, I needed to know he was safe and happy. I needed to know he was free of manipulations that would make him do things he didn't want.

I didn't think that was too much to ask.

Maggi spread her hands wide. "Peace to you both. I do not wish to bring either of you tumult in your hearts. I only wish to save you some pain. Hunt for a way to free him then, and if you find it, I will gladly help you with whatever you may need to make it come together. But be wary of false promises from those who would tell you they could break the ties between him and his kind."

I stared at her, not sure where to go with this dream now. "Is there anything else you think I need to know?"

She nodded. "Many will tell you that you are the one, Zam, that has a chance to bring the Emperor to his knees. I don't know how that would be possible. What I have seen in my scryings, over and over, is that you will meet the Emperor and three times he will make you an offer that will tempt you beyond all you could imagine. Three times. That is all I have seen. But do not let others tell you that you are the one to bring him down.

That path will end with all our blood spilled in the desert sands."

I frowned and closed my eyes, ignoring most of what she said, thinking only of what could tempt me—Bryce of course. My brother's life was the temptation I wasn't sure I could refuse again. The Emperor had asked me to bow to him twice, and twice I'd refused. What more could he offer me to make me say yes?

Of course, I knew the second I thought of the question, what it would be. A way to free Maks. Maks, who'd been at the Oasis battle, who'd done what he could to fight Marsum then when he'd been younger. Was that why he was so tightly bound to his father now, as punishment for daring to question him?

Which led to a new question.

"Why didn't Marsum take me at the Oasis? He had me in his hands. Not once but twice." I looked at Maggi, trying to discern if she was telling me the truth or not. She tucked her hands inside the sleeves of her long dress.

"Your mother is why, I believe. Her bloodline was weaker than your father's and you obviously took after her. In this case, I believe it saved you. When he touched you, he felt how weak you were." She frowned. "You are a mixture of possibility, Zamira. Weak, but destined for things even I do not understand. I have yet to figure out why that is."

"You and me both," I said.

Before I could ask any other questions, I was jerked awake by a boot thumping into my head. I opened my eyes in the real world and found myself staring up at a gnome. His long white beard tickled my forehead and gray worried eyes stared down at me.

"We found the jewels in your bags," he whispered. "We must give them to her, but we don't want to."

I stared at what he held in his hands.

The emerald from Dragon's Ground. The diamond that Bryce had stolen from Ish, and the sapphire we'd taken from Maggi herself.

I rolled, throwing Lila from me as I reached for the jewels, snagging them from the gnome. But not before Maggi saw, her eyes blinking wide, and then narrowing. Confusion and then desire swept over her features.

"My jewel. You . . . did not give it to my sister?"

I tucked them into my shirt, but again, not before she saw all three. Her eyes widened as they landed on the other two jewels.

Inside my shirt they dug into my skin and were super uncomfortable, but I needed them out of sight for what I was going to do.

"You should free the Raven," I said, changing directions entirely.

"No, I need her help yet." Maggi's eyes narrowed. "What are you going to do with those jewels? You have no power to tap into them."

I shrugged. "Trade them for some food, maybe a new saddle."

Her eyes narrowed farther, and the visage of the Ice Witch and all her anger rolled through her. Shit, I did not want to go head to head with her again. I'd beaten her last time, but I wasn't entirely sure it wasn't a fluke.

She stood slowly, her skirts billowing out around her

and she held out a hand, palm up. "Give me my jewel back, Zamira. It is the least you can do for what I have shown you. Your mother and her love for you. The knowledge of what will happen to your lover if you kill his master. The knowledge that you will face the Emperor. Surely you see the value in those things?"

I took a step back. "Yeah, that's all fine and dandy, but there was no deal ahead of time. There was no contract that I would owe you. You offered to help. We took it and now Lila and I really have to go. We've got werehyenas on our asses, and a Jinn tracking us."

The sunlight coming through the window told me we'd slept the night away while Maggi had taken us into la-la land. Balder would be, should be, rested.

Assuming the gnomes were as good as their word.

The gnome tugged on my hand. "Your horse is fed, tacked, and ready to ride, my lady."

Maggi growled at him. "You are my servant. Do not offer her anything."

He bowed to her, his hands clasped in prayer in front of his face. "And I do not want you to have the gem, lady of ours. You are not kind when you hold that power. And we love you. We wish to be with you always, but not like that." The words tumbled out of his mouth and her eyes locked on him.

But she spoke to me, and the strain in her eyes was clear. "You may go. Do not come back with any of the jewels or I will take them all."

That was enough for me.

I spun and bolted, Lila with me. Down the spiral stairs we went, leaping three and four at a time as I scrambled to get the fuck away from the Witch. Maggi had given me some help, and I assumed that was why she'd taken Lila.

"Her addiction to the gem, that's what tipped her," Lila said as we burst into the courtyard. Balder stood quietly waiting, and the Raven sat up on the parapet high above, her head and black eyes swiveling to watch us.

I ran as fast as I could across the stone paved yard and leapt at the last second, vaulting onto Balder's back. He plunged forward and I raised a hand to the Raven. There was nothing I could do for the big bird, at least not now. But a promise in my mind formed, stupid as it was. I would do what I could to free her. Just not right then. Right then, I had to make a run for it before a certain Witch changed her mind about letting us go.

Balder galloped across the courtyard and into the snow. We all but flew across the flat plain, and he stumbled a little when we transitioned back to the rocky firm ground. I let him run as fast as he wished, taking us straight south.

Lila clung to my shoulders. "That was . . . weird. She was so nice before you came, and so nice until she saw the gems."

"Like a split personality," I said. As soon as the words slipped from me I knew they were true. Not unlike her sister, Maggi had multiple sides to her, dependent on the power she held.

"Do you think she really wanted to help us?" Lila asked.

I thought about it a minute. "Yes, I do. I'm not sure,

though, that she told us everything she'd planned on. The arrival of the jewels kind of busted up that party."

We rode hard for half an hour before I felt comfortable pulling Balder up. He snorted and danced. Refreshed even though he'd only had . . . "Wait . . . it was morning when we got here. We were out for almost twenty-four hours!"

"Does that matter?" Lila asked.

Something about it tugged on me like an itch in the middle of my back I couldn't quite reach. "Maybe? Maks had to have been looking for us, and the were-hyenas as well . . . and the Raven said that the Witch's home," I refused to use her name if she was going to be a camel's asshole, "she said her home was hidden from the world."

There was a moment in there when I realized *that* was what the Witch was up to—she had helped us. She'd hidden the three of us for twenty-four hours, which meant we were *behind* Maks and Ishtar's hunters now. She'd given me a chance to get to the Jinn's Dominion without having to face Maks, without having my hand forced. I still didn't know why she'd help me. There had to be something in this for her. What, though?

That question in and of itself made me nervous.

We had a chance to get the pride back now, thanks to her, and maybe . . . maybe we could save Maks at the same time.

I didn't have it in me to hope, to be honest. There were too many factors at play.

The best I could do was a small thing. "THANK

YOU!" I yelled the words into the wind and hoped the Witch would hear them. Maybe she wasn't the camel's asshole I thought. Maybe she was doing the best she could, just like the rest of us, stumbling along, making mistakes and trying to right them where she could, like she said.

I slipped off Balder's back and walked beside him. He didn't need the rest, but I needed the movement and I wanted to think.

Lila scurried up his neck so she sat about halfway, her wings outstretched for balance, the wound from the crossbow bolt scarred but fully healed. "We still don't know how we are going to save the others. Unless you've come up with a plan I don't know about?"

"I know the layout of the Jinn's Dominion," I said as I scrambled over a pile of rocks. "Our father drilled it into us, so if we were ever taken, we'd be able to find a way out." Of course, now that I'd learned that Marsum had wanted to take me to raise me as his own, it made sense why we'd been taught the layout.

The training, the understanding of how the Jinn's lands were set up, none of it had been for Bryce to rescue people once he became alpha. We'd never gone in after someone if they'd been taken, never.

The training had been so I'd be able to escape if I were taken.

"Sweet baby desert god, this is a fucking mess. My whole life is nothing but lies." I grimaced.

Lila grunted. "You and me both."

She had a point.

There was a brush of air to my left and I turned to

see Bryce walking beside me. He was indistinct, but he was there. I shook a fist at him.

"You got something you want to tell me?" I barked. "Like how much Dad knew about Marsum wanting to take me as some sort of freaky-assed adopted child?"

Bryce's image wavered, and he turned his head to me, his eyes more golden than I'd ever seen, his voice deeper, resonating in his belly. *"He didn't want you as a child, Zamira. He wanted you as a mate."*

It took a moment for the words to sink in. When they did, my stomach rolled hard over itself as if it would scramble to get away from me. I pushed a hand into my belly as if I could hold it together. "What?"

His image wobbled and for a space of a heartbeat, I thought he was someone else, an old man in sand-colored clothes, but no, it was just Bryce. *"Do not go to him. He will not kill you. He will bind you to him forever."*

I couldn't help the way I sucked air as if I'd been running, but I forced myself to talk through the panic. "Not possible. He could have taken me when I was a child!"

Bryce shrugged. *"Except he swore he would not. Maggi didn't show you that part. That he swore he would not take you until you were older. That was the deal he made—your mother's life for a semblance of a life for yourself."*

I stared hard at him. "Why are you telling me this now? Why did you not say something before?"

I blinked and Bryce was gone. "Damn it! You could be a little more helpful than that!"

I could have sworn I heard a heavy sigh, but it could have been the way the wind whipped through the rush grass too. And then his final warning. *"Do not go to the Jinn's Dominion, Zamira. Not if you wish to remain free."*

Lila landed on Balder's saddle. "Who were you talking to?"

I struggled to swallow, my mouth suddenly dry. I grabbed a water flask and spun the top off, then sucked down several long gulps before I answered her.

"Bryce. He just showed up." I screwed the lid back on the flask and tucked it into my saddlebags. "He confirmed what Maggi said about Marsum." I filled her in quickly on the exchange.

She was quiet for a beat and then the questions spilled out of her. "What are we going to do? What about the others? What about Maks? We can't leave them there."

I shook my head. "We aren't going to leave them there. Lila, my skills lie in sneaking in and stealing what I want and sneaking back out. This is the same as any jewel heist, only the jewels are our pride." I looked at her. "We aren't turning back."

She grinned. "Good."

We were quiet a few minutes before we hit something that made us both stop in our tracks. Paw prints in the loose soil, easily the size of both my hands side by side.

"That's the hyenas?" she gasped.

"Yeah." I bent and touched one, seeing how degraded the edges were. "Yesterday. We're behind the full pack too." I looked up at her. "This is good unless they turn back."

"Let's go to the water," she said. "They are following

Maks, staying west. If they turn back they might pass right by us."

I nodded, mounted, and turned Balder east, going straight across. When the waves came into view, I saw a few sirens swimming, waving at us. I waved back. They were ineffective on me and Lila, and Balder was gelded so we would be fine.

Along the edge of the water, we traveled in relative ease for the next few days. There were no witches, no Jinn, no dragons, no werehyenas.

No Maks.

No Bryce.

No Shem.

More than once I found myself thinking about the three of them, and how they'd turned things around on me in different ways. How each of them had impacted my life and in some cases turned it on its head.

I shouldn't have missed Shem at all, but I found myself wishing he'd been able to stay closer, that he'd been able to give me a little more insight into what I was supposed to be doing. Because while I was the alpha of my pride, and I felt that truth all the way to my bones, there were pieces of my life I didn't understand. Bits that didn't quite fit. And I suspected my crazy uncle had more information than he let on. A thought formed . . . the dream walking the Ice Witch had done, what if I could do that and reach Shem? "Hey, Lila."

"Yup?" She looked at me from where she coasted on an updraft, rolling to her back as if in water and not air.

I opened my mouth to tell her what I was thinking

about trying and then shut it again. That was ridiculous. I was no mage. "Nothing."

She squinted one eye at me but didn't press. I probably couldn't even do it without the Ice Witch helping me. My hand went to the pouch where I kept the clear diamond . . . and I wondered if maybe there was something else I could do to try to reach Shem.

To ask him the questions I had. But each night I lay down, I told myself I would do it the next day.

By day four on our own, we'd settled into an easy pattern that consisted of food, movement, and trying to stump one another with obscure Shakespeare quotes. That easy rhythm was the only reason I have to explain why we didn't notice the trap until it was too late.

Way too late.

Chapter Fourteen

To be fair, the trap that we sprung wasn't meant for us specifically; at least, I don't think it was, despite who set it. We settled down for the night, later than usual, meaning I didn't check out the area very well. My bad.

I stripped Balder of his tack and set up a small fire. Lila brought back two birds for our dinner and I gutted and cleaned them with speed.

"What do you think Maks is doing?" she asked me softly as I worked. "Do you think he's okay?"

I shrugged as I pulled the last of the feathers out of the birds. "No idea. He's more likely only a day ahead of us now. Batman could not keep up that breakneck pace for long. He'll reach the edge of the Jinn's Dominion in a week, the werehyenas right behind him, and I imagine he'll be just fine."

"Really? After the Jinn left him to die in the mud?" Lila waddled close to the fire, her belly full of the bird innards. She ran her tongue around the edge of her mouth.

I ran a spit through the two birds and set them over the flames to cook. "Lila, I don't know. I don't know how I'm supposed to save him when even the Ice Witch says I can't. She's powerful. I'm not, remember? And what if what he said was the truth? What if he was fooling us all along? We don't know, and maybe we never really knew him." Maybe I never really knew him.

Ahh, that bit hurt the most because I'd yet again let my squishy weak heart follow its own path right into Maks's arms. A path that my head had told me was dangerous and stupid, and I'd followed it even after I learned he was a Jinn. Shit, I would have been better to let Steve keep cheating on me and stayed married to that dumb ass.

"No, I don't think that's true," Lila said softly. "I think you're afraid to embrace what you really are. I think . . . you aren't all shifter. That's what Maggi said. Or was that Merlin? Ishtar, maybe?"

I hunched my back a little. "I know that's what you think. But that doesn't mean it's right."

"What do you feel? Do you think it's possible, though? 'Cause, let's be honest, if you have any sort of hidden powers, now would be the time for them to come to light." Lila moved so she was close to the fire and staring up at me with those big eyes of hers. The weather here was slowly warming and the fire was almost too hot on some nights. And yes, I was avoiding her question by thinking about the weather and the fire in front of me.

"I don't know," I finally said. "I . . . I've always been weak, Lila. As far as anyone else is concerned, at least."

She put her two front claws on my knee and gave my leg a squeeze. "Well, maybe now is the time to try, then. I won't laugh if you can't do anything but squeeze out a fart."

I laughed and shook my head, then lifted both hands covered in blood and a few feathers. "Try what? What am I supposed to try, Lila?"

She frowned. "Yeah, I don't know. I guess you have a point."

I went on, still laughing. "Meditation? Chanting? Singing to the stars? Dance naked under the moon?"

"Not funny," she grumbled. "This could save us one day, you know. You should take it at least a little bit serious."

I rolled my eyes, not so much at her but at the world. At Maggi for putting these thoughts in Lila's head that I was someone special, because the reality was I already knew that my abilities had to do with hard work and a spine of steel, not natural talent.

"Look, I'll close my eyes and do like a . . ." I flipped my hands around and a few feathers floated off, "soul-searching thing. Like when I look for my pride, but instead of looking for them, I'll search me, okay?" I didn't even know if it was a thing, what I was talking about. But by the way Lila's eyes lit up, it would do. And it would settle this hope she had.

"Good. At least try. The miserable have no other medicine, but only hope." She pushed off my legs and curled up next to the fire again. "That's from *Measure by Measure*."

"I know." I rubbed my hands in the loose sand, working the worst of the blood off, then dipped them in the pot we had for cleaning.

Sweet fucking goddess, this was stupid. Dumb. A waste of time. But then again, it wasn't like we were going anywhere until morning.

I sat on the ground, folded my hands in my lap and closed my eyes. I took a big breath in through my nose and out my mouth. I turned my thoughts inward as if I was going to search for my pride, but instead of sending energy outward, I kept it all to myself.

The energy rumbled around in me, pushing to get out, to search for those who were attached to me. I couldn't help it as a flare of energy tugged on me, the color a deep, pulsing green wrapped in threads of black, as if it were sickly. I frowned and let my own energy flow toward it.

My stomach clenched as I realized who was calling to me, to my energy.

"Maks." I whispered his name and Lila grabbed at me.

"What do you see?"

I swallowed hard, understanding now that Maks was part of my pride, as was Lila. He'd sworn his fealty to me as one of my seconds.

And he was sick.

Dying.

How was that possible?

I pressed my fingers into my eyes as if I could block

out the sight, except I wasn't seeing his energy with my eyes, not really. My muscles shook and trembled. Dying, how could he be dying?

"Lila, he's in trouble. I don't know how, but we have to help him. He's sick, and it's killing him." I finally lowered my hands and opened my eyes. "The energy around him is black and it's literally sucking the life out of him."

So much for looking into myself for my own power. Then again, I wasn't surprised. I expected nothing more than to find exactly that—nothing. And now I'd found Maks. And I knew he needed us as much as the rest of my pride.

"Just how are we going to do that? We know he's . . . possessed or whatever it is that's going on. He wants to hand you over to Marsum." Lila paced in front of the fire.

I scrubbed my hands against a tuft of grass. "I know. Maybe we need to find Merlin. He seems to know more about Maks and the Jinn than he should. Maybe he can heal him?"

Lila bobbed her head once. "And if we can't find Merlin?"

She had a point. Merlin wasn't exactly known for showing up when needed. More like showing up when you least needed him. Or when he wanted to try to kill you and then explain that somehow that was really helping you.

I frowned, drew in a big breath and got a distinct whiff of rotting compost. I wrinkled my nose and twisted around. "I smell garbage. Do you smell that?"

Lila turned her head into the wind and then shuddered and gagged. "Gods, that is awful. What is it?"

My brain kicked in, labeling the scent about two seconds slower than it should've as the strange shape sailed toward us through the black sky.

Woven ropes bound together, knotted with iron straps. I saw it all in a flash as the net landed on us with a heavy thud, pinning us to the ground. Or really, just me. Lila sat in the middle of a square of empty space, her luck so good that it landed neatly around her.

The rope and weight of it was across the back of my neck, my spine, my legs, and pretty much everything was held down—after my experience of being squashed and nearly killed by the werehyena because I was in my cat form, I wasn't about to shift.

Already the struggle to breathe was a real thing; I fought for each breath.

"Shift! You've got bigger problems than the net!" Lila yelled as the ground rumbled under me.

"If I shift, it will crush me!" I yelled, fighting to get out from under the weight, but damn it, it was heavy. That's what you get when being hunted by giants.

"I wanna wanna eat!" an all-too-familiar voice boomed from not far enough away.

"Balder." I snapped his name and then let out a hiss. How he'd managed to avoid the net, I have no idea. I struggled and fought the bonds as Lila swooped around my head.

"What do I do?" Lila yelled.

I gritted my teeth, knowing I had no choice. If Balder stayed, the giants' queen would eat him. She would crush Lila. I had to send them to safety. There was no way I was going to live through this. But Lila didn't know that.

"Take Balder, find Maks!" I managed to get the words out while my lungs felt as though they collapsed within me.

He would come, if for no other reason than to take me to Marsum—assuming he was within distance for her to find. Assuming I could dodge the queen of the giants long enough to survive. The sound of hoof beats and then a roar from the big three-titted bitch told me Balder and Lila were out of range already. If they pushed hard, they might get to Maks if he'd stopped for the night. Maybe. I just had to hang on until then.

Two hours maybe? I knew I was being hopeful. Two hours was what I held in my head as the time I needed to survive.

Right, no problem. One house cat against the queen of the giants. I could do this. I could; no, strike that, I had to. There were too many others depending on me. I had to find a way to survive. And if Lila brought Maks back, maybe we could figure out what was wrong with him.

The net stayed on me as the queen leaned low and close, her breath as vile as I remembered. She sniffed a few times and my hair fluttered toward her. A sneeze came next, coating me with slime.

"Fuck off!" I yelled or tried to yell. It came out more like a wheeze with the weight of the iron balls.

"Oh, kitty, kitty, I remember you. You is a thief, thief." She whipped off the net and I scrambled forward, fighting to get my legs under me fast enough to stand and face her. A thick finger flicked me in the middle of my back and sent me sprawling onto my face.

I rolled to my back and looked up at her, then grinned and waved. "How you doing, queen bee?"

She glared down at me, thick green snot dripping from her nose and her eyes. Sweet baby goddess, she was sick as . . . well, I would have said as a dog, but I felt bad maligning dogs like that. She wiped a hand across her face, smearing the bright green and now a strand of dark yellow snot all the way from her nose across her cheek to her ear. "You take my jewel, jewel."

"Yeah, well, to be fair, you weren't guarding it that well." I reached slowly for the flail. Only it wasn't there.

She held it up by her finger and her thumb. "You looky, looky for this, pretty?"

The flick in the back made a lot more sense now. She'd taken the one weapon that could do damage to her.

I raised both hands in surrender. Shifting forms would buy me a bit more time, but I'd leave that until the bitter end. I had more pressing matters. "What are you doing outside your territory? You lost, you big dummy?"

She flopped down so she sat across from me. "I kill, kill you in little time. First. Talk, talk." She sucked in a deep breath and I realized she was winded. This sickness of hers might actually save my ass. But I wasn't about to let my guard down. I watched as she placed the flail next to a meaty thigh.

I didn't lower my hands. "Yeah, that's what I was

doing, asking you a question. So, let's talk. What are you doing away from your territory?"

She shook her head and . . . shit, was she crying? "Giants dying, dying. All dying, dying."

My jaw dropped open. "What, how?" Much as I disliked them, they were part of the ecosystem of our world. Even I knew that taking out a giant's tribe would have consequences on the rest of us.

Her eyes narrowed and a bubble formed on the front of her nose as she breathed in and out. "Emperor does this to us, us."

That first word was enough to make my knees weak and I had to lock them to stay standing. "The *Emperor* did this?"

"He come, come to me in dream. Say I owe, owe him. I say no. He takes lives." She shrugged as if it meant nothing. "He make land dead, dead. Not just giants, land sick, sick."

If not for the fact I was discussing this with the queen of the giants, I would have wanted more info. But I wasn't sure how far I could push this conversation of ours. The sun had fully set now. As a black cat, I had the best chance of slipping away while the night ruled. I looked longingly at my saddle and my bag of gear. There was nothing I could do about it. I would have to leave it all behind if I wanted to have even a chance of surviving.

I had only one goal. Get to the flail and shift faster than I ever had before. Maggi and the Raven said I needed the weapon, and I wasn't about to let it go so easily.

"You sure it's the Emperor?" I tipped my head to one side. "Maybe could it be someone else? Some other mage? Merlin? The Jinn?" I was throwing the names out to keep her brain busy.

Not a lot of brains was going to work in my favor, and I could scramble said brains quickly if I forced her to think hard with all the questions.

She frowned and confusion was written in clear bold letters across her face. She snorted and a hunk of snot flew out of her nose and landed between us, the size of a goat. I stared at it, unsure if it was snot or a bit of her brain with the meaty deep red consistency it had going on it. For a split second, I thought it moved and I took a step back. My gorge rose and I struggled against the heaving that my body was sure it needed to do. I looked up at the sky, away from the glob of snot as I struggled to keep my shit together.

"I sure." She breathed out. "I sure." The wheeze in her lungs was audible now as she rested. Her eyes were on me, never moving from her prey even as sick as she obviously was. Her stomach rumbled, giving me an idea.

I pointed at the fire and the roasting game hens.

"You can eat those if you want. Two birds, cooked up nice. Probably not more than a snack for you, but you should have them." I gave a quick wave of my hands to point as I stepped away from the fire. Her eyes left me for a split second and that was all I needed. I launched toward her right thigh, diving for the flail next to her.

I hit the ground hard, knocked the wind out of my lungs and still managed to get a hand around the wooden shaft. I forced the shift from two legs to four and the flail absorbed into me, as did all my weapons and clothes. On four legs, I had nothing but a metal collar woven with scraps of material that indicated my clothing.

Before I could take another full step, I'd already spun and on four legs sprinted away from the queen of the giants. With the wind ruffling my fur and my heart beating double time so loudly, I could hear nothing else. That didn't last.

I counted to ten before a scream erupted behind me, the sound deepening into a phlegm-filled roar that sent a flock of night birds high into the air. I wasn't going to be fast enough to fully outrun her. I'd need Balder for that, but if I'd kept him close she would have eaten him first.

I was on my own.

I raced toward a pile of rocks and skidded around behind them, peeking out. The ground rumbled hard enough that the pebbles jumped and danced next to my paws. I crouched low and kept my eyes on her while she thundered toward me, her arms flailing left and right.

"I kill, kill you!" she roared and then coughed, hacking and choking on her own spit. She went to a knee and thumped a fist between two of her three breasts until she cleared her lungs. I didn't move, despite the stench of her breath wafting over me.

A weird rush of emotions caught me off guard and I had to fight to keep myself still and not stand up.

I felt bad for her . . . and she'd tried to kill me. I hunched tighter to the rock, my mind racing. What the hell was this new emotional shit? I shouldn't be feeling bad for a giant, certainly not one who would tear my head clean off if I so much as gave her an inkling as to where I was.

Yet I couldn't stop the feelings. I couldn't stop seeing the tears trickling down her face, mingling with the snot.

She sat back on her ass and I realized she was dying, right in front of me. She fell to her back and flopped her arms out to the side. Her chest heaved with such effort that her bones creaked.

I shifted back to two legs and slowly stood. "Queen Bee." I didn't know her name, but it was the best I could do. "How did the Emperor do this to you?"

Her eyes found me and the pain in them cut through me as if it were my pain, which was stupid. *So* stupid. Tremors shook down through my body and she smiled at me.

"You . . . not shifter. You magic, magic too. Like Emperor." It was not a question she asked me. Her words did nothing to slow the tremors in my body.

I shook my head. "No, no magic. How did the Emperor do this?"

Her breath rattled. "In dream world. He poisoned my land, land. Nothing will live now." Her eyes closed. "Name is Destry."

I was close enough that she could have grabbed me. I bent to a knee and put a hand on her arm. She didn't flinch.

"Destry, I can't help you," I said. "I have no magic."

Her laugh was wet and pain-filled. "You do. You like mother. Powerful, powerful. I recognize you. Think you her." Under my hand, I could feel her heart beating, but it slowed with each second that passed.

"Dying, dying," she whispered. "Emperor will destroy all land. Your mother stop him. You stop him."

I pressed harder against her arm. "I'm just a cat."

"No. You magic," she whispered.

"Magic cat?" I asked.

She gurgled and it took me a moment to realize she was laughing. "Magic pussy."

I snorted and shook my head. "Dirty to the end."

"Destry last of clan Bonebreaker." She lifted the hand across from me and reached under her loincloth. I watched warily until she pulled from underneath it a small drawstring bag. "Give you this, this."

She held out the drawstring to me and I took it. As it touched my hands it shrunk from the size of a large boulder to the size of an apple. Still warm from being against her skin, I rolled it in my hand.

"What is it?"

"Magic dust . . . make you see the magic in you. Sprinkle on skin. Make you strong, strong."

I stared at the pouch and her arm flopped to the ground. I pressed a hand against her arm again. Her heart stuttered. I would have been her last meal. Her last attempt at survival.

And now she'd given me something that was important to her.

Fuck, and now I was tearing up. "I'm sorry for stealing your jewel."

"No sorry." She breathed out. "Jewel bad, bad." Her

eyes flicked open and she looked at me. "Sorry I try eat you. Can't help it. Giant stomach."

I smiled and she smiled back and the light flickered and died behind her eyes. In the night, the black of her iris gave one last final flare and then faded. Silent.

Her body shuddered and a new stench filled the air as her body let loose the last of its hold on life. I backed away, clutching the small bag to me.

I stood there a long time, close enough to watch over her, but not so close the smell reached me unless I took a deep breath. Destry of the Bonebreakers was a queen who'd died because the Emperor demanded his dues, and she refused.

I'd refused him twice now.

Shit, I was in trouble if he asked me again.

The pouch she gave me I tucked under my cloak. Magic dust; it was probably ground-up psychedelic mushrooms. But you never knew when a little magic would come in handy.

I took a few steps back from her. All I had left was a verse I remembered from when someone died of old age in the pride. I put two fingers to my mouth, then knelt and pressed them to the ground. "May you meet your ancestors in death, Destry, and may they hold you tight and not turn you away from your final place among the stars."

The ground rumbled and cracked around her body, splitting in all directions. I stepped back fast, my eyes locked on the vines that erupted out of the ground and wrapped around her body.

Whispering vines that spoke of blood and power.

Laughing softly as they drove into her body like spears. Horror froze me as I watched them suck her blood, the vines bulging as they gulped her down, and her body shrinking right in front of my eyes.

This was the Emperor.

This was the death he would bring to our world if he were released. Which meant I couldn't kill Marsum. I couldn't take his jewel, no matter what anyone else said.

The sound of hoof beats turned me around. "Lila?" I shouted for her, thinking that maybe she'd turned around and come back without Maks. Because she'd not been gone long enough to have found him.

"Run!" Lila screamed. "He's got other Jinn and the hyenas with him! They've got Balder."

Chapter Fifteen

ila's shout didn't give me much warning. But the idea that Maks had already hooked up with other Jinn was bad. Worse than bad was that they'd somehow snagged the hyenas.

I gave a low whistle for Balder. He whinnied off to my right as the three horses and riders circled me, a hyena chained to each. The werehyenas were, to say the least, pissed. They snapped and snarled, lunging at the end of their long chains.

I let my eyes go to Maks first. He was not on Balder, but another Jinn was. I glared at him. "That's my horse."

I gave a three-toned shrill whistle and Balder reared up, going from well-trained war horse to bucking bronco in 2.2 seconds. The other Jinn I didn't recognize shot forward on a big black horse. That Jinn held his hand out and mist poured from his fingers.

Lila screamed and I twisted to find her held tightly

by Maks. He held her in front of him, wrapped up so her wings were bound flat against her body.

I reached for the flail but the mist hit me first, pinning my arms to my ribs. I shifted to my cat form and howled as I fell on my face, my front legs stuck back to my sides. I squirmed and fought, shifted back to two legs and booted the Jinn in the face as he bent close.

"That's right, keep fighting. It'll give me something to blame the bruises on." The Jinn leaned over me, pale blue eyes visible and all but glowing in the dark. I snapped a knee up and caught him in the side, flipping him away from me.

"Vic, I told you to just pin her down." Maks sounded tired, and then the bands on me tightened and my eyes shot to him. His hand was held out to me and thick gray sparkling mist danced around his fingers. My legs jerked together and my hands were forced to my back as tightly as if they were using iron bands.

Lila let out a roar that was both pitiful and heart-breaking. Defeat was not a good look on either of us. I closed my eyes so I didn't have to see Maks's face. I couldn't look at him. Couldn't think about the betrayal he was clearly showing us. Maybe it was all Marsum. Maybe it wasn't.

"Kill the dragon, Maks," one of the Jinn said.

"NO!" I screamed the word and my eyes popped open wide. Whatever defiance and strength left in me came surging to the surface. I rolled around so I was on my butt, then rocked back onto my shoulders and flipped up onto my feet.

The werehyenas chattered their maniacal laughter at me.

I wobbled. "No, I need her with me."

"*We* don't need her," the Jinn that went by Vic said. He looked at me. "What will you give me for her life?"

"The flail," I whispered. "Take the flail."

"No!" Lila yelled. "You need that!"

Vic tipped his head to the side. "What flail?"

I twisted so he could see my back. "The flail of Marsum."

He crowed and I was jerked off my feet as he snagged the flail. I whispered softly, "Take his life, please."

The flail left my back and Vic swung it around, testing the weight. I dropped to my knees and the twin spike balls barely missed my head.

"It's light," Vic said. "Too light for battle. This can't be the flail of Marsum."

I held my breath. I needed to save Lila. "Flail, I know you can hear me. If I am your master, if you belonged to my mother, then you can do as I say. Take his life!" I yelled the words and Vic laughed.

"Kill the dragon," Vic said.

"PLEASE!" I screamed. I was desperate. Because Maks wasn't going to save her. Because I had no pride when it came to saving the sister of my heart.

I whipped my head around to see Maks still holding Lila, but his eyes were blank, and his hands hadn't moved.

"Maks, you know you can't do this! You can't kill her! She saved us both! Please, Maks, if there is anything left of the man I knew, you won't do this!" I begged and didn't care that I begged. I had no pride left to me if it meant I could save her.

His throat bobbed with a heavy swallow, but he didn't move to do anything, so I counted that as something. Lila sobbed, her body shaking even while she was pinned down. The sapphire stone, along with the other two, were in my bag, tucked away because that had seemed like the best idea. If we got out of this, I was never letting her take it off.

"Remember the țuică, Maks?" I said. "Remember that night we almost died in the snow? When you helped me out of the river? You are not a killer, Maks. You aren't. You aren't like them." His eyes flickered closed as I kept speaking. "Please, hate me all you want. Take me to Marsum. But don't kill her. She doesn't deserve to die."

The third Jinn approached him. "Give her to me, whelp, if you can't be a man and do as you're told."

Time seemed to slow, and I wished with all I had that there was some magic in me, that *somehow*, I could free Lila, that I could undo the magic that held her.

Please, please let me be something more, not for me, but for her. To save her.

There was a moment where Maks and I locked eyes. And then Lila let out a screech and her wings snapped out from her body, unleashed as she shot into the air, winging hard for height. "Shoot her!" Vic hollered.

"GO!" I yelled up at her. I didn't know where she'd go, only that she had to. But she was as fierce as she was little and she listened about as well as I did when it came to running from a fight.

There was a rush of something falling, the whistle of wind over her body, and then she was just there, dropping out of the sky, barrel rolling and avoiding the Jinn's mist. She belched as she went over the nameless Jinn, and green acid poured from her lips, sparking and dancing as it fell on his upturned face.

He screamed as the droplets hit him and then she was away again, heading for camp. "In the bag!" I yelled after her.

If she could get the sapphire then maybe we could get out of here. Maybe. Hope whispered through me.

"You mean these?" Vic held up the three stones. Clear diamond, blue sapphire, and deep emerald winked back at me.

I slumped. I knew Lila wouldn't leave me, but I didn't know how to keep her safe. Vic hauled me to my feet and then lifted me with ease so I was draped across his saddle, my ass not far from one of his hands.

He laid a hand on my butt. "I can see why you wanted to fuck her, Maks. She really does have a nice ass." He gave it a squeeze, then a swat, and I gritted my teeth. A low hiss slid out of me and the horse under us shied to the side.

Vic gave me a sharp slap on the other cheek. "Knock it off, cat."

I made myself stay still as the third Jinn managed to gather himself up. He mounted Balder again, wobbling, whimpering, one hand to his face. I grimaced at his unbalanced seat, knowing how much it would throw my horse off.

"Let's go. That dead giant is stinking the place up," Vic growled. "Bart, stop your whining and get your head in the game."

"It fucking hurts!" he howled. "I can't make it stop burning."

I laughed even though the laughter jammed my gut against the rounded pommel of the saddle. "It'll burn until there is nothing left to burn, dumb ass. It's acid. It will eat its way through anything. And don't try to help him, Vic. If it gets on you, then you'll be missing fingers in no time. Strike that, fucker. Help him all you like."

He swatted my ass for the third time and from across the way came a low growl. I lifted my head enough to see Maks staring hard at Vic. Even in the dark, the way he watched what was happening said it all.

Maks was still in there, somewhere. He'd let Lila go, and now seeing Vic spank me repeatedly was giving him some serious issues about just who was touching me.

"You think he'll save you yet?" Vic laughed and urged his horse forward, obviously unbothered by the fact that one of his buddies was whimpering in pain and clawing at his own face or that the other was obviously pissed at him and had death in his eyes.

The thump of a body hitting the ground caught my ears. I twisted to see only a glimpse of Bart as he writhed on the ground. Maks caught Balder by the reins and tugged him along.

"He let Lila go. That means something," I said finally. Vic grunted.

"No, he didn't."

"Um, yeah, dumb ass, he did." I squirmed as if trying to get comfortable when really, I was trying to see if I could get my fingers near either of my blades. Besides having my arms pinned, they were clamped in the middle of my back. I had a small blade tucked tightly to my lower spine, but I wasn't sure if I could reach it, if it would do me any good. A blade against magic was not really something I saw going well for me. But I couldn't stop trying.

"You are exactly what Marsum said you are," he muttered. "Which is bothersome. Because if he was right about you, then perhaps the rest of his words are true."

I wasn't sure if he was talking to me or not. And for the first time in a long time, I figured it might be best to stay quiet.

Maks rode up beside Vic. "It means we need to be careful. One on guard at all times. One watching her at all times."

"You think I'm a fool? As soon as Bart heals, it will be two watching her at all times. I don't trust you, Maks." Vic put a hand on the back of my head and ran his fingers through my locks. If not for the way he gripped at the tangled mess, I would have said he was trying to be seductive. "And you still want her, which means she can control you yet."

He jerked my head up sharply, putting a bend in my back that had me whimpering. I didn't try to bite back the noises. If I let Maks see the trouble I was in, then maybe I could get him to save me yet. Control him, no.

But maybe if he saw me suffer, it would spark the protectiveness I knew was in him. A foolish hope, a part of me knew that, but I still wanted to try. I didn't want to totally give up on him.

Vic let my head go and I slumped again. Time ticked by. The rolling gait of the horse lulled me into a sleep that was fitful and far from restful. They rode through the night and at dawn they stopped and made camp.

The werehyenas were staked at the edge of the camp, their chains tied down by Vic's magic.

"I think Marsum will like these new pets." He patted one of the oversized canids on the head. The creature's deep gray eyes met mine while it suffered itself to be treated like a mutt. I gave it the slightest of nods and it narrowed its eyes at me. I shrugged. If the werehyenas didn't want my help freeing them, then I wouldn't when I got free. And I would be damned if that wasn't going to happen.

"Four hours to rest, then we go again," Vic said.

Maks nodded and went about setting up the camp, not unlike how he did when we had traveled together.

"Well trained, isn't he?" Vic sat next to me and the mist rolled from his fingers. He moved my arms to the front and bound them once more, my fingers laced and unable to respond to even a small command from me. Best I could do was glare.

"Fuck you."

"I'd like to, but Marsum made it clear the only person getting your sweet ass is him. That being said, anything else goes as far as I'm concerned." Vic leaned in close and I let out a small growl as I bared my teeth. I might not have the jaws of a lion, but even on two legs, I had overly sharpened canines. He laughed, caught my head and kissed me hard, plundering my mouth with his tongue. I fought to get away, but bound as I was, there was not much I could do but bite him. I twisted my head and cut his lip with my canine, tasting blood as he pulled away—magic, that's what he tasted like, magic and the desert, and I didn't dislike the flavor, which bothered me. I grimaced and shook my head. "You taste like shit."

He licked his lips and ran a hand through his hair. "You taste a little like a clear spring after a year in the desert. I might have to take another drink later." He grinned at me, his eyes full of lust.

I stared up at him, hating him. Hating the Jinn. Hating everything that was happening.

A sound I knew well lit the air and I forced myself not to move, not to react to it.

A blade coming free of a scabbard.

Vic turned and dropped to a knee as said blade whistled through the place where his head had been only a moment before. He reached for the flail.

"Are you insane? You just lost the bounty on your head. Do you want your father to kill you?" Vic roared as he launched at Maks, the flail coming free. I pushed off and slammed my body into the back of Vic's knees, dropping him and bringing the flail to the ground as well.

Maks sidestepped the two of us and brought the handle of the long sword down hard on Vic's head. Vic rolled to the side, groaning, his hand releasing the flail.

The bonds on my arms and legs wavered and then were gone. I lurched forward and Maks caught me with one arm. He lowered his forehead to mine. "Run, Zam."

I reached for his face, not hesitating for a second. "Come with me, Maks."

"No, he'll take me again if he thinks you've gotten away."

He, meaning Marsum. I cupped his face. "Please tell me we can undo this."

Maks shook his head. "I will always love you, Zam."

I pulled him to me, kissing him hard and he kissed me back as fiercely as he ever had. A part of me hoped that like any fairy tale, the kiss of your true love would be enough to save him, but I knew it wouldn't. Love wasn't enough.

It was never enough.

I let him go, bent and scooped up the flail, then went to the bags where the three stones were. I took them back. Maks watched me as I considered Vic on the ground.

"Goodbye, Maks. I will always love you," I whispered.

The pain in his face and eyes tore at me like claws dragged through my flesh. Good gods, this ache in my heart was like nothing I'd ever felt. Not even losing Bryce could compete with this pain of knowing Maks was trapped, that there was no saving him from a madman. I ran for Balder and leapt onto his back, put my heels to his sides and bolted away before I could say anything else.

Before Maks could say anything else.

The werehyenas howled after me. But what did I care? They would kill me and take the stones. It was obvious they did not want nor need my help.

From above me came the sound of leather-clad wings, and then Lila slammed into my chest. She knocked the wind out of me as she clambered to wrap her wings around my neck. I leaned over her, leaned over Balder's neck and let him have his head.

The Jinn behind us would not give up now that we were in front of them. And there would be no second chances for us.

There was no more time to be subtle.

We would race into the desert with death and enslavement in front and behind.

What a fucking day.

Chapter Sixteen

B alder, Lila, and I galloped for a solid hour as fast as he could take us. Sweat foamed along his neck and down his sides before I asked him to slow. Even then, he plunged forward as if he could keep going. He probably could, but we were a few hours ahead of the others now, I had no doubt. The other horses didn't have the build for speed. They were warhorses meant for carrying big men and armor. I frowned, thinking of Batman. What had happened to him? Maks loved that horse.

I leapt off Balder and walked beside him, giving him a rest. The terrain was shifting into a more desert-like look even here near to the water. The ground was sand in places and the heat of the day had begun to climb even in that short span.

"Lila, are you okay?"

She was still curled tightly to my chest, and she'd been quiet the whole time we'd galloped away.

"No." She shook her head. "I'm not okay."

Panic lashed me and I put a hand to her back. "Injured?"

"I thought we were both dead there," she said. "And that Maks would be the one to do it." A shudder went through her and I knew why. Her own father, her own siblings, had been sent to kill her. To weed her out because she was weak. I looped Balder's reins over his neck but continued to walk beside him. I reached for my bag and pulled the sapphire stone out. "You need to wear this, Lila. It gives us an edge."

"I don't want to be like the Ice Witch," she whispered. "I don't want to go mad with power like my father."

"And I don't want to end up bound by the Jinn again. You carry the sapphire, and for now, I will carry the diamond. We will leave the emerald in the bag."

I pulled the blue stone out first. The sapphire was about the size of my fist. I took a piece of leather strapping from my bag and wrapped the stone until there was no blue showing. Then I slid the thong over her head and set it up like a harness so the stone didn't move and shake. "How's that?"

She leapt off my shoulder and into the air, flew around a few times and then came back. "I barely feel it. Shouldn't it be heavy and make me unbalanced?"

"Was it heavy and unbalanced when you used it against the gorcs?" I asked.

She shook her head. "No, but I thought it was a heat of the battle kind of thing where I just didn't notice it."

Even as I looked at her, the stone seemed to get

smaller and blend in better with the leather straps and the scales on her body. I frowned again. "Well, it looks to be making itself at home."

"I want a safe word," she said suddenly. "Like if you start to see me go crazy, a word that tells me I have to take it off."

I raised my eyebrows at her. "Okay. Banana pants."

She laughed. "What's a banana?"

"My dad said it was a kind of fruit that was yellow and looked like a dong." I grinned, knowing full well we were avoiding all the messy stuff that had just happened. That our joking hid the ugly truth of the day.

"Banana pants it is." She shook her head and moved to my shoulder, wrapping her tail around my neck, her tiny claws clutching the edge of my ear. "That was nasty back there, Zam. That was scary."

"Yup."

"Marsum will try to use me to hurt you, just like he's using Maks," she said. "We need a plan."

She was right on both counts. "We're still a week from the edge of the Jinn's Dominion." I paused and looked behind us as if we could see the Jinn on our tail. "If we go east again, we could hug the shoreline. That'll give us drinkable water for a few days yet. It doesn't go completely saline until the southern tip. There are plenty of fish to be had. Footing isn't bad, less likely to get any stone bruises on Balder."

"The storms, though," Lila said.

"Right, but we have to assume the Emperor now has his sights on Shem, and Shem is headed the other way."

She tightened her hold on my ear. "Maybe. I don't

think we can assume anything."

Her words reminded me of what Destry had said. I quickly filled her in on the giant queen's belief that the Emperor had poisoned the land and wiped out her clan because she wouldn't buckle to his whims.

"You think she was right?" Lila asked.

I pulled out the magic dust Destry had given me. "She believed it enough to give me this."

I held the leather bag out to Lila and she poked at it with the tip of her nose. "What is it?"

"Magic dust, apparently. No idea if it's anything or just ground-up mushrooms." I put it back under my cloak. "But she thought it was important. She said if I sprinkled it on me I would be strong, strong."

Lila blew out a breath. "I don't like any of this."

"Neither do I. I can't turn away from the others, Lila. But I won't be mad if you—"

"Don't even think it," she growled and pinched the edge of my ear hard enough to draw a yelp from me. "We're in this together whether you like it or not. You're my sister."

I smiled. "Thanks." I mounted onto Balder and moved him into his ground-covering trot. We couldn't really slow down. I had no doubt the Jinn would ride their mounts into the ground, fueling them with their magic to keep them going until they dropped dead.

I kept Balder to the east, along the seashore. The ground was hard enough that following us would be difficult, and I had Lila sweep the hoof prints with her wings, flying back and forth across the sections that showed a scuff or a turn of soil.

We rode between the hills, pushing hard to the south. I kept looking back, fully expecting a cloud of dust announcing the Jinn on our asses yet again. I swallowed, my throat tight as I thought of Maks. He'd hurt Vic and let us go. There was going to be hell to pay for him. Was that why they weren't on us? Because they were too busy hurting Maks?

I let myself find the energy that was Maks. It was the same pulsing colors as before, wrapped in sickness. I'd not even asked him how he was dying, why he hadn't said anything about it in all the time I'd known him.

It felt as though a hand wrapped around my heart and squeezed it hard enough to slow its beating. Lila, flying beside me, must have seen my face change. "What is it?"

"Thinking about Maks. He'll be punished for letting us go. And he's sick, Lila. So sick."

"It wasn't him," Lila said softly. "He didn't change anything. I could feel his magic holding me."

I looked at her and frowned. "But then how'd you get away?"

She grinned, her eyes sparkling. "You happened. You did something and his magic was gone and all I felt was warmth, and a burst of energy that . . . well, for lack of explaining it better, it felt like you. I could feel how much you loved me, and it set me free."

My jaw dropped. "Are you shitting me?"

"Nope, not one little bird turd of shit." She grinned. I stared.

"Lila, that isn't possible. I didn't feel a thing." I stumbled over the words. There had been a brief moment, but it was there and gone before I could say it was anything.

"Well, it's what happened." She shrugged her wings up and then winged ahead of me and flew backward. "Maybe that's how magic works for you. You just don't feel anything."

I snorted. "That's ridiculous. How can that even be?"

"I just know that Maks didn't let me go, Zam. You freed me."

I wanted to deny her again, but she turned and flew behind to check our back trail. "I don't have any magic, Balder," I said and patted his neck.

He blew out a big breath and bobbed his head. I stared between his ears, seeing the glitter of the water in the distance. The Jinn had really gone way to the west. I hadn't even realized just how far until now.

The sirens saw us again, waving. That was likely why. Even the Jinn were not immune to the sirens' calls.

That wasn't really what I wanted to think about, though. What if Lila was right? What if I did have magic? I shook my head even as I wondered. Maks had to have let her go. That was all there was to it. Sure, I loved her to pieces, but I knew without a shadow of a doubt that Maks loved her too.

That had to be what she felt. There was no other answer. Because what was magic when you couldn't feel it? Nothing, that's what.

The problem was I couldn't fully deny what everyone around me was saying. Maggi, Destry, and now the Jinn saying I was more than what they thought.

I gritted my teeth and stared ahead. No, they were wrong. I would know if I had magic running in my veins . . . wouldn't I?

My hand went to my neck, but there was no necklace anymore. The one I'd worn for years, the one that had blocked a curse laid on me by Marsum.

A curse that nothing would ever go right for me, that I would fail at everything. I frowned as my thoughts jumbled together. If nothing went right, and I had magic, would that suppress the magic? Would that be what I was dealing with?

I rubbed a hand across my forehead. "This is giving me a damn headache," I grumbled.

The whoosh of wings told me Lila was on her way and I turned to see her flying hard for me. I squinted my eyes. There was no one behind her, so she wasn't being chased.

She tipped her wings and landed on Balder's rump, and he gave a little buck hop.

"I saw them," she breathed out. "The three of them are riding hard for the south. They went right past our trail."

"They didn't see you?" I asked.

She grimaced. "Maybe Maks did, but he was the only one looking up."

"So he's okay?"

Lila rolled her shoulders. "I'm not sure. I didn't get close enough, but he's upright on his horse. And those horses aren't going to last long. Maybe another six hours and then they'll start dropping."

"Maybe it's a good thing he lost Batman," I said.

"Maybe he let him go knowing what would come," she replied. She had a point. There was enough of Maks left that he was fighting where he could. Defying the other Jinn with little acts of rebellion.

Leaving his horse behind so he didn't run him into the ground was something the Maks we knew would do. I smiled to myself even while my heart struggled around the painful beats and my eyes watered.

"We don't have to ride as hard now if they passed us by already. If they were smart, they would have let the hyenas loose to track us," I said.

"They think they are better than everyone else," Lila said. "They would never stoop to use someone else to do a job they believed they were better skilled for. Those hyenas won't last, though. They'll drop and then we could be dealing with them again."

She had a point.

I eased Balder to a walk. We reached the shoreline a short time later, filling our water bags and letting Balder have a deep drink. There would come a point where the water was no longer fresh, but salt, and we needed to take advantage of it while we could.

"Tell me about the layout of the Jinn's Dominion," Lila said. "Maybe we can come up with a plan that will actually work for getting in and out."

I laughed, but there was no mirth in it. "This will be like walking into a lion's den with bloody steaks strapped to our asses. Just in case you were wondering."

"Yeah, I figured as much. But if they think we'll come roaring in like lions to face them, they don't know us all that well." She preened as she spoke.

I laughed for real that time. "You have a point, Lila the Fierce."

I closed my eyes and let the swaying of Balder's steps act as a rhythmic form of meditation. "The Jinn's Dominion is built like a hub with the weaker Jinn on the outskirts, working through four levels of their power structure to the central hub where only the most powerful Jinn sit."

"Well, that's stupid. Shouldn't it be a mix?" Lila muttered. I let it slide, even though I agreed.

I tried to see the maps in my head my father had pored over. Ex-marine that he was, he was all about the strategy of a battle, the lay of the land and how to use it to his advantage.

"Each ring is marked by five towers, so as you draw closer to the center the towers are closer together and so much harder to get by." In my head, I could see the map as my father's hand sketched it out in the sand. I squatted to his left, and Bryce to his right. I spoke the words that he'd given to us then, verbatim. "Going to the middle between the outer towers takes you directly into the path of the next rim of towers. It's much more challenging than just taking the safest path. The watch towers are manned by the Jinn's dead. Great flying creatures that have no purpose except to protect and guard the inner sanctum of the Jinn."

"WHAT?" Lila bellowed the word. "I know all the flying creatures out there. What are they?"

"Like a twisted man, a blend of gargoyle and dead that leaves a body almost impenetrable to traditional weapons like swords, and a soul commanded by only the first Jinn."

Lila grunted. "The first Jinn, meaning Marsum."

I nodded and opened my eyes. "Yeah, I think so. The reality is the four rims of the Dominion are guarded not only by Jinn of varying powers, but these dead Jinn too. Even after they die, they aren't released from service."

Lila shuddered and I had to agree. At least in death, you should have some measure of peace even if you were an asshole.

That was what waited for Maks if we killed him. Not freedom. More enslavement. Maggi was wrong about that much, his death would bring him nothing but more chains.

We rode on, discussing the possibilities, always coming back to only one truth. No matter which direction we took, we needed to go in small, which meant stashing Balder somewhere safe, somewhere we could get back to.

There was only one place I could think of. The Oasis. It wasn't far from the Jinn's Dominion which was why it had been used as a place of parlay.

Night fell and we stopped and set up a small camp, no fire. I didn't dare with the Jinn and their new pets having passed us by earlier that day. I wrapped myself in my cloak after feeding Balder and sharing some of my dried food stores with Lila. Not really all that tasty, but it filled the void in my belly.

"Do we want to set a guard?" Lila asked, yawning and stretching.

I nodded. "I'll stay up for a few hours, then I'll trade off. We'll leave before light." I pushed to my feet and dropped my cloak. The night air was warm enough, I didn't need it if I was going to be up on my feet circling our camp. Lila burrowed into the material still warm from my body with a happy sigh.

I walked to the edge of the sand before it turned into rock and stared south. My heart was torn into little aching pieces, and I hated this new pain as much as I'd hated Steve. I grimaced. "I really have shit choices in men. Either they betray me, or they are forced to betray me. Maybe I need to be celibate after this." I let out a breath and a soft shuffle caught at my ears. I turned and dropped to a crouch, my hands going to my kukri blades.

A thud, and then another of hoof beats . . . I lifted my head as a shape emerged from the southern dunes. Black coat, a limping step, and no rider.

"Batman?" I stood and he snorted and shied to the side, stumbling. "Easy, easy, buddy." I held my hands out, and he sniffed the air in my direction and then hurried to me. I pulled a few oat balls from my pockets, partially crushed, but he didn't care as he took them gently from my palm. I ran my hands over him, checking him for wounds or other injuries. That same bum leg of his was swollen and there was a bone out of place. He grunted as I probed it, a grimace on my face. A fracture then. I frowned and my hand went to my kukri blade on my right thigh. There was no fixing a break in a horse's leg, not out here, not on a horse that was meant to run.

"Oh, buddy, I'm so sorry," I stood and pressed my head against his neck. "Was this why Maks let you go?" He shook his head side to side and his mane flipped over to me, smacking me. A thin piece of material tied in the dark threads was rolled tightly and had bumped me.

I untangled it, thinking it was just some fly-away from him being loose on his own. But the material rolled out in my hands, words etched onto it with charcoal.

I saw the first few lines and my eyes blurred. Maks had left me a note.

"Zam, I know you'll find this because I know Batman will always find you and Balder. He knows where his home is, just like I do. I can't tell you how sorry I am. I thought I was strong enough to resist Marsum's hold on me. I think Shem knew what I was getting into. He suspected at least and he asked me to make the choice for you if I thought it would happen and Marsum would take over me. The closer I get to Marsum, the tighter his hold will be on me. I can feel the noose tightening already. I know I can't convince you to leave your pride and run for the hills, so I will say this. There is a pathway through the four rims that will take you into the inner sanctum. It starts near the northern tower. Watch for the flickers of golden stone beneath the sand. That is your path, and it will give you the best chance to survive both in and out."

I took a breath, barely realizing that I hadn't been breathing, then continued. *"The rest, well the rest is I can only say thank you. For a little while, I knew what it was to be part of a family, to know that you loved me for who I was, and not because you saw in me a conduit to Marsum's power. I will never forget you. I will never forget the night of the țuică. It was then I knew you would be the last woman I ever wanted. Don't try to save me, Zam. I know you're thinking about it. It's that damn heart of a lion you have, but there is no way to make it happen. There is no cure for being a Jinn. Tell Lila I'm sorry. I never meant to hurt her. Tell her I am and always will be proud to call her my little sister. My fierce Lila. Do right by Batman. I couldn't let him be killed by the Jinn. I knew they would do it. But I knew they would make him suffer."*

He signed the end of it simply, *Maks*. Though to be fair, I could barely see through the blurring of my eyes. Batman nudged me with his nose, put his head on my shoulder and tugged me to his chest. I wrapped my arms around his thick neck and clung to him. "Shit, Batman, I can't do it either. I can't just let you go any more than I can let him go."

He held me tightly, his jaw bone digging into my back. I stood there for a few minutes, my heart and mind racing.

Lila thought I had magic.

Merlin thought I was special.

My mother had died to keep me from Marsum.

That all had to mean something more than just being a simple shifter. It had to.

"Screw this bullshit. I'm not giving up." I slid down until I was on my knees in front of Batman. His left front leg was swollen, hot. The fracture would only continue to spread, and that meant it had to be healed right now if he was to go on.

"Lila, let's hope you were right," I said.

I wrapped my fingers around his leg, feeling the crack under my fingertips. He snorted and bumped me with his nose. "Hang on. I don't know if this will hurt or not."

Yeah, I was stalling. Mostly because I didn't want to know that I couldn't do this, because if I couldn't do it then I would have to end Batman's suffering. As merciful as it would be, that was no small thing to do to cut a horse's throat. Especially one that you'd trained and worked with for years.

I ran my hands up and down his leg, massaging the swollen area, working the blood flow as I worked to slow my breath.

I closed my eyes and wrapped my fingers tightly around the section of his leg that was cracked.

Please, I don't know what you are, or if you're my magic or even if you can help me. Batman's leg is hurt. Please fix it. We need him. I repeated the phrase over and over until sweat beaded on my upper lip and my hands ached from holding him so tightly.

He gave a low groan and my hands tingled for just a moment, like I'd buried my hands deep into the sand at high noon, feeling the warmth of the desert. A rush of energy caught me off guard and I opened my eyes to see the bonds of my pride wrapped around me. Not just the lions I sought, but Maks and Lila too. Their energy flowed into me and from there it pulsed into Batman. The colors wove around one another and under my hand the bone cracked, only it didn't crack apart. I could see it under his skin as clearly as any picture, and watched as the bone slid back together with a soft click. Batman jerked his leg up, holding it as if I would clean out the hoof, bobbing it there. The colors soaked into his skin and then they were gone as fast as they'd been there.

I took my hands away and he lowered his hoof, took a step and then another. Perfectly sound, I could see it already.

To say I was shocked was a small understatement.

"Holy shit. Holy fucking shit!" I lifted my hands to the sky, fists clenched. I fought the yell of triumph because I didn't want to wake Lila, but apparently, I'd been gone too long, and she'd taken note.

She flew in beside me, breathless and her eyes wide. "What's happened? Wait, is that Batman?"

The words rolled out of me so fast I wasn't sure she'd understand me. "Yes, that's Batman and then there was a note in his mane and the note was from Maks but Batman's leg was broken and I knew I would have to put him down but I didn't want to and I remembered you think I have magic, and Marsum wants me for some reason and Merlin thinks I'm special and I thought that the only thing that I had to lose was a little pride and really no one would even know if I failed but I didn't fail and oh my gods, Lila his leg healed and it was all of us together, it's not me it's the pride, my pride and it was all of us, all the energy wove together to heal him." I drew a breath and she lifted a wing tip, stalling me.

"Wait, can I see the note?"

I handed it to her. Batman trotted over to Balder and the two boys butted noses and then sidled up to one another, happy to have their friendship united once more. But that . . . I couldn't know that. That they were happy to see one another. I frowned and stared at them. I could read their body language, but there was no way I was picking up on emotions.

I searched myself and there was nothing there, just my own feelings. My own elation at doing something I didn't think possible but that needed to be done.

Batman would be okay.

And then I remembered the rest of the note. Maks saying goodbye.

Ah, gods of the desert and sand, that hurt. Lila finished reading the note and handed it back to me.

"Do you think the way in, is the way in?" she asked. "Or is it a trick?"

I didn't let myself answer right away. I let her question soak in for a moment. The north tower was directly south of the Oasis where the Jinn had wiped out my family. It had a certain sense of coincidence I couldn't deny. "Yes, I think it's a way in. As much as Marsum and the Jinn want us to believe Maks is totally gone, he's not."

We went back to the tiny camp together. Balder's head rested across Batman's back, sound asleep.

Maybe it wasn't much, but it lifted my heart to see them together. They were friends, buddies, and they'd been through a fair amount of shit together. I sat and Lila climbed into my lap and promptly went back to sleep.

I stayed awake all night, thinking about the Jinn's Dominion, how we would get in and out with three other full-sized lions.

Maybe a little bit of magic dust, and the heart of a lion, and a small dragon would be enough.

Because by morning, I had a plan.

Chapter Seventeen

Five days of riding at a quick but not brutal pace brought us to the southern tip of the Caspian Sea.

We saw two more sets of standing stones and one blood vine that tangled itself around a body. A man. "Who do you think got caught?" Lila asked as we stared at the shrunken body.

"No idea. He was naked." I was sure it was a man. The body was too big, too bulky, even after being drained.

She leapt off my shoulder and swept toward it, staying high as she inspected it. A single pass and she was back to me. "Werehyena, I think."

Well, that worked in our favor. I hoped. Except for the fact that it gave the Emperor more strength.

The seals native to the Caspian Sea barked at us as we past headed east, still hugging the curve of the water.

Their barks followed us, announcing our passage as surely as any guard dog.

"Shut up, you ding dongs!" Lila hollered, diving around them and teasing them. Which of course only set them to barking more as they leapt for her.

I glanced over just as she snatched a fish right out of a seal's mouth and flew away, cackling. I grinned. She'd found her chutzpah again, no problem. I, on the other hand, was more and more nervous the closer we got to our destination. I wondered if this was how she'd felt going into the Dragon's Ground. Which meant I needed to suck it up and hold my shit together.

She gobbled the fish up and swung by me, stinking of fish and salt water. We'd lost our fresh water now that we were so far south. "How is today looking?"

I kept my voice flat, emotionless so it wouldn't shake. "We'll reach the Oasis this afternoon. Tomorrow we will go into the Jinn's Dominion."

She landed on Batman who calmly trotted next to me and Balder. He kept up much better with no rider. His leg, despite the harder work, held up as if it had never broken, as if the old injury had never been. I still couldn't believe that he was sound. Broken legs in horses only ended up one way.

"How do you feel about the Oasis? Have you ever been back since that day?" she asked.

I shook my head. "No. I don't even know what happened to the bodies of the lions. Ishtar swept in and scooped us away before I could do anything. Before I could even consider burying them."

She was quiet a moment. "It will be okay, Zam. We've come this far. I can't believe we would fail now."

I wasn't so sure she was right, and a line came to me from one of Shakespeare's plays.

"And so, from hour to hour, we ripe and ripe. And then, from hour to hour, we rot and rot; And thereby hangs a tale." I said the words slowly, feeling the truth of them for the first time.

Lila nodded, her eyes narrowed a bit. "That's from *As You Like It*, isn't it?"

"Yes. This story is far from over, Lila. I feel like we've only just begun to dig through the surface of what is going on in this world. All these fucking assholes before me thought they were protecting me, us, by keeping us in the dark, and all they've done is hamstring me." I shook my head and Balder picked up his pace as he picked up on my irritation.

I struggled to keep my emotions in check as we rode on, and I began to see places from my childhood. At the very least, we wouldn't be going through the village where the women and children were left to rot. I was sure there would still be bones scattered there, bits of huts, old gear worn and half covered by the sands of the desert. Nearly twenty years since that fateful day when our world had been torn asunder.

Near midday, a hill sat ahead of us and I stopped Balder at the bottom and slid off his back. "The Oasis is on the other side. We need to go up carefully since it is a common place for different species to stop and drink. It's supposed to be neutral territory."

Lila hopped off Batman and I set the two horses up,

ground tying them. As well trained as they were, nothing short of a full-on attack would make them leave where they stood, waiting for me to call them. I gave them each an oat ball and then shifted to my cat form, dropping to all fours. The sand was warm on the pads of my paws as I bounded up the slippery slope, Lila at my side.

The last time I'd come this route, I'd chased Bryce, wanting to see the Jinn for myself. I looked to my left, and for just a moment, I was sure I saw him there, in his lion form, racing up beside me. He turned his head, winked, and then was gone.

Not gone, still with me, just not in the flesh.

Seeing him made me think of the Emperor's promise. That he could give me my brother back if I would bow to him. My thoughts slid away as I slowed near the top of the dune and lowered to my belly to creep up the last bit. At the crest of the hill, I flattened my ears to my skull and peeked over the edge. Lila did the same, pinning her wings back to her sides and peering over the top.

The Oasis hadn't changed a great deal, not really. The swaying trees were still thick on top with green foliage, and the palm fronds swayed. The ground was covered only in patches of life-sustaining plants, and there was no sound. Not even of water rippling against a shoreline. The water was near the center of the Oasis, so that part didn't surprise me.

The wind whipped around us in a gust and I narrowed my eyes against the flying sand.

"You see anything?" Lila whispered.

"Nothing. Follow me, stick close." I stayed on my

belly and all but slithered over the top of the dune, sliding down the slope as quietly as I could.

Lila was beside me and as soon as we hit the flat of the bottom, I bolted across the open space to the cover of the first clump of trees. My heart pounded almost out of control and while I might have tried to tell myself it was the run across the open space, I knew better. The past reared its head around me, whispering things I didn't want to remember in clear detail. I could see the lions moving around me, ghosts in my mind, the sound of their roars filling my ears.

Lila pushed against me, covering me with one wing. "Deep breaths. It is in the past, Zam."

She was right, and she was wrong, but I did as she said and managed to get myself under control. I tipped my head up and sucked in a deep breath. There was no smell of Jinn, at least nothing that was recent. But there was something else that both caught me off guard and gave me a burst of hope.

"Lion shifter," I whispered as I crept forward, following the smell. The scent was strong enough that there was no doubt the shifter was still here, but I didn't recognize them. Male or female I couldn't tell, and it was no shifter from my pride. I kept moving deeper through the Oasis until I found the edge of the water, and that was where the lion shifter sat.

Literally, in a lion's form, but holy shit he was not what I expected.

Lila sucked in a breath a little too sharply and he whipped his head around, his solid black mane flaring.

Black fur rippled as he stood and stalked toward us, mouth open as he scented the air.

Easily, he was as big as Bryce had been. Maybe larger, it was hard to say from the angle we stood.

A low growl rumbled out of him, and I immediately put myself in front of Lila. I couldn't help it, my body puffed up and I arched my back, turning sideways. A hiss snarled out of me and I ignored the fact he probably couldn't hear it over his growl.

His eyes widened and then . . . the bastard had the nerve to sit and laugh at me. "Shit, are you serious? You think you can take me on, little cat?"

"You think you want to mess with the alpha of the Bright Lion Pride?" Lila snapped as she shot into the air.

He grinned and yawned. "The Bright Lion Pride was wiped out a long time ago. As were most of the lions. There are no prides left."

I glared at him and shifted so I stood on two legs. I pointed a finger at him. "Shift. Now!"

I put as much command into my voice as I could and he shocked me by doing as I said. He shifted to two legs, his eyes wide like he was as surprised as me.

He had black hair and eyes just as dark with a rim of gold. He was taller than me, built broad in the chest and narrow in the hip. He reminded me a bit of Shem in his form.

Lila squeaked. "He's naked. Damn, I forgot about that part."

I kept my eyes on his, hands on my hips. A naked body didn't bother me. That was part of a shifter's life.

I walked right up to him and jammed a finger in his chest. "Who are you, and what are you doing here?"

He arched an eyebrow over dark eyes. "Who are you?"

"I asked first," I growled, never lowering my eyes from his. I'll give him credit, he tried to keep his eyes up, but he was no alpha. His eyelids flickered.

"Ford. From the Gold Creek Pride." He lifted his eyes and grinned up at me.

"Zamira. From the Bright Lion Pride," I said.

His eyebrows shot up. "Dirk's pride? I heard that's where the slaughter started." I didn't correct him, and he rambled on like the apparent fool he was. "Can I put my clothes on now?"

"No." I didn't look away from him. "What are you doing here?"

"Looking for a mate." He eyed me up suddenly as if assessing my possibilities.

"Fuck off, she's taken," Lila snarled.

Before I could say anything, he threw back his head and laughed. "Oh, shit, I would never want a tiny little thing like you! I was looking because where there is one lion, there's a chance there's more."

I arched a brow at him. "I suggest you leave. There are no mates . . ." A thought crossed my mind. He was looking for a mate. It wouldn't hurt to have an extra pair of eyes at my back. Male lions when hunting for a lady would do anything to get their grubby mitts on them. Including stupid, dangerous things like walking into the enemy's encampment. Assuming I could trust him.

Then again, he was being brutally honest at the moment.

I glanced at Lila and she shrugged, almost like she could read my mind.

"I'm about to go into the Jinn's Dominion. They are holding three of my pride members hostage. Two females, one male." I tipped my chin at him. "Might that interest you, playing the hero to two women?"

His eyes lit up. "Tell me they aren't all teeny tiny like you and you might have my attention."

Sweet baby goddess, he had a one-track mind. "Darcy is a very finely formed woman, but you need to understand something. I am their alpha, which means you need my permission to take her from our pride."

Lila landed on my shoulder. "Oh, this is new. I didn't know that."

I shrugged. "You'll catch on."

Ford looked from me to Lila and back again. "Wait, why would she catch on?"

"She's my second."

He bellowed a laugh again, slapping his hands on his knees repeatedly.

Lila grumbled. "Now? Can you kick his ass now?"

"Give it a minute," I said. We could use him, and I wouldn't feel terrible if he died, to be honest. Not with this attitude. Then again, this was typical behavior for most male lions. Fat lazy bastards who expected the women to do all the work, have the babies, and bring them lunch, then bend over and . . . well, you get the picture.

He dropped his head between his knees as if to catch his breath and I kicked up, catching him square under the jaw with the toe of my boot. There was a satisfying click of his teeth snapping together and then he flipped backward, flat onto his back. As he fell, I leapt toward him, pulled both kukri blades and ended up on his chest.

Ford's dark eyes were fogged with confusion as he stared up at me. "What happened?"

"I kicked you in the face, fool. Now. *I'm the alpha*. You got that?"

I pressed one blade under his chin and I reached back and pressed the tip of the other close to his family jewels.

"Lower and to the left," Lila called out with a little too much glee, but I did as she suggested. The confusion left his eyes and submission rocked through them.

"I got it. You're the alpha. You . . . are you taking me into your pride?" He seemed uncertain.

"You want in?" I raised a brow at him again.

His eyes went thoughtful. "Yeah, maybe I do. You obviously have the balls, even if you aren't much bigger than a desert mouse."

I pressed a little harder with the blade against his balls. "Really, you want to insult me right now?"

His grin didn't slip. "Look, if you were a real lion, I'd be all over you, and you'd be all over me. I'm just keeping this real. I can see you're a leader. I'll give you that. But I won't pussy foot around the fact that you're smaller than any other shifter out there, which worries me."

I hated that he was right, because it was the truth simply put. I was smaller.

And I always would be. I eased up a little on the blades. "Will you be able to hold in your dickish behavior and actually help if you're in the pride?"

He winked. "Of course I can. Can you take a joke when I poke fun at your teeny tiny kitty cat form? I have a terrible sense of humor."

My jaw ticked. "I've been the butt of jokes my whole life, asshole. I can take it, but when I say jump, you'd better ask me how high on your way up."

He spread his arms wide, muscles rippling. "You got it. You're the boss. I want to be your second."

"Nope." I shook my head. His size might work in my favor, especially when it came to Steve being a pig. "You can be the enforcer. Seeing as I'm so fucking teeny tiny."

"Ooh, even better." His grin widened and he rubbed his hands together. "How many members then?"

I stepped off him and sheathed my two blades. "Three in the Jinn's lockdown, with one of the ladies pregnant. Me and Lila. And two others . . . one other, but he won't be around much. The other is off on a mission of his own making."

Maks and Shem were still part of our pride as far as I was concerned. I wasn't about to not count him.

Ford's eyes went wide as he moved into a crouch. "Shit, that's a big pride. I mean, for what's left of the lions. I've never found more than a lone male here and there. No females at all."

I nodded. "Most of us were scooped up as kids and

hidden far from the desert. We lost my brother recently, so we're down one."

Lila climbed my leg, settled on my shoulder, and peered at Ford. "Were you really here looking for a mate?"

He nodded. "I figured my best bet was an Oasis. Everyone comes through them at some point. I've checked out three others. I usually stay a month or better, depending on the location."

I nodded. That made sense. "Well, Ford, you are now the enforcer of the Bright Lion Pride. That means you're on the hook for helping me save the rest of our members."

He clapped his hands together, rubbing them vigorously once more. "We going to kill some Jinn?"

I shook my head. "Not if we can help it. This is a search and rescue mission, not a search and destroy. Besides, have you ever even killed a Jinn?"

He held my eyes a moment, then looked away. "No, but I'd like to."

"I have," Lila said. His eyes whipped to her. "And so has Zam."

His jaw dropped. "You two tiny things?"

I turned my back on him. "Size isn't everything, Ford. You'll learn that eventually. I mean, assuming the ladies haven't already pointed it out." I grinned over my shoulder and his jaw remained dropped as he spread a hand toward his groin area.

"Please, the ladies' only complaint is the ride lasts too long."

I snorted. "Then you aren't doing it right."

Lila laughed and I joined in and even Ford laughed. For Ford being an obvious misogynist, he was funny, and he could take a joke if his laughter was any indication. A little laughter wouldn't hurt, and I'd cure him of the misogyny quickly enough.

"We have a way to get the other members of the pride out. But if we can't get them out, then we can't have a pride, and Darcy will be off the table for anyone, not just you." I turned and locked eyes with him, asserting dominance once more. "Got it?"

He grinned up at me. "I got it, boss. I've never had an alpha before."

"Ever?"

He sat up and rubbed his chin, scratching at the light stubble. "Nope. When our pride was wiped out by the Jinn, those of us who escaped scattered. I was still a cub and I ran until I collapsed. A mother caracal shifter and her son found me. I stayed there until I was grown."

My belly clenched. "You were raised by a caracal shifter?" I wasn't sure I'd heard him right.

"Yeah, they're pretty cool, but they don't tend to have an alpha because they don't run in prides. They're solitary creatures. My mom took me in even knowing that I would one day be a brute to feed." He grinned. "I looked out for her until she finally booted me out, told me I was too much to keep in food even for her."

I shot a look at Lila who was already staring hard at me. It couldn't possibly be the same unusually colored dark lion that Maks had talked about, could it? That he'd dreamed he'd been raised with as a cub.

Only one way to find out.

"Umm. Did you have a brother?" I asked. "Named Maks?"

Ford stared up at me, frowning. "Are you a mind reader? A telekinetic?"

My brow raised. He did know those were totally different things, right?

Lila snorted. "Oh, my gods, you might be cute, but you're kind of dumb."

My lips twitched as he glared at Lila. "We know Maks. He told us, well, he said he'd dreamed he'd had a younger brother he was raised with and he mentioned he was an unusual color for a lion. But he didn't tell us your name or that you were a black lion because he'd thought it was all a dream. I assumed he meant a red lion."

He shook his head. "No, that's not possible. Maks was killed a long time ago. The Jinn came looking for me and he ran out to lead them away. He never came back."

I nodded more to myself than to him. "Yes, that sounds like something Maks would do." And I was betting the connection to his brother was partly why Maks had taken on the job to come to the Stockyards in the first place even if he didn't realize it. That a dream of a brother who'd been a lion shifter would drive him to leave the Jinn.

I rubbed a hand on the back of my neck. "He's still alive, Ford. He's the other member of the pride."

Ford stared hard at me, his eyes closing down, hardening. "Where is he then?"

"The Jinn took him over again. He's part Jinn, part

shifter," I said. "He fought it while I knew him but . . . there is nothing we can do at the moment."

"You'd give up on him?" Ford snarled. "Where is he? I'll find him myself then."

I snapped a hand out and slapped him before I could stop myself, before I even thought of what I was doing. His head snapped to the side and I got up in his face. "I will *never* give up on Maks. Never. Right now, there are members of our pride who are in immediate danger. We save them first. Then Maks. Do you understand me?"

He slowly turned his head, anger burning in his eyes, but he lowered them, just a shade. "I understand, Alpha."

"Good." I twisted away from him, then turned back and pointed a finger at him. "Get some clothes on. We need to bring our horses in and have a chat."

Lila bobbed her head. "Yeah, we need to have a chat right now."

He gave me a mock salute, the anger still there simmering, spun and strolled toward his bag next to the water where he'd been sitting when we first arrived.

I backed up a few steps and then turned and hurried toward the outer edge of the Oasis.

"It seems way too coincidental that he's here," Lila said, keeping her voice low. "I mean, Maks tells you about this dream he'd had, of having a lion shifter as a brother, and then we just happen to run into him?"

I agreed, but my mind raced, because there was nothing off about Ford. Nothing that sent up my red flags other than the fact that he was obviously a dick.

"The Oasis is a well-known watering hole. If we were going to run into anyone, anywhere, this or one of the others would be the place."

At the edge of the Oasis, I let out a whistle for the two horses. A moment later, they crested the hill and slid down, their legs sinking into the loose sand. I caught their leads and they followed me happily to the shade of the trees and the water. They dropped their heads to drink and it was only then that I let myself look around.

The battle had taken place on the far side, and even from where I stood, I could tell there was very little left in terms of remains. The desert had reclaimed the bodies.

"Dust to dust," I said softly to myself.

Ford came over and stood next to me. "Is this where Dirk met the Jinn? There are a lot of bones over there when I checked, and even some weapons still visible."

I had an urge to touch him, so I let myself do it. I reached over and grabbed his forearm. He looked down at my hand as I gripped tightly.

"What are you doing?" he asked.

His skin under my hand was warm, but more than that was the sensation of him sinking into my bones as part of my pride. "Making the adoption official."

"You want me to call you Mom now?" His lips quirked to one side.

"Not so much." I tightened my hold. There was a pulse of energy between us and then I let go. He was there, just inside my head near the bundle of energy threads tied to each of my pride members. His were a dark orange and completely healthy. Unlike Maks's still pulsing with sickness.

I looked at Lila and she nodded. "Yeah, I feel it too, like I want to protect him now, and not just kick his ass for being an idiot."

That was the thing about being an alpha or an alpha's second. You were always looking out for the others; you couldn't help it. Even Steve. Damn it, even Steve was there, needing me to save him. Again.

Ford took a step away, his bag over his shoulder. "I've been here a long time and was about to move on when you showed up. You like ruining plans, don't you?"

Lila snorted. "You have no idea."

She flew over to land on his shoulder and an immediate twinge started in my belly. She took to him easily enough now that he was part of the pride, but that wasn't what gave me the twinge. It was as if Maks was being replaced.

And I didn't like that one damn bit. I shook my head, literally trying to shake the feeling, but it wouldn't leave me. So be it. We weren't replacing Maks, that wasn't possible. But his brother could still be part of the pride. And to be fair, Darcy would be all over him like stink on a camel.

"You're kinda cute for a dragon, Lila. Not the ugly lizard I would have expected." He reached up and poked a finger at her side. She whipped her head around and snapped at him, her razor-sharp teeth missing the tip of his finger by a whisker.

"Don't poke me, ye fat guts!" she snapped. Okay, maybe I was worrying about nothing. She left his shoulder and came back to me. The horses had tucked in tightly behind me and seemed to be eyeing him up too.

"*Henry the Fourth*?" I offered. She bobbed her as she landed on my shoulder. "He's a dick. I thought Maks was a toad. But his brother is a right limp dick."

Ford turned his head. "You calling me names, teeny tiny dragon?"

"Yes! Fat guts!" Lila snapped.

He grinned. "All that hot air, and no flames. Must burn you right in the ass, eh, teeny tiny one?"

She sucked in a breath and a hiss followed. "Oh, I'm going to kill him."

"He's doing it on purpose, Lila," I said, my voice low. "He's trying to rile you up."

I could feel the threads of his energy there, just under my skin if I focused on them. Energy that was nervous and uncertain. He was picking on Lila to cover the fact that he was not sure where he stood at all.

"Stop it, both of you," I said, putting some power into my voice. "Not one more word or I will kick you in the face again."

Once more, he saluted me and the unease in him settled. Lila grumped on my shoulder. "I liked the Toad better than Fat Guts."

I smiled, my heart hurting. "Yeah, me too."

Me too.

Chapter Eighteen

F ord took us away from the water toward the
northern edge of the Oasis. There between a
cluster of trees was his campsite. The sand
had been kicked over the fire pit, and there were
deep marks in the trees where he'd sharpened his
claws. I had to give him credit, it wasn't a complete
pigsty.

He flicked his bag down on the ground. "We can
stay here. The Jinn don't seem to come to this side of
the Oasis."

I frowned. "You've run into Jinn?"

He shrugged. "Yes and no. I'm good at hiding from
them. Much as I'd love to take one on, the reality is I've
never seen a single Jinn on his own. They always ride
with at least three."

I moved to Balder and stripped him of his tack, slid
off his bridle and then removed the rope halter I had on
Batman. They took off, bucking and snorting, heading

straight for the bits of grass that cropped up here and there.

"You sure that's a good idea?" Ford asked.

"I think I know what I'm doing with my own horses, Ford. Keep it up and your name will still start with F, but it will end with *ucker*." I pawed through the bags until I found the few bits of dried food I had left. I handed some to Lila and then raised an eyebrow at Ford. He nodded and I held a strip of meat out to him.

I thought that with his mouth busy, he'd figure out being quiet was a good thing.

Not so much.

"Tell me about this Darcy. And what about the other one? You said she's pregnant?"

I thought for a minute about saying nothing, but what would it hurt? The more invested he was, the better. "Darcy is my age, blonde, blue eyes. She likes the traditional roles for women. Kiara is younger, and dumb when it comes to men——"

"Oh, I like her already." He grinned around his mouthful of dried jerky and I gave him a withering glared that slowly dissolved the smile.

"They are both under my protection, Fucker," I said. "And Kiara is pregnant with Steve's cub. Steve is the one who is going to cause problems."

"Oh, can I bang his head on a rock?" His hopeful tone made me snort.

"Possibly. We've got to get them out first."

The sound of hoof beats turned me around. Mostly because there were three sets, and neither were Batman or Balder by the rhythm.

There was a flash through the trees and even though I didn't get a good look, I knew we were in shit. "Jinn." We had seconds at best.

I shifted and launched myself up the tree closest to me. "Ford, hide!"

"Fuck, where?"

He had a point. I slid down and landed on two legs. The quick shift left me wobbling, but there was no time for any second guessing. I stepped beside a tree and put my back to it. "Lila, be ready."

Goddess of the desert and sands, was I really going to fight a Jinn? My only chance lay in a surprise attack.

The hoof beats thundered toward us.

I counted the seconds as I pulled my kukri blades. The flail would be my last resort as always. Ford shifted into his lion form and let out a roar, drawing their eyes to him.

The flash of a horse's leg beside me was my cue. I leapt up and swung hard for the Jinn's neck. Decapitation was about the only sure thing with these goat fuckers. And I wasn't about to give them a chance to wrap us up with their magic.

In midair, I sliced as I swung both arms out, crossing my blades as they met in the middle of the Jinn's neck. His eyes found me, his mouth opened, and his head rolled from his shoulders, his body still bouncing along with his horse who had no idea it was now riderless.

I landed in a crouch and shot forward as Lila swept down from the trees and breathed on a second Jinn as she flew by him. The sapphire attached to her flared a brilliant blue even under the wrappings and her breath came out in a blast of arctic cold that hit the Jinn in the head. I jumped forward, tackling the Jinn at the waist, our combined weight throwing his horse off balance. I grabbed the horse's reins and pulled its head sharply to one side. The horse squealed and spun, falling, crushing the Jinn's leg.

The Jinn below me didn't move as I jammed my blades into his neck and yanked them sharply through the half-frozen flesh.

"Well, well, what will you do now?" a voice called to me. I spun to see Ford on his knees, blood pouring from multiple wounds on his body. The Jinn that stood over him was tall, over seven feet easily and lean, as though he were part giraffe.

I grinned at him. "I don't really like that one."

Ford gaped at me. "Alpha, please, I'm part of your pride now. You have to protect me."

I shrugged and kept talking while my right arm went behind me. "Yeah, that's the rub. You've been a fucker right off the bat. Being mean to me. Being mean to Lila. I probably would do better to let you die now than have to kill you later."

The Jinn laughed. "Oh, lion, you are in deep shit." He took his eyes from me and looked down at Ford.

I snapped my arm forward, throwing my blade, aiming for the Jinn's left eye. I ran after it, so as it hit the mark, the blood splattered my face. The Jinn screamed, his magic spreading around him. I grabbed him around the arms and kicked him in the back of the knees.

"The knife, Ford! Take his head!"

Ford didn't take the knife, but grabbed the Jinn on

either side of his head and yanked. I dug my heels in to help offset the powerful decapitation. The Jinn's head literally popped off, the noise a combination of bone snapping and flesh tearing.

The body in my arms went limp and I dropped it.

Ford stared at me, and went to one knee, his head lowered. "I swear my life is yours, Zamira."

I patted him on the head, breathing hard, my pulse and blood pounding with a blood lust I'd never felt before. "Don't get sentimental on me now, Ford. I wouldn't have let them take you, but they don't know that."

The three bodies sunk into the sand as I watched until there was nothing left but an indent where they'd been.

He reached out and touched my calf, his head still bowed. "Thank you. Both of you."

Lila hummed happily to herself. "Damn straight."

That had felt almost too easy. Which made my skin crawl with warning. Was it possible that these were scouts? If so, who else might be along soon?

"Lila, go up. See if there are any more Jinn coming."

She bobbed her head and shot into the air, gone in a flash of silver and blue.

I went to my pack and pulled out the hacka paste, smearing it over the minor wounds on Ford, then stitched up the bigger ones before smearing the paste over them as well. As far as I knew, no other shifters healed when they changed forms. They healed fast, yes, but not in an instant. That would be just me.

I took a match, struck it and lit the paste on fire, cauterizing the wounds perfectly.

"That's good stuff." Ford's voice was husky as I took my hand from his arm where I'd put the last of my paste. I was running out. I would need more and soon with the way I went through it.

"Yeah, it is. Now, help me get the horses," I said.

It took us an hour to convince the Jinn's three horses to come close, and it was only after Balder and Batman showed up that they let us gather the reins.

"Why are we doing this exactly?" Ford asked. He'd been remarkably quiet the last hour. Nearly dying had apparently shook him more than even he'd realized and he'd lost some of the attitude.

"We're bringing three out of the Jinn's Dominion. We're going to need mounts. Even though I'm not picking up on any injuries, there will be fatigue for sure." I tied two of the Jinn's horses to Balder in a long lead line manner, one on either side of him. He wouldn't let them go anywhere they shouldn't. The third I tied to Batman for the same reason. Then I let them go. They pranced away, heading straight to the water.

I turned back to Ford. "We'll give the horses a few hours break before we gear them up. We're going to have to leave them here, unattended." And of course, if we died facing the Jinn, they would die to. Maybe not right away, but they would still die.

I grimaced and pushed that thought away. "Come here, let me show you what I've got planned."

I marked out the four rims of the Jinn's Dominion for him and showed him the north tower. "That's our pathway in. We look for a shimmer of gold under the sand, and that's the path we follow for our best chance."

"Who gave you that information? Can you trust him?" Ford raised an eyebrow.

"Maks gave it to me," I said. "So yeah, I trust him."

"You love him." It wasn't a question. I nodded.

"I do. But it's complicated."

"No shit, if he's really Jinn." He frowned and shook his head. "He saved me. Jinn don't do that. They won't even save one of their own. Are you sure he's a Jinn? I only remember him as a caracal."

He was right, of course. Maks didn't follow the Jinn's rules at all and wherever he could, he bucked them. "Yes, I'm sure he's at least part Jinn." Saying those words hurt far more than mere words should have. But thick as he was, Ford didn't notice.

"How are you planning to deal with the Jinn exactly?" he asked. "Not that today wasn't total proof of your ability, but if what you're saying is true, then we aren't going to face only Jinn but their dead as well."

"That's why we need to go under the cover of night," I said. "You've seen how small I am. We're going to dull Lila's scales with ash from your fire and if all goes as planned, no one will see us going in or going out."

"What about me?" Ford shook his head. "There's no way I'll be able to slip by."

I nodded. "I know. You'll wait here." I put my finger on a spot in the sand drawing that was just outside the outer rim of the Dominion. "You're our backup. If you see us coming at speed with Jinn on our asses, your job is to swoop in and be the hero. You help us cover the ground we need to get back to the Oasis."

He frowned. "You sure?"

"It makes the most sense," Lila said. "If the others are injured, or slow, we're going to potentially need some muscle to pack them back."

Slowly he nodded. "Okay. What if you need me to come in sooner?"

I swiped a hand through the four rims I'd drawn in the sand. "If you see shit exploding, you can come find us."

His eyebrows shot up and his lips twitched like he wasn't sure if I was serious or not. "Exploding?"

I laughed, but it died on my lips. "I am kidding. If everything goes as planned, this will be a routine extraction, quiet going in and quiet going out." How many times had I heard my father use those two words? *Routine extraction.* He would never not be a marine even years after he'd lost his men in the desert.

The next two hours crawled, and I didn't feel like talking so I leaned back and closed my eyes, pretending to sleep. In reality, I sunk myself into the energy that tied me to my pride. Kiara, Steve, and Darcy, all bundled together to the south. The best I could get from them was they were cold and hungry, but otherwise unhurt, though Kiara was the weakest of the three. That they were cold was an odd thing and a good clue as to just where they were. I wasn't sure how well I'd be able to track them inside the Dominion. Cold meant they were likely underground.

Finally, I let myself look for Maks, finding him easily.

He was in the Jinn's Dominion too, but farther to the east. Like the others, he was uninjured but still sick. Still dying. For the moment, he was alive. That was the best I could find. Ford lit up as he moved around, his energy buzzing orange, and Lila's soft colors as she rested with me.

I let myself sink a little deeper, and I found the horses near the water, their energies the same color of silver, but with variations that allowed me to pick out Balder and Batman from the small herd with no problem. Funny, but I'd never considered them part of our pride, but it looked as though they were as tied to me as were the others.

Deeper yet, the sands around me shifted and danced, vibrating with an energy I'd never noticed.

Deeper again and the water called to me.

Deeper again, and against my back, the flail warmed, humming with energy. I paused there. The magic in the flail was hot, the heat of fresh blood spilled, of the last breath of life escaping a mouth, the heat of a burning fever before death claimed a new soul.

My eyes didn't open and yet I could see the desert. The same place I'd been before.

The Emperor stood in front of me. "Zamira. I'm surprised to find you here."

"You called me here, didn't you?" I snapped as I moved to away from him. Once more I was stopped by something at my back, something that followed me around.

"I did not. You are finding a deep well of power in yourself, aren't you?" His face was kindly as he smiled.

"You killed Destry and the giants," I snapped.

"I did not." He shook his head.

Well, what did I expect? That he'd take ownership? "Then who?"

"The one who would take my power for his own. I may be the monster in the dark, but the monster in front of you that wants my power is far deadlier to this world." He sighed. "The choice will be yours soon, to decide the fate of our world." The Emperor watched me closely. "What will you do? Will you kill Marsum and remove his jewel, freeing me? Or will you let him live and become the new ruler of your world?"

"I choose neither," I snarled.

My hand reached up to the flail on my back.

"Damn it!" roared Ford, snapping me out of the trance as surely as a bucket of ice water doused over my head. I jerked upright, breathing hard as if I'd been running flat out.

I stared across at Ford who clutched his left hand. A new wound there, one that looked self-inflicted. I couldn't help the exasperated snort that escaped me. "How exactly did you survive on your own?"

He shrugged, and I approached him with the hacka paste while I struggled to put together the vision I'd had.

I took his hand and turned it over, getting a good look at it. "It's not deep. We need to save the paste for those we're bringing out. There's a good chance they'll need it."

Ford nodded. "Right, of course." He took my hand in his good one, holding onto me. "I really am sorry about the things I said before. About you and Lila."

I arched a single eyebrow, not sure if I believed him. Color me cautious when it came to men suddenly reversing their positions, but it smacked of him being up to something. "Sure. Thanks for the apology."

He smiled and winked at me, then arched both brows high. "You think Darcy will like me?"

The question shouldn't have surprised me. I took a step back, looking at him through the lens of a woman who sought a mate. He was tall, strong, well put together with a smart-ass attitude. And he was a black lion, which made him unique if you could deal with the cheek.

"Possibly. I honestly don't know what her type is." Which was true. My brother had loved her, and she had fucked Steve believing she should because he was the alpha apparent. I wasn't sure that either had her heart.

He sagged a little. "Well, I'll just have to convince her then, right? Any suggestions on how to show her I'm a good guy?"

"How about we get her the fuck out of the Jinn's Dominion first before you start the courtship?" I walked over to my bag and dug around in the pack. "I'm going to get a pack ready for you. Then you're going to shift to four legs, then you're going to carry me all the way to your hold position at the edge of the Jinn's Dominion so I don't burn energy I don't have to. Got that?" I dug through the gear, making sure there were a few clothes the girls could wear. "I need a pair of pants from you, besides those you'll need."

He threw a pair at me and I stuffed them into the bag. Extra weapons, a blanket, the last of the hacka paste, three water bags. On my own body, I tied the bag of magic dust to my belt, made sure the kukri blades and the flail were firmly attached and adjusted the straps over my chest and shoulders. The diamond was wrapped in a leather bag and I hefted its weight. On a whim, I looped it through the middle of my bra so the stone hung against my belly. Less noticeable than if I'd hung it from around my neck. I put a hand on the emerald stone, and at the last second tucked it into the bag.

The green stone was meant for Maks. I wasn't sure I should give it to him, but I took it anyway.

From there, I got the five horses ready, and that took up the last of the daylight. I stroked Balder's nose as I finished tacking him last. "You wait for me, buddy, but if I'm not back by tomorrow night, run back to the Stockyards."

He snorted and pushed his head into my chest. I repeated the instructions to Batman. Both horses watched me with dark, serious eyes, as if they completely understood. I hoped they did.

"Lila, you ready?" I turned to find her buried in the ashes of Ford's campfire. She popped her head up so only her violet eyes peered at me surrounded by painted black scales. I stared at her, my heart racing. "Shit, you look like your dad."

She grinned and snarled. "Good, 'cause he's a major fucker, don't you think? Maybe they'll fear me."

I laughed and she flew to my shoulder. The coal ash clung to her scales. I waved a hand at Ford. "Strip and shift."

He pulled off his clothes and threw them to me one

at a time. I stuffed them into the bag and then he shifted into his lion form. He stretched and yawned, showing off his teeth.

"We're like the eastern wall's ninjas." Lila giggled. "Scourges of the night!"

I laughed and went to Ford. I put a hand under his belly and he squirmed. "Stop that, I need to get the straps on you, fool."

"Sorry, ticklish," he grumbled.

Lila leapt from my shoulder to his, then up to his head. I quickly looped the wraps between his front legs and back up over his shoulders and tied them to the bag. "Feel good?" I asked him.

"Not bad. I can run with it on." He turned his big head to me and I reflexively scratched under his chin the way I had with my brother how many times? Too many to count.

For just a moment, I felt him there with us. I looked to my left, the image of a ghostly golden lion pacing the Oasis. Only I wasn't sure it was Bryce.

Blue eyes stared up at me from the golden lion.

My father's ghost stared back at me.

I hoped to hell it wasn't the bad omen it felt like.

But I had a feeling things were not going to go as planned.

Chapter Nineteen

Merlin did not like it in the box. He did not like it with these rocks. He would not care to have his ears boxed, or be forced to eat dirty socks. He grimaced at the foolish rhyme, but the reality was he needed something to keep his mind busy.

A box like he was jammed into was meant to drive the occupant mad. It was meant to break your heart and soul, to strip you of your humanity so you could be used by your captors. To be fair, Marsum didn't understand he was dealing with a man who'd survived several such torture techniques over the years, and as such, he'd prepared himself so if ever he faced it again, he would come out in better shape than before.

After all, he'd been the one to create the infinity box, just like the one he'd stuffed his father into, though that one was much larger. Marsum wasn't strong enough to make anything larger than the box Merlin had been jammed into.

From where he sat with his head resting on his knees, he could see Flora next to Marsum at the high table. Their voices were foggy, but the words were clear enough.

"What do you mean he's back without her?" Marsum slammed a hand on the table as a messenger, a low-level Jinn, bent into a full bow.

"He said she escaped. She used her own magic and they killed Bart with acid and escaped." The Jinn dared to lift his head.

Marsum swung around to glare at Merlin. "You think Zamira could have unlocked the binds on her bloodlines on her own? I opened her to her grandfather's magic so I can train her, and use it for my own. But not the rest."

Merlin tried to shrug, but otherwise said nothing. There was nothing Marsum could do to make him speak, or at least nothing worse than this stupid box.

Marsum glared at him. "Tell me, Merlin!"

Merlin yawned and closed his eyes to mere slits. Marsum grabbed Flora by the neck and held her up. "It bothers me not one whit to kill a priestess of Zeus if it means I will find your obedience with her death."

Merlin opened his eyes. "And then when she is dead, you'll have nothing to threaten me with, you fool."

Marsum snarled and then a slow smile wrapped across his face. "And how would you like a first-hand view of your woman enjoying my pleasures, then?" He let Flora go and Merlin's eyes shot to hers.

The flicker of anger in them was all he needed to

know that she would not back down either. "I'm sorry, Flora."

"Not as sorry as this one will be," she snapped, and a roll of thunder crashed through the room. Marsum turned as a bolt of lightning danced from her fingertips and blasted him across the hall, slamming him into the stone.

Merlin stared. "Why didn't you do that sooner?"

Flora ran to him and a second blast of lightning hit the box, shattering it. He all but fell out, his limbs crying from the length of time he'd been forced into the unnatural position. Flora helped him up and then they ran through the main tower.

"To the Oasis," Flora said. "Can you take us there?"

"I can, but my father—"

She snapped him around. "He's awake, Merlin, and he knows you are here. There is no hiding now."

He gave a single nod, still shocked that she could break the infinity box, then wrapped his arm around her and stepped through the ether, leaving the Jinn's Dominion behind.

The boom and ruckus of the scrambling Jinn was gone in an instant.

He went to his knees in the sand around the water of the Oasis, breathing hard. "Sweet baby goddess, Flora. Marsum is stronger than the last time I met him."

"So I gathered." She dropped to her knees beside him. "But that was no infinity box, or I would not have been able to smash it. More to the question, why didn't you stay with Zam? You were supposed to be helping her."

He closed his eyes, unable to look her in the eye. "I couldn't leave you. Not when I convinced you to come to this hellhole and help me. Not when it was my fault you were captured because I didn't trust you with all the information. This was . . ."

"Not all your fault," she said. "Merlin, thank you for trying to save me. Even if I had to save you in the end."

He looked up to find her smiling at him, a distinct twinkle in her green eyes. "Are you sassing me already?"

Before he could understand what was happening, she leaned in and kissed him. Soft and sweet, spicy and full of fire, the kiss didn't last nearly long enough.

She pulled back first. "We need to find Zamira. We know she is the key. We know she needs to take the Jinn's stone, but there is so much at odds here, so much contradiction. Did you see Maks?"

"What?" He looked into her face, still more than a little stunned from her kiss. How long since a kiss had set him back on his heels? A hundred years? More?

She patted his cheek. "Pay attention. Maks stepped in the room right after the messenger. He was back with the Jinn. Though I doubted he wanted to be."

"What did his eyes look like?" Merlin forced himself to pull it together.

"Like he was stoned on poppy juice." Flora stood and walked to the water, knelt and rinsed her hands off and patted her face.

"Then he isn't himself. Marsum has him in his control again." He frowned. "That does not bode well for Zamira. She might go in to save him rather than take the stone, and she needs that stone to deal with my father."

"All well and good, but if you'll recall the last two stones were not on her radar either. She seems to find them whether she wants to or not." Flora glanced back at him and her eyes widened.

A breath of warm air ghosted across the back of his neck, right before a pair of hairy lips nibbled at the base. He let out a yell and rolled forward, coming up with hands glowing, magic suffusing his skin.

The gray horse stared at him and bobbed his head once. Merlin frowned and stood. "You couldn't have said there was a horse behind me?"

"Funnier to watch your reaction." Flora chuckled.

He grimaced and drew his magic back into himself. "Wait," he leaned over to see two horses tied in a long line behind the gray. Next to him was a black horse with a horse tied behind him. Five horses.

"That's Zamira's horse," Flora whispered. "But she's not here."

He looked the horses over. They were ready to go, to bolt from danger. He turned slowly and faced the south. Searching the ground, he found what he was looking for.

Big lion paw prints sunk into the sand, and there beside them, a tiny set of paw prints far harder to see in the dark.

"She's here all right, just farther south. Her pride is in there, Flora." A chill whispered down his spine. "She's walking right into a trap."

"Then we have to help her!" Flora said.

"We can't. You know that." He turned to look at her.

"Or at least, I can't." He moved to untie one of the horses, a chestnut with flaxen mane and tail. "Ride, you can get there. You can help her."

"Aren't you afraid of me being caught again?"

He shook his head. "No. I think you are done playing nice. And I . . . I have someone else I must face."

She reached out for him. "Your father."

He nodded. "I will do all I can to slow him down. Stay with Zamira, help her. Once the magic is unlocked, she will need the guidance of someone she can trust."

"She won't trust me."

He grinned. "Not right away, but she will. She has to —she needs you to be the mentor she has never truly had."

He dared to reach over and pull her into his arms, locking his mouth over hers for a brief moment before he pulled back. "I've waited my whole life to find a woman who matched me not only in strength, but in meddling."

She burst out laughing. "Damn you, Merlin. Go, see if you can subdue your father. And I will save you once you get caught again."

Flora swung onto the horse's back and gave it her heels, sending it into a flat-out gallop. The other horses watched them go, as did Merlin.

"Be safe, Flora," he whispered as he opened the ether and stepped through to a dark and dead land. Ahead of him was a temple, a pyramid made of bones and rock.

He drew himself up. This was about to get interesting.

Chapter Twenty

B efore we'd left the safety of the Oasis, I'd lifted a hand to my father's ghost, but otherwise didn't acknowledge him. This was not the time. The Oasis had been the place of his death, where he'd defended his family and his pride, but it would not be my reckoning ground.

I'd shifted, dropping to all fours. Next to Ford, I was the size of a cub at best. I leapt up and onto his back, hanging on to the bag of clothing and emergency supplies.

"Let's go," I said, and Ford jumped forward, racing straight south. Around the eastern side of the water he went, and as the sand kicked up from his huge paws, the flicker of sandblasted bones winked up at me. A glimmer of steel. A chunk of leather.

It was a graveyard that had gone untended for many years. I drew a deep breath, holding the smell of my home in my lungs. The water, the sand, the heat of the day, it all was an imprint that would never leave me.

I hunched down, clinging to the bag as Ford ran, bursting out of the Oasis. He was strong, and obviously used to running in this form because he never slowed or even broke stride. There was no moment where I thought he was going to give up and tell me he needed to walk.

"Ford, how long have you been roaming the desert on your own?" I asked.

"Since Maks was killed. My mother . . . she said I had to leave because I was too much to feed, but I was already moving, already wanting to go," he said. "I'd stayed because I felt responsible for her."

Classic alpha lion, and rather interesting. There was more to him than I'd thought. "Looking for him even though you believed he was dead."

He nodded. "Maybe a part of me knew he was still out there."

I lifted my head into the wind, breathing in the scent of the desert. Partly because I looked to pick up on any Jinn that might be coming our way, but also because I'd missed this place I had been born. It called to my soul in a way I couldn't explain even to myself. Like I belonged here.

I wrinkled my nose at my attempt at prose.

Ford began to slow, and I realized we'd covered a lot of ground and were nearing the drop-off point for him. He dropped to his belly, panting. "Here we are, ladies."

I hopped off and Lila grabbed at a water skin for him,

managing to get it open and pour it into his mouth. Really, it was quite the scene, and another time I would have been snickering with the way his head was tipped and how her tiny claws gripped the water skin so carefully.

When he was done drinking, I stepped out in front. Though we couldn't see them from here, there were two towers waiting for us in the dark.

"You ever been this close to them before?" I asked.

He shook his head. "Nope."

I shook my body as if I could shake out the nerves. "Lila, fly low."

I put a paw on Ford's nose. "If we aren't back by morning, go to the Oasis and get the fuck out of here."

"And where am I supposed to go?" He didn't pull away from my paw. "Maks is in there too. If you aren't back by morning, I'm coming in after all of you. Maybe they'll make me alpha for being the hero."

I laughed. "Nope, you'd need balls as big as mine for that."

He snorted a laugh and I spun, and sprinted away from him, headed straight south.

The sand gave under my feet, but because I was so light, I didn't struggle with it like the bigger cats. Then again, Ford had moved in it at a decent clip, far faster than I would have thought.

"Zam, do you think we'll be able to do this?" Lila asked softly.

I glanced up at her. "Do you want my honest thoughts, or some sort of *made up, make you feel better about the stupid thing we are doing* kind of shit?"

She snorted and then laughed. "I think that answers my question."

I sighed. "I think we have a chance. I'd say we have the best chance at getting in undetected. I'm almost sure of that part. They won't be looking for us. It'll be getting out where I'm not sure we'll be able to move without being caught." That was the only part of the plan I didn't have a set idea of how to make it happen.

She winged beside me, our pace next to one another easy. "What about moving them one at a time?"

I frowned. "More chances to be caught."

"But easier to hide one rather than three," she said.

Lila had a point. "I don't know, Lila. Let's see what we see when we get there." There was not much more I could plan for at this point. We were going in. It was going to get ugly. And hopefully I could get everyone out. That was my only goal.

Lila landed ahead of me and I slowed my own pace. Ahead, lights glowed in the distance, lights that ran into the sky to the far left and the far right.

"Which tower did Maks say?" Lila asked as we walked forward, our dark bodies not exactly blending with the sand but it was the best we could do. At least Lila's scales weren't all glittering, picking up the light like they so often did.

"We stick to the right northern tower and look for a glitter of gold."

"That's going to be a bitch to see in the dark."

I nodded. It was, but again, it was all we had, and still it was more than if we'd tried to figure it out on our own without Maks's note.

I had a moment to wonder about Merlin. He'd been a pain in my ass as we'd worked our way through the Witch's Reign, and I'd seen him briefly when he'd gone to speak to my mentor Ish, but that had been in a dream.

A funny twist in my gut caught me off guard. Not that he'd ever been that helpful, but what if he'd been killed? He was the one who put the Emperor to sleep all those years ago. If what he was telling us was true.

And why the fuck would I suddenly be thinking about him now?

A boom rattled well inside the rims of the Jinn's Dominion and lightning arced through the sky, striking into the heart of their hold. Lightning on a clear night? That was anything but natural.

"Now, Lila!" The distraction was exactly what we needed. I shot forward, belly to the sand as I drew next to the northern facing tower.

I caught a glimpse of what exactly the tower was made up of as I zipped past it. The individual speckles of sand could still be seen, but they'd been heated until it was a tower of golden glass that reflected the light. A screech from the top made my hair stand on end and I couldn't help my entire coat puffing up like I'd been touched by the electricity dancing through the empty sky.

A glance upward confirmed one of the Jinn's dead crouched on the tower, looking back at the chaos in the center of the hold. Its wingspan was maybe twelve to fourteen feet, and the wings attached to the arms so they were all one limb. A thick tail lashed off its muscled back, but it was the face I couldn't look away from. Human, but sunken so far that the teeth protruded and the eyes sat deeply into the skull. Gray skin covered the entire thing, clinging to the bones and muscle, showing each clearly, even in the dark.

I wasn't sure if it was baring its teeth or if that was just how it looked.

"Deadshits," Lila muttered. "That's what I'm calling them."

I shushed her and looked away from the deadshit—hell, it was a good name—and to the ground. A glimmer of gold caught my eye and once I had a bead on it, I raced along the line. The gold flickered and beckoned, and I kept my paws tight to it for fear of what would happen if I dared to step off.

The pathway took us through the first four levels of the rims with only a pause here and there. The central holding was boiling like a beehive that had been kicked. I pressed my body against the base of the last tower between us and the central stronghold. I stared up at the clear building. The glass was not what I expected; wouldn't it be easy to break?

The lightning was gone as suddenly as it was there, and I knew whatever distraction we had was over.

"Deep breath, Lila." I closed my eyes for a moment, orienting myself with what I recalled of the maps my father had drawn. The dungeons were deep, at least three levels down from the main floor. I let myself connect with my pride, finding them easily.

And Maks . . . he was there too, only he was on the main floor.

"Should we get him first?" Lila asked and I glanced at her.

"Can you see the energy?"

"I can feel it," she whispered. "I can feel Maks closer than the others."

I shook my head. "We can't."

And with that, I shot forward, Lila sticking close to me as we raced across the final open space. There was a moment where I looked up and was sure one of the deadshits flying across looked our way and my heart stuttered.

But before I could duck or dive away, he was gone, winging toward the north.

I slid to a stop against the central tower and the smooth glass. Well, shit, I hadn't considered this.

"How the hell are we getting in there?" Lila whispered.

I gritted my teeth, thinking. "I could use the flail, but that will be loud and we need quiet."

Lila stepped close and the sapphire glowed between the leather covering as she lifted the tip of her claw and flew upward, drawing a line of blue ice. The glass cracked, but it was quiet, a crackle of freezing water. I shifted to two legs and pushed against the center of the doorway she'd drawn. Four feet high, it wasn't too big, and hopefully not too noticeable.

I shoved against the glass cube, the edge crackling as it split and the chunk slid inward in one piece.

I went to the end of the chunk and pushed, spinning it open wide enough that we could both slip through. Darkness greeted us, and I put my back against the chunky glass door and scooted it partway closed. I could still get my fingers around the lip, and that would have to be enough for when we came back.

I crouched and shifted onto four legs, a tiny groan escaping me. Too many shifts, too close together were not what I wanted to be doing, but no choice. I bit back on the rolls of pain and let my eyes adjust.

Lila tucked in close. "I can't see anything."

"Hold onto my tail," I whispered and then I took a step forward. We were in a room, and ahead of us was a door with the slightest glimmer of light under it.

"Something touched me," Lila hissed.

I whipped around. And then snickered. "It's a dress, I think. We're in someone's closet."

She giggled, nerves getting the better of both of us.

"Maybe Marsum dresses like a lady when no one is looking?" she whispered.

I grinned to myself. "I'd like to see that. Though I suspect he'd make an ugly woman."

Lila tucked her head against me. "Horribly ugly."

I hurried toward the door. It wasn't closed tightly, and I slipped a claw under the bottom edge where there was a good gap and pulled it open. The lights outside the closet were not particularly bright, and we were indeed inside someone's room. Flowers and perfume, it was a woman's room. I hurried out and scooted across the room to a large bed. The smell in here was familiar, but I couldn't quite pin it down as it was mixed with the heavy perfume of what could only be someone trying to hide bad body odor.

I grimaced and went for the main door as the handle twisted.

"Shit." I hissed the word and shot under the bed, Lila right beside me. The door swung open and . . . Maks stepped in, followed by a curvy blonde woman who pawed at him. "I knew you'd come back. I knew you would."

He didn't answer, didn't so much as look her way. "Go away, Nell. And stay out of my room when I'm not here. It stinks like your perfume." Well, that explained the smell.

"I will not. I don't know what happened to you out there, but do you think it was easy for me here without you? You said we'd escape together."

"And you told Marsum, didn't you?" he countered as he spun and grabbed her arms. "You are not my mate, Nell. We never bound ourselves together because you always hoped for more. I'm guessing Marsum turned you down? So, now you'll settle for me?"

I could hardly believe what I was seeing, what I was hearing. This woman . . . she'd been with Maks? I wasn't even jealous because it was obvious he wasn't interested, and let's be honest, he'd had to see me deal with Steve, someone I cared very little for even though he was my ex-husband.

She whimpered. "It's not like that, Maks. You're a caracal shifter, like me. I thought . . . I thought you'd be able to protect me. That's why I came here."

Maks snorted. "You were a diva from the time you realized what a diva was. Get out of my sight."

She gave a huff and stomped out of the room. I

stared at Lila and her wide eyes said it all. We were alone with Maks. Did we dare try to steal him away?

Would he fight us?

There was only one way to find out.

On my belly, I shifted, cursing that I was doing it again. But if this worked, then I wouldn't have to shift again.

I rolled out from under the bed and pulled my blades as I stood. Maks lay on the bed, his eyes closed.

"Hello, Zam."

So much for surprising him.

Chapter Twenty-One

I pressed a blade to Maks's throat while he lay on his bed with his eyes closed. "You ruined my surprise, Maks."

His lips twitched, but his eyes didn't open. "Did I?"

Lila sucked in a sharp breath. "Zam, you don't want to kill him."

I didn't dare look at her. Here, deep within the Jinn's Dominion, well inside the enemy's territory, I didn't know what to expect from Maks. "I love him, Lila, but he could still turn on us. Marsum could come through him, just like before. And if Marsum dies, then his power and assholeness goes straight to Maks."

"If he's not possessing me, he can only see through my eyes. If he's possessing me, he can hear and feel everything I hear and feel," Maks said softly. "So right now, he thinks I'm sleeping because my eyes are closed. He can't hear me."

That was good enough for me. I dropped the knife

to the floor, and jumped on top of him, planting my mouth over his. He wrapped his arms around me and kissed me back, rolling me over so he was on top of me, taking the kiss deeper. Lila groaned and I caught movement from the corner of my eye that told me she crawled back under the bed. That and her voice.

"You two . . . seriously? We are in deep shit and you two are making out like teenagers?"

Maybe she was right, but what was I fighting for if not the ones I loved? I ran my hands through his hair and breathed him in, as if I could hold this moment forever. I made myself pull back, pressing my forehead to his. "Maks. You're sick. I can see it on you."

He rubbed his cheek against mine, first one side and then the other, but he didn't address my concern. "They're in the third level below. The door to the dungeon is not far from Marsum's quarters. I can help you get there. He's leaving me alone for the moment."

"Yeah, because your eyes are closed," Lila muttered from under the bed. "Aren't they?"

I ran my fingers over the closed lids. "Yes, they're closed."

Maks smiled, but the tension in his face was anything but happy. "Zam, if you cling to my back, and Lila too, I can keep you covered with my cloak. I can walk you past the door. Next to it is a heavy statue you can crouch behind."

I kissed him again and he pushed off me, sitting up, eyes still closed. "Marsum thinks you're faking only being able to shift into a house cat. He believes you are hiding your strength on purpose. He believes you are the female lion shifter he's been waiting for."

"I'm not," I said.

"I know, but it gives you an edge. He knows you will come for the others, but he thinks you'll come in guns blazing because that's how lions do things." He held his hand out and I put mine in it. His fingers closed over mine and he raised my palm to his mouth.

"I need to give you the emerald stone, Maks," I said. "Maybe it can help you. Maybe it will stop Marsum and you can come with us."

"No, if he knows I have it, he'll take it from me," Maks said.

Lila shot out from under the bed. "But my grandmother said you had to have it. And Zam is right. What if it helps you?"

I nodded, and then said, "I agree. That stone belongs with you. Can you use it against Marsum?" I took it from my bag and pushed the stone into his hand. "Try. Please."

"If he feels me using magic, he'll come looking," Maks said.

I leaned my head against his. "Maks. I can't leave you here. I can't. You're dying."

"I know," he whispered. "It is because . . . well, it doesn't matter now why."

"Yes. It does," I said.

Lila leapt up and landed on his knees. "Tell us what happened. Please."

Maks took a slow breath and then shook his head.

"Marsum left me alone for a great part of my life because I was seen as weak, lesser, because I wasn't as strong as he wanted. He had other sons, full Jinn far ahead of me. None are left. He killed them. When he sent me to the Stock-yards, I was already sick. Ishtar's necklace she gave me, it stemmed the illness. Victor took the necklace off me."

"He wants you dead too," I said. "Is he next after you?"

"He is." Maks nodded.

I looked at Lila. "Maks, do you remember your mother?"

"Jinn don't have mothers," he said. "Or at least they aren't kept around. As soon as they give birth they are removed. That way the next generation of Jinn are kept separate from any outside influence."

I frowned. "Okay, look, long story short because we are running out of fucking time. We ran into your brother, a black lion who had been adopted into your caracal family. I know that sounds crazy, but he . . . he remembers you being taken by Marsum. They thought the Jinn had come for him, being a lion, but they'd come for you, Maks."

His eyelids twitched and I slapped a hand over them.

A tremor went through his body and I felt the change in him as Marsum dropped into him. "Lila, hide," I whispered.

I leapt off the bed and slid underneath, grabbing my blade as I went. This was not what I'd call the best act of bravery of the day, but we needed to get to the others. I shouldn't have spent so much time with Maks.

But I knew this was the last chance I'd get. In my

gut, every instinct said there would be no more after this, that this was the final goodbye.

He stood and did a slow turn, speaking to himself. Sort of.

"What are you up to, Maks? I thought for sure you and Nell would have gone back to your usual fucking." He tapped a toe, a move that was not something I'd ever seen Maks do. "You're hornier than a two-peckered goat. Did she leave you wanting? Nell never was a tease before."

He strode around the room, and for a heart-stopping moment, I thought he'd open the closet and see our exit. I reached for Lila and drew her to me. Maks did a full turn around the room and then went to the door. "To my chambers, boy. I need to speak with you."

The door opened, and we watched as Maks left.

I scrambled out and stood, tiny cobwebs drifting off me.

"You think with all that magic they could clean a little more." Lila let out a sneeze. I looked at the closet and the long cloaks of varying colors. All cloaks worn by Jinn.

"Lila, I have an idea."

She groaned. "Why do I get the feeling I'm not going to like this?"

I hurried to the closet because I didn't want to think about losing Maks—again. Inside were a variety of clothes, all made for Maks, far too big for me. I grabbed three shirts and slipped them on, one after another.

"Are you cold?"

"No." Hell, I was already sweating with the added

273

material. I next went for the pants. Three pairs of pants. Three thick cloaks.

I was weighed down with the clothes as I shifted into my four-legged form. I stumbled forward as my four paws touched the ground. The chain around my neck was much heavier than usual, which wasn't terribly surprising.

Lila nodded. "Good idea. For once."

"Shut up, you, and open that door." This was going to be the tricky part.

We knew roughly where we were going, even without Maks telling us the doorway to the dungeon was near Marsum's personal quarters. Lila flew to the door and sat on the handle, turning it easily. I grabbed the edge with my claws and pried it open. There was no movement in the hall and a few places we could hide if need be.

"Let's go," I whispered and slid out the door. Lila dropped to the ground and jogged along beside me, bouncing a little side to side. Good thing she'd not eaten yet today or her belly would have been dragging the floor.

At the T-intersection at the end of the hall, I again checked for movement before stepping out. We wove our way through the building, deeper and deeper until we were at the final doorway.

I was out of breath, and it wasn't just the clothes. The tension around us rose with each passing second. Not once had we run into a Jinn. Not even a flicker of movement. Surely, they should have been crawling all over the place.

"The door," I whispered to Lila and again she hopped up on the handle and it twisted open. Too easy, this was all too easy.

I swallowed hard and slid through the doorway. The interior of the hall was lit by torches set in the walls as they wove down a circular staircase. "Stay against the ceiling," I said.

Lila shot up and I raced down the stairs, hugging the inner wall of the curve. Still no Jinn.

Three flights down, there was another door and this one had a guard. Before I could even shift, Lila was on him. She swooped down and touched the Jinn on the head, freezing him, then pushed him sideways. His head hit the stone footing and shattered.

An eyeball rolled toward me, chunky like a painted rock.

I shifted onto two legs. The extra clothes were not as much of an issue this deep underground, but the shift was. It left me breathing hard and seeing spots as I searched the guard's body, found the keys, and pulled them out. I did a quick check of the energy of my pride. All three were in there, far to the north Ford tugged on me, and somewhere above my head was Maks.

I stripped off the extra clothes and piled them on the floor.

"Lila, watch my back," I said.

I put the key in the lock and twisted, a dull click sounding like a gunshot to my straining ears.

The door moved easily as I pushed it open. The dungeon was not made up of cells, but tiny boxes that my eye and mind couldn't make sense of, at least not right away.

Inside the box closest to me was the barest shift of movement and a golden eye caught mine. Horror like a wash of cold water rushed over me. "Darcy." I breathed her name as I ran to the box.

Like ice, the glass box was slick and my hands skimmed it quickly as I searched for a way to get in. Darcy was crunched inside, her head pinned to her knees. Tears streaked her face as I tried to find how, how to get this fucking piece of shit open.

"Incoming!" Lila hollered.

There was no time to be nice about this. I took a step back and grabbed the handle of the flail.

"Darcy, close your eyes."

Her eyes widened and I stared hard at her. "Trust me and close your eyes."

They flickered shut and I swung the flail at the corner of the box behind her left shoulder. The twin spiked balls slammed into it and stuck. Just like before. When I'd fought to free myself of Ishtar's hold on me, the flail had freed me.

Black mist poured out from around where the spiked balls dug in. I didn't yank it out. "It's magic, you should be sucking that in, you bad boy."

The flail shuddered under my hand and a pulse of light shot out around the spikes. I closed my eyes as the box shattered. I turned my head away, catching a shard across my cheek.

I swung back around to see Darcy sprawled out, tiny

cuts all over her. I handed her one of my blades. "Clothes by the door. Help Lila defend it."

Darcy blinked up at me. "What?"

"Now!" I snapped the word, pushing a tiny pulse of my own energy into it and she leapt to her feet. I was already headed toward the next box. Kiara was in this one. I repeated the instructions and she closed her eyes right away.

I tried not to notice the blood in the bottom of her box. And the realization that her extreme fatigue was partially depression.

The flail shattered her cage and she sprawled out as Darcy had. I put a hand on her arm and helped her up.

"Kiara," I said and pushed the handle of my blade into her fingers. "Take it, clothes at the door, defend it."

Her eyes flickered with pain and then I saw a spark of something she'd never carried before. Rage mingled with the pain. She drew a slow breath. "I want to kill them all, Zam."

I tightened my hold on her. "Wait for me. We'll do it together."

A tear slipped down her cheek. "Yes, Alpha, together."

She walked away, ignoring the cuts on her body, on her feet. I turned to face the last of my pride members.

I stood over the final box to see Steve glaring up at me. Yeah, glaring, like it was my fault he'd been caught.

Then again, I had sent him after Kiara.

I lifted the flail above my head and gave it a slow swing. "Close your eyes, Steve-O."

Chapter Twenty-Two

Steve's head tipped, and for a moment, I thought his mouth was moving but I couldn't hear a word he was saying inside the magic glass box. For just a split second, I thought how nice it was not hearing his voice.

But he was part of the pride, even if he was a limp dick. I brought the flail down on the corner of the box, behind his shoulder like I'd done with Darcy and Kiara.

The glass exploded and he came out swearing a blue streak. But for the first time in a long time, it wasn't at me.

"Those motherfucking Jinn!" he roared, and I held a hand out to him. He took it and I yanked him up and away from the shards of glass. He landed lightly beside me and I didn't let go.

"We have to get them out of here."

His whole body tensed. "You are not my alpha."

I nodded. "Then perhaps you are not part of this

pride. But how about we discuss that after we get the hell out of here?"

There was a scream from the hall and Lila let out a tiny roar. I left Steve standing there and ran for the door.

Kiara and Darcy circled a Jinn, and another body was on the floor. "Take his head," I said.

The Jinn's eyes shot to me and he went to his knees. "Please, I don't want to be here. I'm like you."

And then he shifted into a lion, his fur a ruddy gold. He stayed on the floor, his body in total submission. Darcy and Kiara stumbled away from him.

Steve snarled behind me and came out of the room in full-on lion form. I put a hand out. "Steve, if you attack him I'll drop you with this flail right now and just count the loss as necessary."

The Jinn, or lion shifter, trembled on the floor. Golden eyes rolled up to look at me. "Please don't leave me here. Please."

Well, shit, this was not as I'd planned. I reached out and held a hand to him. "Swear your loyalty on your life."

He shifted back to two legs, clothes intact. Just like me. I fought to keep my face neutral.

"I swear it on my life, to give you my loyalty until death." He put his hand in mine and without even realizing what I was doing, I took hold of his energy and wrapped it into the pride. He sucked in a sharp breath.

I blinked once. "Okay, kid, let's go."

Steve grabbed my arm and spun me around. "Are you insane? He's one of them!"

Darcy thrust clothes at Steve, and he took them,

dressing as he glared. I waited until the three of them were clothed. I pushed Steve out front, still not acknowledging his questions.

"Lila, ride with Steve, direct him back to the escape hatch. Darcy and Kiara, go with him." I did a quick calculation of the time. We'd be coming up on dawn soon, which meant we had to move.

Lila shot a look at me. "Where are you going?"

I looked at the kid. "What's your name?"

"Benji." He stared at me.

"Benji, are there others like you, part Jinn, part shifter?" Like him. Like Maks.

Like me?

He bobbed his head. "Yes, and they don't want to be here either."

I looked back at Lila. "Benji and I are going to get who we can." I shook my head at her before she could argue. "It will be easy with two over five, you know that. Go. We'll be right behind you."

Steve didn't wait, but I grabbed at him. "Hold. I have something for you."

I pulled the diamond out from under my shirt, still wrapped in leather, and slid it over his neck.

"What is it?" He touched it and frowned at me.

"Lila, you explain it to him," I said. There was no time for more than that. I could feel the clock ticking down.

Benji and I followed the four of them up the stairs. They turned to the right at the top and Benji beckoned me to the left. We hurried, and even so, we were lucky not to run into any Jinn.

"Where is everyone?" I asked the gangly youth at my side.

"Marsum called them to the main council hall. Except for those of us who are half-breeds. Minus Maks, of course. He's . . . they don't treat him like a half-breed. Not like us." He glanced at me and then stopped in front of a door. "There aren't many half-breeds left."

I motioned for him to go ahead and open it. The door swung inward and Benji went first. His voice was low, but I could still hear his words, hushed and filled with anticipation.

"We're going. Come on, get your stuff, quick. Just like we practiced." There was a shuffle of bodies and the sound of cloth being rustled, the sharp intake of breath.

I stayed just inside the door, watching the hall to either side, glad it was empty, and . . . still bothered by that very emptiness. Even with all the Jinn being called away for a meeting or some such stupidity, shouldn't there have been someone left to guard the halls? Was this supreme overconfidence on Marsum's part or something else?

My gut twanged with anxiety because I suspected something else. I just didn't know what.

"Hurry," I growled.

Benji came first, holding the hand of a young boy who couldn't have been more than five or six. Skin as smooth and dark as the night sky reflecting the lights of the torches, and huge golden eyes stared up at me. "Hello, little cub." I crouched down to him. "We're going to get out of here, okay?"

His lower lip trembled and then he bit it, holding it

still. "Okay," he whispered. I touched his chin with a finger and stood. I looked over the rest of the escapees and had to do a double take. Nell was behind Benji, her eyes rimmed in red, a bag clutched in her arms.

She looked at me a moment and then looked away. Of course, she hadn't seen me in Maks's room.

Two others were next to her, both girls. I drew a quick breath, scenting them. One more lion shifter. Nell was a caracal and the final was a cheetah. I nodded. "Stick close. If any Jinn come, fight for your life. Do you understand?"

They all nodded, and I turned, leading the way through the tower. I kept scenting the air, but it was thick with the soured tang of the Jinn and I struggled to pick up anything past that. A hint of lion, of Steve's distinct musk finally reached me and I picked up my pace.

Too easy . . . those two words kept reverberating through me, and I couldn't shake the feeling that perhaps I should slow down. But slowing was bad too. The last thing we needed was to sit around with our thumbs up our butts waiting for the Jinn to capture all of us.

Maks's door came into view; I jogged to it and pushed the door open. Lila and the others waited inside. "I told you to go."

Steve grinned. "Lila said she was in charge in your absence and she said we were waiting."

My jaw dropped. "You actually listened to her?"

Darcy smiled. "She threatened to freeze his balls off and shatter them on the floor."

That would do it.

I opened the door wide and ushered the newbies inside. "Through the closet, there's a door. Steve, you pull it open; everyone wait at the base of the tower."

I stood at the door and did a final sweep of the hall. I should have felt relieved. We were almost out.

But . . . no, there was no relief here. There was no weight coming off my shoulders.

"Fuck," I muttered under my breath. The little lion cub looked up at me. I grimaced. "Sorry, kid. Ignore me."

"They like traps," he whispered.

He might as well have tossed me into an ice-cold river for the way my breath shot out of me. "Do you know what they're planning? Did you hear something?" I dropped to one knee in front of him.

He stepped close to me and tucked his head under my chin as any cub would do with an alpha seeking protection. "I heard them talking. They like traps."

I wrapped an arm around him. "Can you shift yet?"

He bobbed his head and shifted right in my arms. His fur was not black like Ford's, but speckled, almost like a leopard with deep brown overtones and lighter highlights. I scooped him up into my arms. "Anyone who can shift, shift now. We're going to run as fast as we can. Steve," I lifted the cub to him, "you're carrying him."

Steve didn't so much as blink. He took the boy and set him on his shoulders, then shifted onto four legs. The bulk of lion filled the closet space and I squeezed by him to open the stone break in the wall.

It was damn well heavier to pull in than to push. "Darcy."

"I've got it." Kiara stepped up beside me and together we pulled the door open. I did a quick scan outside.

"We've got very little of the night left for cover. We have backup to the north. Run hard, don't look back. Do you understand?" My eyes went to the slim girl in the back. "Cheetah chick, you first. Turn on the speed, you got it?"

She grinned at me, showing off perfectly filed teeth. "On it, boss." She stepped forward and shifted. Like me, her clothes went with her into a bit of a collar around her neck. She crept past Steve and he gave a soft chuff of encouragement. Maybe this time his experience had made him realize what an ass he'd been.

Probably not, but one could hope.

Everyone else shifted, and Lila flew to my shoulder. "You aren't shifting, are you?"

I shook my head. "We're going to cover them."

I went back to the bed where Maks had left his shotgun. Four shots, two grenades. Enough to draw the deadshits to me and buy my family some time.

At the closet, I slipped out through the door. My pride stayed on their bellies, many of them blending with the sand. "Wait for it," I said as I turned to the east and jogged into the open. My heart was in my throat and fear like I'd never known whispered through me that this was it. I was going to die. But I'd die for my pride. I'd die knowing they had the best chance at safety that I could give them.

I'd die, and Maks would be not long after me with the sickness that coursed through him. Lila . . . she'd likely be along for the ride.

I would not cry. I would not cry.

I jogged until I was closer to the edge of the second rim of the Jinn's home. Two deadshits sat on top of the tower, their backs to me. "Hey, motherfuckers, what's going on?" I lifted the gun and sighted down it as they turned.

One breath out and I squeezed the trigger, the boom of the gun breaking the deathly silence of the early morning. The deadshit on the right screeched and fell to the side, his wings barely catching him as he fell. I didn't know if it was dead-dead or not. Frankly, I didn't know if you could kill one of those things. But he was out of the sky and everyone's attention was coming at us.

His buddy launched straight toward me.

"What an idiot," Lila said.

I shifted my stance and squeezed off another round. The stock bucked into my shoulder and the deadshit howled as he spun in a circle until he hit the ground. Screeching erupted from all over and I broke into a run, racing to the east and the south, drawing them away from my family. I didn't expect to kill the deadshits, but we'd draw them away and slow them down.

"Lila."

"Yeah?"

"This is probably not going to end well," I breathed out as I switched the gun to the grenade launcher.

"It's not over till the fat dragon sings," she said and

shot into the air. I aimed the grenade at a cluster of deadshits swooping straight for me.

The thump of the gun going off, and then the dead-shit in the middle *caught the grenade* and just stared at it. "Not smart," I yelled as I skidded to a stop, then dropped to the ground as the grenade went off.

The percussion of the blow was enough to send the cluster of deadshits flying in bits and pieces in all directions. The ground around me looked like it was raining body parts. A screech so close it might as well have been right in my ear sent me scrambling forward. I pushed to my feet as something large and black tackled me back to the ground.

"Stay down!" Ford snarled as a deadshit swooped over us. Before I could say anything, he leapt into the air, grabbed the deadshit by the leg and dragged it down, shaking it hard to the side, smashing its head into the tower.

Above, Lila worked with the sapphire, freezing the deadshits in bits and pieces. Not their whole body, but here and there, enough to throw them off balance, to make it hard for them to come after us. There were too many.

But I'd known that going in.

I spun, lifted the gun on sheer instinct as a deadshit swooped down for me. I pulled the trigger, the gun went off and the slug took him in the belly, but he didn't slow.

Those dangling back legs gripped my one arm and yanked me into the sky. I twisted hard, and reached for my knives, only they were gone with Darcy and Kiara.

The deadshit looked down at me, its face pock-marked and caved in as if eaten with acid.

"Lila, I've got your friend!" I grabbed hold of the flail with my free hand and swung it over my head, driving it into the deadshit's belly. He roared and his wings stopped moving as his body pulsed and danced while the flail pushed its way into the dead flesh.

As we fell, he spun, screaming to the sky. I dared to look up.

The morning light had given enough glow to the sky that the mass of dark gray deadshits swooping toward us made it look as though night had not lifted.

"Well, that's a fucking stinky shit." I yanked the flail out, the handle warm to my fingers. "No killing me yet." Maybe it wouldn't cost me anything since the deadshits were already dead?

I could hope.

The deadshit let me go and I twisted, shifting as I fell.

Static electricity coursed over my fur as I dropped out of the sky. The scent of lightning was there a breath before it crackled through the air around me.

Everything happened in a rush. I hit the ground, lightning blasted the deadshits left and right, hoof beats, shouting, Ford roaring, Lila joining him.

"Are they out?" I yelled up at her.

"They're clear!"

"Time to go! Ford, let's move!" He ran toward me and I jumped onto his back. Lila swooped down next to us and flew hard as he raced north. The horse and rider

287

spun and galloped next to us though the horse gave the big lion some serious side eye.

I looked at the rider, and for just a moment, I thought she was someone else. Long black hair and eyes as green as my own . . . but her body was petite, and curvy where my mother and I were both lean and taller.

"Who are you?" I yelled across to her.

She turned her head and grinned, lightning dancing in her eyes. "Your new fairy godmother."

Ford grunted and Lila said nothing. The woman had helped us. That would have to be enough for now. Twenty minutes later, we caught up with the slower members of the pride.

"Ease off," I yelled up at those in the lead. Steve and the cheetah girl. They circled around to us and I did a quick head count. Everyone was here.

How was it possible that we'd gotten everyone out?

Well, everyone except Maks.

"Where are all the Jinn?" Kiara sidled up next to me and Ford. Her eyes were gaunt and her ribs showed through even under her fur. She would need time to heal, to gain her strength back.

"That's a good question," I said. "They aren't giving chase though, so that means it's time to go home."

The lions and other shifters roared their agreement. The cub dropped to the ground and leapt and ran amongst the others. Different coats, different builds, different packs, but for now we were one family.

Why then did it feel as though I was still waiting for the ax to come down on the chopping block?

My earlier premonition when we fought the Jinn at the Oasis would suddenly make sense in the worst possible way.

Chapter Twenty-Three

We moved slowly northward, pacing ourselves so the cub could walk, and even Kiara who struggled was not pushed too hard.

I shifted to two legs, and nearly fell over. How many times had I gone back and forth now? I put a hand on Ford, letting him take my weight for just a moment before I got my legs under me fully.

"I'm impressed," Flora said. She'd introduced herself, and said she knew Merlin. Other than that little tidbit, she'd given no indication that she was going to talk much.

"About what?" I looked up at her.

"That you got them all out. Marsum puts too much faith in his dead ones. Where he was during all that, though, I'd truly like to know." She shook her head, a grimace on her face.

I shrugged, wishing I could throw the sensation that we weren't out of the frying pan yet. "A lot of luck."

Her hands were easy on the reins and she was careful with her horse, which made me like her almost as much as what she said next. "Luck is a crock of shit. The harder you work, the luckier you get, girl. But I think you already know that. Don't you?"

I grinned. "Maybe you are my fairy godmother. If that's the case, what are we doing next?"

She rolled her eyes. "Fairy godmother does not a psychic make me."

"You mean telekinetic?" Lila said and winked at me as she landed on my shoulder. I laughed, recalling Ford had thought they were the same thing. He grumbled something that sounded like "show off" under his breath.

Flora looked past me to the bigger lion, then back to me. "What happened to your male caracal?"

Her question caught me off guard and it struck far too sharp a chord. "Nope, not going there," I said.

She shrugged, rolling her shoulders. I stared up at her, and the white flowing dress with slits up to her hips, and I realized I'd seen others wearing similar attire. "Were you a slave?"

"For only a moment," she said, and there was a sound of thunder in the distance. "I am a priestess of the thunder god himself. So, while I can't call on his power regularly, in times of great need I am able to make a rather lovely showing of the weather."

"Do you need time to recharge?" Lila asked. "I do. The sapphire draws from me in order to work."

I lifted a hand to her. "You didn't mention that before."

"I barely used it before. But I can feel it now. I think if I tried to use it again I'd pass out."

That tingling sensation of the ax above us grew and I was sure the blade was pressed against the back of my neck. I turned and looked to the south. Even with the sun up, I couldn't see the Jinn's Dominion, the towers, or the deadshits. And still no Jinn.

Had they been waiting inside the tower where Benji said they'd all been called? Were they there still, thinking that we were coming to them? How had they not heard the fight with the deadshits?

I chewed on the inside of my cheeks, thinking about that possibility. "We rest for one hour when we get to the Oasis," I called out. Eyes turned toward me. "One hour, then we're going to have to double up here and there to make sure everyone who is struggling is being carried."

Ford bobbed his head first, then the others slowly followed. I noticed he hadn't taken his chance to cozy up with Darcy on the walk. Then again, Darcy was all but glued to Steve's side. Kiara . . . I found her on the edge of the group, walking with her head down.

Before I could go over to her, the cheetah gave a chirp.

"Water ahead," she called back.

I really needed to get names so I didn't offend them by calling out species. I sighed to myself. Once we were resting at the Oasis, I'd do a roll call and see who everyone was. Maybe they didn't all want to be part of this suddenly mixed-up pride.

We went in as a straggling group, right to the water. Everyone dropped to drink, including Flora and her horse. Lila winged off my shoulder. "Zam, you going to get a drink?"

I held back, nose flared. "Give me a second." I turned slowly, looking through the sparse trees to the more eastern side of the water. Once more, the ghost of my father rose through the sand, his massive jaws open in a silent roar, a single word I knew as well as I knew my own name.

Run.

Jinn . . . the Jinn were here even if I couldn't smell them. "It's a trap, get the fuck out of here now!" I spun back to my pride as I yelled.

Most were face down in the water, unconscious. I bolted forward, grabbing at them and yanking them back, so that at least they wouldn't drown. Lila, I lifted and cradled her with one arm.

The slow clap of hands turned me around. From the edges of the Oasis, emerging from the sand like mist, were the Jinn.

The ax against my neck fell.

My hand went to the flail on my back and I yanked it out. Marsum, tall, blond and smirking, strolled toward me. "Really? With my own weapon, you'd attack me? That seems rather foolish."

"It was my mother's, you piece of shit," I snarled and settled into a defensive crouch.

"Well, perhaps, but I made it for her, did you know that? Before she let herself be seduced by your father. I

293

really thought she'd stay with me." He shook his head and made a tsking sound.

He snapped his fingers and from behind him stepped Maks. His eyes were the hard, violent blue that told me he was not the man I loved.

"Maks, would you die to secure our place as rulers of this world?" Marsum asked softly.

"Yes," he answered without even a moment's hesitation.

Marsum held his hand out and curled it as if Maks's neck were within his grasp. Maks gasped and his hands went to his throat.

I laid Lila on the ground. "Let him go. Now!" I roared the last word and Marsum lifted his eyebrows.

"No. You see, I want you at my side. Your family line is far too dangerous to have you floating around out there on your own."

Maks struggled, but only in the sense that he fought to breathe. With a scream, I ran at Marsum and swung the flail as hard as I could. He didn't move. He didn't so much as flinch.

The flail froze an inch from Marsum's chest. He smiled at me. "The flail knows its master, Zamira. And it will not harm me."

The handle under my fingers was warm and I clutched it harder. "No, you are not its master," I growled. "I am."

He laughed at me and Maks slumped, forgotten. "You are the flail's master? You think so, do you? Then why did it stop before hitting me? That was no magic of mine, pussy cat." He licked his lips. "Your mother was a cagey one. I won't make the same mistake with you that I did with her. Your leash will be as short as I can make it."

"Challenge him," Maks whispered. Marsum snarled and I didn't hesitate.

"I challenge you." I snapped the words, trusting Maks as I yanked the flail back to my side.

"Boy," Marsum snarled and flicked his fingers at Maks, flipping him end over end until he slammed into a tree trunk with a thick, sickening thud.

He slid down and I couldn't take my eyes from him. The other Jinn didn't move, except for one I recognized. Vic.

"You can't challenge Marsum. You have to be Jinn to do it," he growled.

Marsum tensed and then slowly turned to face me while he addressed his cohorts. "That's just it, Vic. She is part Jinn. To be exact, she is one quarter Jinn. And only half lion. The Jinn blood," he strolled in front of me, "is from her grandmother. A fucking half-breed slave of no importance."

The half-breeds we'd helped escape had the same ability I did to take their clothes with them, and the truth hit me square between the eyes. They were just like me. Or really, I was just like them.

But there was no time to process the thought that I was part Jinn, or what it meant for me, or how it happened. Marsum held out his hand and a weapon materialized, solidifying in only seconds.

A spear with a wicked curved end he spun lazily in a

circle. "Challenge accepted. If I win, you will be mine in *every* way."

"And when I win," I circled with him, sweating already, "you will be dead as a fucking doornail."

He grinned. "Oh, I like the sass. I really do. I hope you keep it once I'm between your legs."

I snarled and lunged at him, swinging the flail toward his legs. Marsum jumped into the air and the twin spiked balls passed through where he'd been.

The Jinn landed lightly. "Don't think I'm going to go easy on you just because I want to fuck you. You need a lesson about who is in charge here."

He flicked his fingers at me and the flail flew out of my hand, ripped away from my skin. I screamed as bits of my flesh went with it. There was a splash as it hit the water of the Oasis.

Marsum chuckled. "Yes, I think the flail likes you, but you are not its master." He strode to me, spun the spear toward me, right at my head. I dove and rolled as the point of the spear slammed into the ground where my belly had been only a second before. I snapped up to my feet but stayed in a crouch.

My entire focus was on how to get to a weapon. Marsum, on the other hand, seemed only too happy to chatter on.

"Have you figured out yet who you are?" He quirked a brow and then swung the spear again, first at my left side and then to my right. I caught it with my hands, deflecting the blows some, but not enough to avoid them completely. The blows to my ribs sent shockwaves of pain through me, and I struggled to breathe around them.

"Fuck you," I snarled as I stepped back toward my pride. Darcy and Kiara had my two blades. I would have to make do with them. They'd not failed me before.

"All in due time. Though I do think that's going to make Maks very cranky to have you in my bed. As soon as I get a child in you, I'll kill him. Put him out of his misery." He grinned.

My foot bumped into a hand and I dared a glance down. Darcy was there, her eyes wide. She blinked once.

Not unconscious then, but unable to move. Unable to fight.

I looked back at Marsum who—fool that he was— had turned his back on me. I bent and scooped up the blade I'd given Darcy and sprinted at Marsum's back.

At the last second, I leapt, aiming for his head. One clean cut, he'd be done.

But then Maks would be bound forever.

My wrist rolled, changing the trajectory of the blow to maim but not kill . . . and that was the mistake that cost me everything.

Chapter Twenty-Four

I was in midair when Marsum spun, not with his spear but with his hand coated in the black mist that was his Jinn magic. It wrapped around me, pinning my arms and legs together so fast and hard that my own blade sliced into my thigh.

I screamed both with the pain of the cut and with the knowledge that I'd lost. Just like that, because I couldn't condemn Maks to the life that waited for him if his father died.

Marsum slowly turned, laughing. "You see, I knew you couldn't do it. Not that. You'd lose your precious Maks."

I used the only ace I had up my sleeve. "The Emperor wants you dead, limp dick."

His smile slid only a little. "So, your grandfather has been chatting with you, has he?"

My whole body seized up, the air rushed out of me

and I saw nothing but the vision of before. The vision of the kindly-looking old man I'd thought seemed like a grandfather. And he was.

"Oh, you really didn't know?" He chuckled. "It doesn't matter. As long as I have you, the falak will remain quiet. Once you give me a child, I'll finish the Emperor with your help. As it was meant to be." He drew me close with a crook of his finger. "You lose, pussy cat."

I pulled my head back as he leaned in for a kiss. I snapped my head forward, slamming it into his nose. There was a satisfying crunch of cartilage shattering and then the sweetest sound to my ears as Marsum howled.

"Little bitch!" he roared.

"That's queen to you!" I roared back. "I am a lion of the Bright Pride. I will not be held down. I will not bow to you. I am a queen in my own right!" The words were a flood, the power of my life and bloodline through my father singing through me. "I would rather die than give you anything, let alone a child."

He snapped his head around to stare at me, blood dripping from his now seriously crooked nose. "That can be arranged."

He flicked his fingers at me and I flew backward through the air until I was over the water. And then he let me go.

I dropped fast, hit the water, gulped a last breath of air, then sunk as though a stone were tied to me. My arms and legs still bound.

My eyes adjusted to the shadows in the water quickly

as I sank to the bottom. I hit lightly, my lungs already protesting the lack of air.

I rolled to my belly and right in front of me was the flail, half sunk in the soft bottom. I wriggled forward, fighting with the water and the wound in my leg. I had no hands to touch the flail so I laid my head against it.

Take the magic around me. Please.

The flail warmed under my head and the bonds on my legs and arms released. I reached forward and grabbed the flail. It wouldn't work for me against Marsum, but I had nothing else.

And if he thought I was done fighting, he was about to get the surprise of a lifetime.

With the flail in my left hand I fought to get to the surface of the water, my body demanding air. I broke the surface, gulped a breath and something shoved me back under.

Well, something being Marsum.

His laughter reached me even through the water. "So, you broke the spell on your limbs? That is interesting. Maybe you aren't the weakling everyone has been telling me you are?"

I swam to the other side of the water and broke the surface again, only to be shoved under once more.

Over and over, I fought to get out of the water, would manage a breath and then be pushed deep again.

He was tiring me out.

Making it so I would be easier to deal with.

I don't know which time he shoved me under when I let myself just float. My body was hungry for more than a gulp of air, and fighting through the water with the flail in my hand was exhausting me far faster than I wanted to admit. Even if I got out, I would not be able to fight him with any sort of skill or speed.

Marsum had won.

I would have groaned had I any air to escape me. I slowly pushed to the surface and this time there was no gulp of air. Marsum's power pushed me back under the water.

I clenched my hand around the flail. What had I left to me to fight? My weapon wouldn't hit the bastard. I couldn't kill him because of Maks. My pride members were flat out.

I felt the darkness come for me, and in a blink, I was no longer in the water, but standing in the middle of a desert, my—fuck me—grandfather, the Emperor, in front of me.

His eyebrows were quirked upward. "Facing Marsum, are you?"

"Are you really my grandfather?" I realized I was dripping water all over the sand as if I were truly there. I *knew* I wasn't, but the lines between reality and vision were nearly invisible to me.

He gave me a single nod. "I am. But perhaps now is not the time to discuss your genealogy, seeing as your heartbeat is slowing, and I doubt Marsum is smart enough to realize he's actually killing you."

I just stared at him.

He pointed at me with a single finger. "You have connected to your pride more than any other shifter.

Use it, use their strength to feed you, to break the hold Marsum has on you. Use it to connect to the magic in the flail. Only then will it be yours when you face him."

"It won't fight him!" The words burst out of me as the scene began to fade.

"He threw it away, cast it aside. A master does not cast aside his protégé. Connect with your weapon, Zamira. And be stronger for it." His voice faded and the water was in my mouth, up my nose, filling my body.

The darkness around me was not that of a vision now, but of death. I sunk into it, connecting with my pride. They were all there, including Maks and Lila. I stretched my senses further to the flail in my hand. Power rippled through it, the power of the Jinn who'd made it. I tightened my hand on the haft.

I will never throw you away. That was the only thought I had.

A sharp pang in my hand resonated outward and I stared as blood from my palm swirled around the weapon. The red bloom was there and then suddenly sucked into the weapon, gone.

My lungs ached and my muscles screamed for air. I could only hope I'd done enough to connect with my flail.

I drew my pride's strength to me, their energy flooding my limbs like light cutting through a storm cloud.

It filled me, and in it I saw their hearts. Strong, wild hearts that were meant for freedom and love and loyalty to their pride and packs. A roar of affirmation bubbled up in me, but I held it back as I pushed for the surface, lifting the flail above my head with both hands.

I broke through the water and Marsum's magic so hard I shot out so my upper body was free from the water before I sunk back. The power of Marsum on me rolled off my shoulders and I swam to the shoreline. My fatigue was gone. The flail was light in my hand.

And I'd never been so angry in my entire life.

I stood and turned to see Marsum on the other side of the water. His eyes were wide, and he was staring at me with a grin plastered on his face. A grin that said it all. He thought he'd beaten me.

"Are you done fighting me?" He started around the edge of the water, the mist wrapping from his fingers and shooting toward me. I twisted the flail, spinning it so the two balls whipped through the ribbon of mist.

Like watching a spinning wheel weave wool, the flail snagged the mist and spun it all on its own, and it sucked the magic into the metal and wood. I smiled back at Marsum. "No, I think we're just starting."

I ran around the edge of the Oasis, straight for him. I already knew what I had to do. Bind him. The way he'd bound me. Which meant I needed someone with magic.

I diverted some of the energy coming into me into Lila through the threads of energy that connected us. "Lila, wakey wakey!" A little bit of freezing all around his body should do the trick. At least until I could come up with something better.

Goddess of the desert, let me come up with something better.

The flail hummed under my fingers as it sucked

Marsum's magic deep into it. Marsum just stared at me as I slid to a stop in front of him. A moment passed where we just stood and then all hell broke loose. I pushed enough of the pride's energy back to them that they all woke. And they were as pissed as me.

I snapped the flail forward, going for his belly—and the twin balls smashed into him, sending him to the side. From the ground, he spun the spear, the blade nicking my left arm. I flinched and Marsum used the advantage to his fullest, running flat out at me.

I backed up as fast as I could, keeping him in front of me.

"You can't kill me," he snarled as he swept his spear at me. "And I will have you one way or another."

He drove the point of the spear to the left of my legs and then swept it outward, slamming me onto the ground. The wound in my leg and arm were slowing me down, even with the strength of the pride running through my veins. Those veins were running out of blood.

Marsum dropped his weapon and leapt onto me, his body pinning me to the ground.

He clamped his hands on my wrists and lifted them above my head. "You stopped fighting me." He tipped his head to one side. "Why?"

I smiled as Lila swept by and touched the middle of his back. The cold shot through him and into me but didn't freeze me.

He roared and the ice on his back shattered, his magic ghosting around us. "Nice try, but the fire of the desert will always save me."

Before I could move, he slammed his mouth over mine and kissed me. Well, kissed maybe on his part. I writhed and fought to get away from him, driving my knees into his side, twisting and fighting to get him off me.

Heat, fire, the desert, roared inside me in answer to the magic he shoved into my belly. Fire I didn't understand, yet instinctively knew came from my mother's side.

He was lighting the fire of my Jinn blood. That was what he'd been trying to do before, using Maks.

Marsum wanted me to connect with him, to make me want him, which would never happen. I managed to shove him off. "What did you do to my curse? Why is it not trying to kill me?"

He grinned at me and ran a tongue over his lips. "It was never meant to kill you. The curse was meant to send you back to me to have it removed. Assuming you were alive. And once I realized you were alive, I changed it. I made it so you would be drawn to the desert, that everything in your life would bring you here. To me."

I stared at him, my jaw hanging open as I saw the last leg of my journey replay in fast forward. How everything and everyone seemed to be sending me to Marsum, albeit for different reasons.

I stood there too long.

His magic wrapped around me and I screamed as he pulled me toward him once more.

My arms were pinned again. He took advantage of it and slammed his mouth over mine, his magic shoved deep into my body, lighting things I never knew were there.

My blood boiled under the heat, under the power we held together.

I started to sink into myself. To feel I could change things for the better if I but embraced what Marsum offered.

His fingers slid into my hair, holding me to him.

As suddenly as Marsum was on me, he was yanked off. My eyes remained closed as I struggled to understand what was happening. I opened my eyes and blinked up at Maks standing over me, one of my own kukri blades in his hand. Blood dripped down the side of his face and those blue eyes held all the sorrow in the world.

"Goodbye, Zam," he said softly.

Without another word, he rammed the blade into Marsum's throat, cut through his spine and took his head. Just like that, my heart shattered.

"NO!" I screamed the word as an explosion of magic sent me flying through the air. I tumbled head over ass, and a tiny pair of claws dug into my arm. I shifted as I fell and Lila took the weight of my smaller form easily.

"To the horses!" Lila yelled to the rest of the pride and they scrambled, mounting and following Lila as she flew us out of the Oasis to the east, deeper into the desert. Away from the power that flattened the trees and sent up a sandstorm that swirled out of nowhere.

I stared back at the Oasis where Maks stood, his body disappearing under the black of Marsum's magic and soul as it moved into him. His head tipped back and he roared to the sky, deep and guttural as the Jinn around him went to their knees. A new power had been born.

And I'd lost the one man whose soul matched my own.

Chapter Twenty-Five

Lila flew with me until we could no longer see the Oasis. She lowered me to the ground and I shifted and mounted on Balder. It took all I had not to break down in front of those I was meant to care for.

I drew a breath and forced the words from my mouth. "We need space between us and the Jinn." I looked to Flora. "Any suggestions, fairy godmother?"

She smiled but there was pain in it. "No."

Ford cleared his throat. "There's a watering hole about a day and a half from here. That would be closest."

I tipped my head at him. "Lead the way, Ford."

No one argued, no one suggested going back to Ish and the Stockyards, not even Steve. I watched them all. Five horses were not enough, but we made do. Kiara, Darcy, Flora, and Nell rode the four remaining horses. The cub—Frankie was his name—rode with Kiara.

Steve, Ford, Benji and the cheetah—Asuga—stayed in their four-legged forms and ranged around us.

Asuga was happy to lead the way with bursts of speed, then waited for us well ahead. Ford traveled next to me and Balder, quietly at first. But Ford, being who he was, couldn't contain himself.

"Maks isn't coming back to us, is he?" he asked.

I glanced down at him. "I don't know."

His eyebrows dug deep. "You think there is a chance?"

Lila looked back at me from her perch between Balder's ears. I let myself follow the energy of my pride.

I found them all easier than I ever had before. Lila, Ford, Steve, Kiara, Darcy, Benji, Shem way to the north, and even the cub Frankie . . . the others were there on the periphery, and it would be up to them if they joined us or not.

My lower lip trembled as I realized there was no connection pulling me to the west. There was no connection to Maks at all anymore, though my desire to ride to the desert was there, at my back. The curse of Marsum still in play maybe? A tremor stumbled through me. Flora rode on my right and she reached out and touched a hand to my arm.

"If you love him, he's not lost. Love is the only power that can truly save a soul," she said.

I drew a breath and nodded. "You're wrong. I know what it is to lose people. I see my brother even though he's dead. He's gone but not. Maks . . . is the same." I looked back to Ford. "We have to go on, Ford. He's gone."

"For now. He saved you because he loves you, Zam. Because he loves us," Lila said. My eyes went to her again.

Before I could say anything, she lifted off and shot into the sky, tiny crystalline tear drops falling from her eyes like sparkling jewels.

She was right about that. Maks had done what he'd done so there would be no guilt on us, but also because Marsum would have kept coming. He would have kept chasing us. Maybe Maks could hold back those urges?

Only time would tell.

And until then, I knew my heart would remain as it was, shattered.

THE WATERING HOLE Ford led us to was smaller than the Oasis, but it was fine for our needs.

We untacked the horses, rubbed them down and fed them before our group huddled around a fire. The first night, I bade them all sleep, and I would take the watch. I couldn't sleep. Every time I closed my eyes I saw Maks and heard him whisper goodbye.

The fire we lit burned bright against the dark of the night, and the flames hypnotized me. I know, because I blinked and Ishtar was there, standing at the edge of it. Around her was the ghostly edges of her room.

"You . . . how did you call me here?" she asked softly.

Both my eyebrows shot up. "I did not call you here."

She stared hard at me. "You did, Zamira. How is it that my hyenas have not caught you?"

I shrugged. "Never send a dog to do a cat's job, Ish. You should know that by now. They're all dead."

Her eyes narrowed. "You think to mock me?"

"I think you're a fucking douche," I snapped. "Which means you have something up your sleeve."

"Give me the jewels and I will leave you to live in peace. You cannot understand what needs to be done. You are a child, and a weak one at that."

Oh, she just had to go there, didn't she?

I made myself smile. "You can have the jewels—" her eyes lit up, "over my dead and rotting corpse."

The smile slid. "That can be arranged."

"Not if I get to you first." Shit, shit, shit, where did that come from? I was not going to take on a desert goddess! But my blood was boiling—that same heat Marsum started as he kissed me had lit me once more. I snapped my fingers and waved a hand as if dismissing her, and the vision was gone.

Only it didn't just erase her, it replaced her with another person who liked the visionary shit.

The Emperor did a slow turn while his ghostly image stood in the fire. "Interesting that you can do this so soon after being awakened. I suppose I should not be surprised." He nodded slowly. "What is it you wish to discuss?"

I frowned. If he thought like Ishtar that I'd called

him here, then I didn't want to look like a fool as I'd done with her. "I didn't take your fucking jewel from Marsum."

He closed his eyes. "That is rather bad news."

I frowned. Why didn't he flip out? Where was the monster everyone told me he was? Was this a game like Ishtar where he would try and lull me into believing he was something he was not?

I tried another tactic. Prove him wrong. "You said I would die without your help."

"I've been known to be wrong once or twice in a thousand years." He smiled as if some inside joke were being shared between us. Seriously, what the fuck was his game?

I went on. "And that if I killed Marsum, with your help, you would return my brother to me. Marsum is dead. I want my brother back. Now."

He shrugged. "You didn't kill Marsum. That was the deal."

I took a step toward the fire. "You fucking dirt bag!"

He held up a hand. "Peace, granddaughter. There is always a way to return the dead to life. Within the wyvern's lair is a way to do so. That is all I can tell you."

I opened my mouth and another question popped out. "You were impersonating my brother. Weren't you? To motivate me?"

He smiled. "Ah, perhaps my skills have gotten rusty. Yes, that was me."

The Emperor had used my own grief against me. I gritted my teeth, struggling to talk evenly. "And my brother in the strange box?"

"That was real. His soul is trapped. It's the only way of possibly bringing him back if he is not allowed to move on." He sighed. "I am tired, and my fool of a son is here. I must go."

He made the same hand wave motion that I'd used to dismiss Ishtar and I was once more the only one awake at the campsite, no vision haunting me.

I sucked in a sharp breath and stumbled back a few steps. "How the fuck did I do that?"

The question was not meant to be answered.

"Your magic, much of it is instinctive," Flora said quietly from my right. I turned to her.

"Instinctive?"

"You will need some training, to tap into it, but much will come to you as you need it. That is the way of some magic." She shrugged. "But try not to get into a pissing match with Ishtar. She might have loved you once, but she has lost her marbles as she gained stones."

I didn't disagree. But I knew Ishtar and I were far from done.

Flora and I spoke at length, quietly, throughout the remainder of the night about what we should do next. The next morning, I was ready to move us on.

I waited until their bellies were full and their guards were down before I stood. I'd been unable to eat, my stomach churning with the thought of what was coming.

"We cannot go to the Stockyards. Ishtar has returned to the land and that is her home." I felt the weight of their eyes settle on me. "The Emperor is not yet free, but it could happen. And then there is the falak

313

to consider. If someone were to kill the Emperor, then the falak would be freed onto the world. We can't have that. But the Emperor is growing in strength and it may be a matter of time before he is free. Unless something is done about it." I drew a slow breath, trying not to think of the falak, the one monster bigger than even the Emperor. How the hell he kept it from devouring us, I would have to find out in order to keep it from happening. But that was not today. Today was about pulling our shit together and standing tall. "I am the alpha of the Bright Lion Pride, a family whose calling was to give protection to those who needed it. The world needs protection now more than ever, and I intend to do something about this." Fucked if I knew what, but those words needed to be said. I drew another breath. "Those who wish to stay with me may stay. Those who wish to go may go."

Steve stood. Of course, the dumb fuck did. "I'm not bowing to you."

I curled my lips. "Didn't ask you to bow, dipshit. I said you could come with me, or you could go your own way."

He glared at me. "You're saying that you're going to save the world? That's what you're saying?"

I swallowed hard once, pushing the doubt away, and then nodded. "Yeah, something like that."

Ford looked up at me. "And how do you intend to do that?"

Lila sat on my shoulder and tightened her hold on my ear. "We have a journey ahead of us. One that will be fraught with danger and death."

I rolled my eyes to her. "You really think that's the way to convince anyone?"

She shrugged and I saw the glint of humor in her eyes. "Well, I think that some of them need to understand how bad it could be. This is not a game. This is a real as it gets."

Slowly, they all stood. Even Benji, even Nell, Frankie and Asuga. Shit, even Steve. That was going to be a fucking gong show the first time he decided to challenge me. And I was sure as the sun rising in the east that it would happen.

Fuck my life, it would only be a matter of when.

Kiara locked eyes with me. "I want to make this world better. Safer for all of us."

My heart swelled as their energy fed into one another, as their strength buoyed each other. I nodded. "Then we're in for a wild one. We still have Ishtar's hunters to contend with, as I'm damn sure she's going to send more. The Jinn to the west. And then whatever we are going to face to the east."

"East?" Steve growled. "Those are dead lands. Why are we going to the east?"

I locked eyes with him. "Because there is only one person, one creature who can help us untangle this shitty mess we find ourselves in."

He frowned. "Who?"

Here we go, I thought, *time to put on my weapons, my armor, and dig in for a long fight to find her.*

"The Oracle."

Afterword

Coming Fall 2018. . . .

"Oracle's Haunt"
(The Desert Cursed Series Book 4)

"Karma. It's pronounced 'Ha-ha' you know."
~Lila